In the Shadows of Love

Memories of Dusk, Volume 1

Damion Thaxton

Published by Damion Thaxton, 2023.

This is a work of fiction. Similarities to real people, places, or events are entirely coincidental.

IN THE SHADOWS OF LOVE

First edition. July 26, 2023.

Copyright © 2023 Damion Thaxton.

ISBN: 979-8223535171

Written by Damion Thaxton.

Table of Contents

Author's Notes

THIS NOVEL CONTAINS subject matter that some people may not feel comfortable with. Subjects include physical assault, physical abuse (of an adult woman), alcoholism, familial abandonment and neglect, and homophobia/slurs.

These subjects are treated with the requisite seriousness they deserve and should be seen as a look into everyday struggles that some people contend with.

Reader

discretion is advised.

Chapter 1

FRIDAY MAY 22ND AFTERNOON

The school bell rang, signaling the end of the last day of school for the year. Isolde made her way out of the classroom and into the crowded hallway. A short walk later, she arrived at her locker.

Her best friend April was already waiting for her, twirling her shoulder-length dark brown ponytail with a finger. Her round, rather plain and pale face lit up with a smile when she saw Isolde coming.

"So, another year comes to a close. And dare I say," April's tone of voice took on a distinct note of sarcasm. "I for one will miss this wonderful place over the summer break." She watched as April rolled her eyes for good measure.

Both girls broke out laughing as Isolde opened her locker, and removed her backpack. "Like, tell me about it. Oh my god girl, Mrs. Ramirez was a fucking bitch. Go on, ask me what she did, right before the bell rang." Isolde said as she began rummaging around in her backpack.

She heard a distinct pair of footsteps approaching them from behind as she pulled an oatmeal creme pie from it.

"Pulled her last-minute summer essay prank on you, did she? Got me with it last year too." The voice came from behind her. Isolde turned to see her other best friend, Jessica.

Her medium-length, curly, and frizzled blonde hair draped over her freckled face clashed with her school uniform. Its gun-metal gray color with a single white tiger emblem, complete with the school name, clashed with all of their hair, she couldn't help but notice.

"Like what the hell was that, right? I got enough on my plate already this year to be worrying about some sadistic old woman's summer homework. Isolde said, slamming her locker door.

She ripped the wrapper off of her treat and took a big bite. The sweet, and somewhat bitter flavor of the cookies complimented the almost cloying creme filling. *Just what I needed after that so-called prank*. She thought.

Jessica gave a hard laugh at Isolde. "Like what? Let me guess, you are finally gonna publish your junk food pyramid?" She moved her hands in a large, exaggerated triangle as she spoke. She pointed to the top of her imaginary triangle. "Isolde's grand food pyramid, the junk food files. And right at the top, no less than four servings per hour, is the infamous oatmeal creme pie.".

Isolde rolled her eyes. "Yeah, yeah, yeah, you girls are like totally just jealous of me and you know it." She ran her hands along her lanky figure in a mock dramatic fashion. Her waist-length, purple-dyed hair flicked as she shook her head for dramatic flair.

April shook her head as she spoke. "Uh huh, keep telling yourself that, Ducky." Despite her friend's words, Isolde couldn't help but notice the grin fade from her face at her words.

Jessica sighed before speaking. "Well, I certainly am, you damn bean-pole. If I ate one of those things they'd have to turn every door in this building into a double-wide so my fatass could get to class." All three friends burst out in laughter at the imagery.

"Anywho, I gotta head out, don't want to be late. You know how my father gets if I'm not home before school is even out for the day. Catch you girlies later." Jessica turned and headed off. Isolde felt a brief pang of sorrow as she watched her friend walking off, knowing the girl was in for an earful, for no fault of her own.

Isolde turned back to April. "Well, then there were two. Shall we?" As she spoke, she held out her naturally, permanently tanned and skinny arm in a mock invitation for April to take it.

Her friend just shook her head again and laughed. "Isolde? You know you're a dork, right?" Isolde feigned offense at the jab.

"Oh no, no, no. Me, a dork? Say it ain't so. Oh, my poor heart can't take it." She put one hand over her forehead and the other over her chest as she spoke, prompting a chuckle out of April.

"Like more seriously though, guess it's time to head out ourselves." Both girls turned and began the short walk toward the main entrance of the school. They were some of the last students to leave the building. Their destination was just outside the building, and the pair quickly made their way to the bike rack.

Both girls set to unlocking, and then mounting their respective bicycles. April was on a blue, vintage-style beach cruiser. Isolde had a green and black multi-speed mountain bike. She watched as April began pedaling down the sidewalk, before turning onto the street.

She felt a little sorry for her friend, on a single-speed bike, but was not about to pass up the opportunity. She shifted into a faster gear and took off, making up the short head-start April had. She rode a bit ahead of April, and stopped, turning to face her.

"You know what would be so, so, so fun? If we raced home. Last one there has to buy the snacks." She watched as April took the bait and began pedaling as fast as she could. Not one to go out without a fight, she began her own furious pedaling.

The houses of the neighborhood whizzed by in a blur as the two girls raced their bikes down the street. Then after turning a corner, down the next one after that. Before long, their respective houses were in sight. She pushed her legs as hard as she could, overtaking April, and speeding off ahead.

The brakes on her bike gave a nasty squeal as she came to a stop in front of her house, forcing her to grit her teeth. She turned to see

April still a few dozen feet up the road. She hopped off the bike and began moving it up on the porch as April was approaching.

"Wow, it's been too long since we did something like that," April said between bouts of stopping to catch her breath, her face flushed red from the excursion. "Though, next time, I'm taking Rachel's bike. This thing is just not fast enough to keep up with your sugar-hyped ass."

Isolde sympathized with her friend. Her first bike had also been a single-speed, and she hated it so much that it was taken back and she had another within a month. She couldn't even begin to imagine how April made it up any of the fairly steep hills around town on that thing.

"Good. How else am I to get better if I have no one to beat over and over." She joked as she finished locking her bike up. "Like, every good athlete needs her rival after all." She struck a pose as April laughed and shook her head.

"Whatever her royal dorkiness says. Anyway, I'll swing by later, like you asked. My stomach is really bitching at me, and unlike you, I can't buy it off with junk food. Later." April waved as she turned and made the short walk home, right next door.

Isolde let out a heavy sigh, once April was out of earshot. She turned towards the door of her own home, dreading the revelation she had for her friends later that night.

AFTER CHAINING UP HER bike, April made her way inside. She had to step over her sister Rachel's big black lab, Buster, who was lounging on the porch. He turned his head to look at her as she moved, a big dog grin on his face, as she patted him on the head on the way in.

She looked around the empty living room. *Guess everyone's busy.* She thought, turning to head up the stairs. After making the short trek, she came face to face with her younger sister, Cassandra. She was the polar opposite of April, being skinny, more so even than Isolde, with a long thin face. She kept her light brown hair in a braid.

"Outta my way chunky." The young girl pushed herself past April and made her way down the stairs. Moments later April could hear their mother admonishing Cassandra as she turned and headed into her room. Sighing, she locked the door, dropped her backpack against the wall, and laid back on her bed.

She squeezed and rubbed her lower legs, letting out another sigh as she did. They were aching from Isolde's impromptu race, as fun as it had been. More than that, they were another reminder of her weight gain over the last couple of years, a fact Cassandra loved to hone in on every single day.

She thought back on the conversation her friends and she had earlier. Something Isolde had said, or the way she acted was nagging at her. She couldn't place it, but something had seemed off about Isolde today.

She reached over and grabbed her backpack. She removed her phone from it and quickly dialed up Jessica. A few audible rings later, her friend picked up.

"Heya girl, you make it home in time to avoid the wrath of he who must not be named?" Her question caused Jessica to chuckle before she answered.

"Not a chance. Where were you? School ended twenty minutes ago, young lady." Jessica mocked her father's overbearing attitude, forcing a grin out of April.

"Anywho, what's up?" April hesitated a moment, her grin fading. She wasn't even sure if she had indeed picked up on anything, but decided to ask anyway.

"Oh nothing much. You know, besides Cassie being her usual charming self." She closed her eyes thinking of her sister's jab. Thinking about how much it hurt, despite hearing some variation every day.

"Anyway, I wanted to ask you something. Did anything seem, I don't know, off about Isolde today?" Jessica gave a long pause before answering.

"No, I can't think of anything that comes to mind. Why, she say something to ya?" April opened her eyes and took a deep breath, feeling a bit relieved. Perhaps it was all in her head after all.

"Nah. I don't know, just seemed like maybe something was bugging her." She thought back to how Isolde had slammed her locker. She knew her friend sometimes had anger management issues, but she hadn't seemed angry, more frustrated.

"Well, aside from her challenging me to a bike race, which we haven't done in years. Wanted to see if maybe she had said something to you or not." Jessica laughed at the comment.

"Really, that's all? Girl, I think you been spending too much time together." April had to frown at the comment. As fun as it was to hang out with Isolde, it wasn't always by choice, a fact she was soon to be reminded of.

"Yeah, maybe. But I mean, better over there than here." The sound of someone stomping up the creaky stairs made her shake her head, knowing what was coming as Jessica replied with a "Yeah, I hear you girl."

She could now hear the sounds of Cassie and their mom arguing in the hallway. *Just once, Cassie, could you at least try to act like a human being instead of the demon you really are?* She thought, gritting her teeth at the racket.

" Ugh, it's family feud time again. I'll hit you up later." After Jessica said her goodbye, April hung up the phone. The mermaid oil painting on her wall shook from the vibration as a door was slammed. Followed by more shouting from her mother.

Not wanting to get caught up in whatever drama her sister had started this time, she got up and walked to her closet. She spent several minutes picking out an outfit, grabbed her phone, and headed out of her room.

"If anyone needs me, I'll be soaking in the bathtub." She yelled as she walked down the hallway toward the upstairs bathroom. Her mom only nodded her head before opening Cassie's door, and more shouting.

Making sure to lock the door, she walked over to the large white porcelain bathtub. She turned both the hot and cold sides on, before walking to the mirror. She reached up and removed the hairband from her ponytail, and stood there looking at herself in the mirror.

She spent several minutes running a comb through her hair, as the tub filled. Afterward, she picked up her phone, and opened a music app, setting the volume of the country music track to the max.

She walked back over to the tub and took a small box from behind it. Removing a small bath bomb, she tossed it in the tub, before turning the faucets off. She disrobed, placed her school uniform in the hamper, and climbed into the tub.

The warm water immediately began soothing her leg muscles, still aching from the race. As she settled into a more relaxing position, her thoughts once again turned to Isolde. She couldn't remember the last time the two of them had raced their bikes. Come to think of it, she couldn't remember the last time she had seen Isolde even act competitively at all.

She made a mental note to bring it up sometime, as she closed her eyes, letting the bubbly water soothe and relax her. As she soaked, all of her thoughts, and worries melted away, enjoying a rare moment of pure, uninterrupted peace.

ISOLDE MADE HER WAY inside, passing her foster father, Mr. Needen, on her way to the kitchen. The man, bald except for a large black mustache, blending into his dark brown-skinned and wrinkled face, gave her a warm smile. She had to look up to him to make eye contact.

"Afternoon, young lady. School go well enough?" She nodded and gave a brief overview of her last day of school for the year. The man gave a warm laugh, to which she couldn't help but smile, despite her apprehension.

"Well, sounds like a right lot of fun. Well, you get some relaxin in this weekend you hear? Don't want you being late and upsetting Mrs. Burke on Monday." He patted her back as he made his way into the living room.

She rolled her eyes and sighed as she liberated a cola from the fridge, and made the trip upstairs to her room. She tossed her backpack down and sat on her bed, taking a moment to enjoy the pop and hiss of the can as she opened it.

Her eyes fell on the small plastic object on her desk and she picked it up., staring at it with a look of disgust as she enjoyed her fizzy drink.

As she sat on the edge of her bed, she took several deep breaths, trying to calm her nerves. She looked across the room at the uniform that hung on her closet door. A single-piece, short-sleeved top ending in a long and flowing skirt. Its alternating red and white stripes were hideous and tacky.

She flipped the small plastic nametag around in her hand. She ran her fingers across it, feeling the deep-cut letters that spelled out her name. In bright white letters running along a red stripe across its top were the words Family Diner.

She threw the small thing across the room and downed the last of her soda in one gulp. Her seventeenth birthday was last month, and her foster parents had made her apply for a job. Mr. Needen knew the proprietress of the nearby diner, a woman named Daisy.

This family connection had landed her her first-ever job, as a waitress. She fell back on her bed. *Of all the ways to spend summer vacation.* She thought.

She looked at her phone. It was Friday, and she began on Monday. She dropped her phone on the bed beside her, as she wondered how her friends were going to take the news. How April was going to take it.

She raised an eyebrow, as the thought puzzled her. Even though April was her best friend, She felt odd over the stray thought focusing on her.

If anything, April will probably be the supportive one, Jessica is the one I need to be concerned over, what with her smart mouth. She thought, pushing the odd train of thoughts from her head.

Forcing herself to get back to her feet, she walked over to her closet and minutes later had changed out of her school uniform into sweatpants and a t-shirt, both shades of light green.

On her way back to the bed, she stopped at her desk, retrieving a box of chocolate brownies. Now comfortable on her bed, she ripped the packaging off of one of the treats and took a big bite. Its decadent and sweet fudge flavor soon had her forgetting her worries. She finished her treat, she tossed the wrapper into the waste bin next to her bed.

As she was preparing to open another, her phone's notification went off, making her jump a little. After composing herself from her unexpected jump scare, she picked the phone up. It was a text from Jessica.

"Heya girlie what up? Just got off the phone with April. Is everything good with ya? She seemed to think there was something off with you today or something." She couldn't help but laugh. Of course, April would be the one to pick up on her concerns, though she was still surprised by it.

Thought I did a better job of hiding it. Eh whatever, she'll find out in a short while. She fired off a quick response, letting Jessica know that they'd be calling her later, once April came over.

She swiped through her phone, landed on a music app, and set the hard rock tracks to random. Throwing herself back on the bed, she decided to take a short nap until April arrived.

Chapter 2

DRYING HERSELF OFF after her long soak, she could still hear her family arguing. A slammed door echoed through the house, followed by another round of shouting as she dressed. A knock on the bathroom door knocked her out of her thoughts as she began making her way to leave.

"Gimme a minute." She shouted, before reaching the door. Opening it revealed her much taller, slightly older sister Rachel. She wore a long-sleeved shirt over tight jeans, her light brown hair falling past her shoulders.

"Enjoying a nice bath while the hatebirds go at it?" As if on cue, Cassandra's door swung open, and she stormed out, slamming it before heading down the stairs. "You know it. Anyway, I'll be going over to Isoldes in a bit. Good luck with Casszilla."

She stepped out of the bathroom allowing Rachel free entrance as her older sister gave a mocking laugh. "Uh huh, Why does that not surprise me? Well, have fun with your own little lovebird." Laughing as she moved, Rachel closed and locked the door before April could respond.

"Hardy har har, you loser." She shouted at the closed door before heading back to her room. She grabbed her purse after slipping her casual shoes on, and headed back out into the hallway.

She was just in time to get shoved to the side as Cassandra stomped her way past, towards the bathroom. "Rach is in there sis." She hollered after her. A move that prompted yet another tantrum from the girl.

"Oh my god, can't anyone use the damn bathroom in this house? you two take so damn long in there." April couldn't help but feel a little bad, as it was true. She often forgot about the time when she was in there, and she was sure Rachel just liked sitting in there to piss everyone else off.

"What about the downstairs bathroom?" She asked her sister, prompting an eye-roll from the child. "Mom is in there right now, and she took a bottle with her." April's heart sank. Their mother suffered on and off bouts of alcoholism, and lately, she had fallen off the wagon again, hard.

She wondered how much of it was Cassandra's fault. At thirteen years old, the girl was a menace. She had a chip on her shoulder that had a chip on its shoulder. April tried to think of a time in recent memory when she hadn't been a rude little brat, but none came to mind.

Over the last year especially, her arguments with their mother had escalated tenfold. There was rarely a day that went by without the two of them fighting about something.

"Great, well it looks like I'll be staying over at Isolde's again tonight. Let her know for me will you, thanks sis." Cassandra just rolled her eyes, gave a "Whatever." and stomped off into her bedroom.

April made her own way back downstairs, once again having to step over the dog, this time laying at the foot of the stairs. Making her way into the small kitchen, she rifled through the freezer, settling on a frozen sandwich.

She removed the wrapper, tossing it into the microwave. As she stood there, waiting for it to heat up, she thought about her mother, and about their dysfunctional family. *Why'd you have to go and die, Dad?* The thought brought a tear to her eyes as she thought back to her childhood.

How she had first met Isolde, as the young girl was sitting by the side of the road, crying and missing her own father. *At least her real dad is still alive out there somewhere.* The thought brought a question to her mind, as the microwave dinged. Which would be worse, having your father die as a child, or being abandoned by him?

She pushed the dark thoughts aside, and grabbed her sandwich, and stood there enjoying it. Enjoying the momentary silence in the house, a rare luxury..

After finishing her meal, she checked her purse, making sure she had her house keys, before heading out the door. Within minutes, she was knocking on the door to Isolde's house. After a few moments, the door opened, with Isolde's foster mother standing on the other side. She was shorter and plumper than her husband, with a much lighter shade of brown skin and blond close cut hair.

"Why hello again, April. Isolde hadn't told us you'd be coming over. She's up in her room, I'm sure you know the way." She let April in as she spoke. April gave her a nod.

"Yeah, thanks for letting me in Mrs. Needen." As the woman closed and locked the door, April made her way down the hallway, and up the stairs, where she knocked on Isolde's door.

A LOUD KNOCKING ON her door shook Isolde awake. "Coming." She yelled, pulling herself off of the comfortable bed. She noticed that her music had stopped, and wondered if the phone had died as she opened the door.

As expected, she found herself letting April in, and watched as her friend took a seat at the small oak desk across from her bed. She closed her bedroom door and turned to face April as the girl spoke.

"So, assuming it's alright with your folks, I'll be staying over again tonight." Isolde recognized the tone in her voice at once and shook her head.

"Like, your mom's drinking again? What the hell." She leaned back against her bedroom door. As if she didn't have enough stress, her best friend's mom just had to make things worse.

"Better believe it. No sooner than I walked in the door, Cassie started it up with Mom. They only stopped right before I was headed out." Isolde had little trouble believing that, as the few times she'd met the girl left a very sour impression.

"Anyway, I'm here. What's this big thing you wanted to talk to me about." Isolde steeled herself, before walking across the room towards her open closet. She dreaded what she was about to do.

"Do me a favor, get Jess on a video call." She leaned against the wall as she waited for Jessica to answer. She must have been busy as it took several moments for her to answer.

"Heya girlies, what up?" Isolde noticed that Jessica was wearing her pajamas, despite it only being about five-thirty. She and April often teased her about the teddy-bear designs all over them, and their banana-yellow color that blended well with her blond hair.

For once, she wasn't really in the mood for friendly banter. She cleared her throat, getting both girls' attention. Jessica looked pretty neutral, while April held a slight grin.

"Well, to answer your greeting Jess, there's actually a lot going on." She took notice of the look of concern on April's face, while Jessica's remained neutral.

"I've, like, got some kind of news for you two. I actually have something to show you, girls." She turned, and closed the closet door, revealing the waitress uniform to her friends.

She watched their reactions, April had a look of confusion, while Jessica seemed unfazed. Isolde expected another wise-ass remark from her and was not disappointed.

"Wow, girl, red and white stripes? Didn't know you were that into candy canes. Don't you think that'll clash with that purple mess you call hair?" Wisecrack aside, she knew Jessica was right.

Just one more reason to hate this new chapter of her life. She reached down and picked up her nametag, and showed it to the others. This time it was April who spoke.

"Wait, is that? Did you get a job or something?" Isolded nodded her head. "Yup, yup, yup. Not exactly by choice or anything. The Needens thought it would be good for me, to build character or something."

She rolled her eyes as she spoke. She couldn't help but notice that April was looking down at the floor. She realized she had gotten it wrong, April was the one to worry about after all.

"So, is this a part-time thing or something? You aren't going to go full time and disappear from our lives or anything are you?" Isolde was expecting any number of reactions from her friends, but that one wasn't one of them.

She could tell her friend was genuinely concerned. She walked over and put her hand on April's shoulder to reassure her.

"Like hell. It's going to take a hell of a lot more than a summer job to get my ass out of you girls' hair." She noticed April's mood lighten up almost instantly.

Jessica on the other hand, once again relied on humor, or at least her brand of it. Isolde braced herself for the coming jab.

"Your ass? Did that come with the uniform or something? Didn't know any bean-poles ever had an ass." All three girls laughed at Jessica's comment, as Isolde walked over to the bed, to settle in and have a nice long conversation with her friends.

THE DISTANT PAST.

The thick hard leaves scratched her skin as she ran. The jungle was denser in these parts, few members of her tribe ever ventured this deep, this far from the tribe.

Even the hunters never strayed so far. The warrior stopped to catch her breath and gather her bearings in a small clearing. She squinted in the dim light, scanning the trees.

It didn't take her long before she spotted her mark. Off in the distance, a good thirty paces, sat a building. It struck her as odd. Its walls were slick and smooth, like the surface of water, but not at all clear. Rather, they were as crimson as blood.

She set off towards the strange building, thinking of the wood and thatch huts of her own village. Before long, she arrived at her destination. She felt the wall of the structure. It was smoother and harder than anything she knew of. What stuck out the most was how clearly she could see her reflection on it, like she was staring into water.

The walls were slanted, down from the top, and out to a point. From which it slanted back inwards, and down into the ground. She looked over it as far she could see, before it vanished into the dirt a short way away.

She looked around the structure, finding what she was looking for. She moved towards the opening, and made her way into the dark structure. She waited for several minutes, for her eyes to adjust to the darkness before moving further into the mysterious building.

Her senses were heightened, as she pushed her emotions out of her mind. The further in she ventured, the worse the air tasted on her breath. It was stale and left an odd taste in her mouth, not unlike blood.

With each passing step, more of the strange and unfamiliar shapes and objects stood out. She stopped next to one of the walls. It had platforms, made of the same strange material as the rest of the place, running across it.

She noticed many small objects, not unlike the clay jars of her village, as she reached out to grab a hold of one. It was smooth, and hard. She squinted her eyes in the dim light, noticing that the object was as clear as the still waters of a pond.

She moved on ahead, leaving the strange object behind. She stopped after a short while, as she noticed the ground didn't feel right. She looked around, squinting in the darkness as she took measure of the walls, and the ground.

She deduced that the reason it felt off was because she was walking at an angle, like she was walking down a fallen tree trunk. *This unusual cave must reach deep beneath the dirt,* she thought as she moved on.

Before long she had arrived in a small room, where she saw the objects she was here to collect. She reached out to take a hold of one, it was smooth, and rough at the same time. It reminded her of stone, or maybe a bone of some sort, but none she could recall.

She picked up a few more of the strange things, and began making her way back to the entrance. She gulped the fresh and humid air, hoping to clear the taste from her mouth as she set off towards her village.

SATURDAY, MAY 23RD Middle of the Night

Isolde woke in a cold sweat. The remnants of the dream still clouded her mind. Looking around the dark room, she noticed April sleeping on the futon next to her bed.

Shaking her head, she removed her covers, and got out of bed. Being sure to make as little noise as she could, she left her room. Continuing to be as stealthy as she could, she descended the stairs and made her way to the kitchen, where she poured herself a glass of water.

She stood there for a while, drinking her water and thinking back on the strange dream. It hadn't been the first of its kind. As long as she could remember, she'd had similar dreams, where she was in a jungle of some kind, always alone.

This one was the weirdest she could recall, as she was thinking back on the ones she did remember. Her reminiscing was interrupted, almost causing her to drop her glass.

"Can't sleep either, huh? She turned around to see April walking towards the sink, before getting her own glass of water. Isolde finished her water and rinsed out her glass.

"Like, not really, just had another of those weird dreams. What about you?" She leaned back against the counter as she spoke, watching her friend.

"That's funny, cause I was having a weird dream too." She let her friend finish taking a drink before asking. She was curious what kind of dream April had, given how often she claimed to not remember her dreams.

"Oh, well do tell. What kind of dream did you have, miss I don't remember my dreams?" She watched as April finished her drink and rinsed the glass before turning back to Isolde.

"Uh, nothing much. Nothing so interesting as running around a jungle, assuming those where the dreams you meant." Her voice carried some kind of tone that Isolde didn't recognize. She decided to press further.

"Like nope, nope, nope. I want more details girl." Was it her imagination, or did she see April shifting uncomfortably? "Wait, like, was it about a boy? You gotta tell me who."

Definitely not her imagination, as April was biting the knuckle of her finger. Something she only rarely did. "Umm, no, not really." Despite the darkness of the room, she was certain she saw April blushing as the girl turned away.

"It was, just, us, you know. You and me hanging out." Isolde raised an eyebrow, "Oh and yeah Jessica was there too. "April added hastily. "Yeah, umm the three of us were hanging out at that old park downtown and all. Nothing really to it, just weird you know?"

April gave a small chuckle as she finished speaking, one that Isolde couldn't help but notice sounded a bit nervous. She watched the girl putting her glass up, almost dropping it in the process. Isolde was starting to wonder about the odd behavior when she heard footsteps behind her.

"Well, what are you young ladies up to at this hour?" Mr Needen had entered the room. She watched as he followed the herd, going for the sink to fetch a glass of water.

"Oh, nothing much, Mr Needen, we just came down for some water is all." April's voice was back to normal, though Isolde was still curious about her friend's odd behavior. Something to question her about later, she thought.

"Like yeah, just had another of those jungle dreams, and came down for water. Guess I woke April up on the way or something." Her foster father gave a nod after looking between them.

"Ok, well you lot get on up to bed, ok? Especially you Isolde. Don't want to throw your sleeping cycle off and be late for your first shift on Monday."

His words hung in her ears. Her first shift. *This summer is going to suck.* The thought was interrupted by April's hand on her back.

"Ok, will do, Mr Needen. C'mon Isolde, let's get back to bed." She said a quick "Goodnight" to the man as she followed April back to her room. As she watched April return to the futon, Isolde checked her phone.

It was three-thirty in the morning, with her alarm set for seven. Another brilliant idea from the Needens. She rolled her eyes as she climbed into bed. She laid there for a while, thinking about how Monday was going to go.

About how, despite being summer vacation, she was still going to have to get up early every morning. Before long, she was drifting off to sleep.

Chapter 3

MONDAY MAY 25TH MORNING

Isolde rolled over in bed, looking for her phone. She spotted it on the corner, and grabbed it, silencing the alarm. It was seven in the morning, and time to prepare for her first day of work.

All she wanted to do was lay back down and sleep. Even getting up at this time the past two days did nothing to prepare her as she tried to clear the sleep from her mind.

She forced herself to get up and off of the bed. She knew if she didn't she would fall back asleep in moments. *Ugh, why'd I have to stay up so late talking to Jess.* She stood up, and stretched, before walking towards the closet.

The gaudy uniform still hung on the back of the closet door, with her nametag now pinned to it. With a heavy sigh, she removed the garment from its hanger, and left her room.

The morning light was still dim, as it filtered through the window at the end of the hall, as she made the short trip over to the upstairs bathroom to have a quick shower.

Twenty minutes later, she emerged from the bathroom, in her work attire, and made her way down the hall to her room, where she gathered her purse and work shoes, a pair of dress shoes, in that same hideous red and white striped pattern.

As she finished lacing the shoes she began to make her way out of the room before stopping to look in the mirror over her desk. *Well, that does it, my social life is dead when I walk out that door.*

Pushing the thought aside, she made her way out of the room, and down to the kitchen. As she was waiting for the toaster pastries to warm up, Mrs. Needen walked into the kitchen.

"Morning sweetie, glad to see you up and ready for work." The woman gave a smile that Isolde couldn't help but return, despite how anxious she felt inside.

"Yup, yup, yup. Time to go make a fool of myself, and look like a candy-cane while I'm at it." The pastries popped up, as Mrs. Needen gave a warm laugh.

"Oh shush you, you'll do fine. I'm sure Mrs. Burke will spend the day teaching you the ropes. You'll do fine sweetie." She leaned in and gave Isolde a kiss on her forehead before moving on towards the coffee pot.

"Like, I hope so. Anyway, I'm going to finish my breakfast and head out." She grabbed the warm pastries, and headed out to the porch, where she set into them. The chocolate fudge flavor hit every sweet spot she had, and as she finished and was unlocking her bike, she felt ready to take on the day.

She walked her bike down off the porch, and mounted it. The air was a bit chilly, with a steady breeze blowing as she pedaled off, wishing she had grabbed a jacket.

Another twenty minutes later, she was locking her bike up out behind the Family Diner. Mrs. Burke was standing in the employee doorway waiting for her.

"Pleased to see you made it on time, young lady." She gave Isolde a warm smile and a curt nod. "Now, Mr Needen assures me you are a bright and dedicated young lady, so I expect good things from you." Isolde took a deep breath, and turned towards the doorway.

"Yes ma'am, Mrs. Burke. I try to give my best at everything I do." She heard a tsk from the woman as she was walking towards the doorway.

"Oh no, that'll never do. Call me Daisy, darlin. Now come on, we gotta get this show on the road." Isolde followed the short and plump woman into the kitchen. Her own uniform, identical to Isoldes, did little to conceal the woman's love of the food her husband, the cook, prepared.

Isolde wondered if the woman's wrinkles as well as the streaks of gray in her short blonde hair were only from age, or from the stress of running one of the only restaurants on this side of town. Daisy stopped, and pointed to the large, middle-aged man with short jet-black hair in a net, manning the large griddle-top stove.

"That there hunk of a man is my husband, Larry." Not turning away from his stove, he gave a "'Pleasure to meet you, young lady," before pouring a glass of water on the griddle. As it began to sizzle, Daisy continued the tour.

They next stopped at a small room, with a few fold-up metal chairs, and a desk with a computer in the corner. "And this here's the employee room darlin. That there computers gonna be how you clock-in, and out. Come along and I'll walk you through it. She did as instructed, and a few minutes later, was officially on the clock for her first shift.

An hour later, Daisy had finished the grand tour, and Isolde had a loose grasp on how things would go. She looked at the clock, which read eight-fifty-eight, and prepared herself.

In two minutes, the show begins. She fiddled with the apron Daisey had given her to wear, and felt around in the pockets. A handful of napkins sat in one pocket, and a notepad with a pen rested in the other. Movement outside the window caught her eye.

A blue minivan pulled up, and a young woman exited the driver's side, before going around to let her young toddler out. *Like great, first customers of the day.* She thought as she made her way to unlock the main entrance.

THE SOUND OF A DOOR slamming shook April awake. She sighed, rolling her eyes as she grabbed her phone. The notification light was flashing so she woke it from sleep mode. It was a quarter past ten am.

Wonder how Isolde's liking her new job. She wondered as she checked her notifications. A group text for her and Jessica, from Isolde.

"Like morning bitches. Yours truly is off to work. Wish me luck, like all of the luck. Text you girls later." She opened the message and saw Jessica had already replied. "GL girly, you got this."

She fired off her own message of encouragement as another slammed door startled her into dropping her phone. Followed by the start of another shouting match.

She climbed out of bed, realizing the futility of trying to go back to sleep now that Cassie was on the warpath again. She left the room and made her way downstairs, toward the kitchen. She spotted Rachel at the small white plastic kitchen table, eating a bagel.

"Mornin sis." she said, not looking up from the book she was reading. April admired how Rachel was able to keep her cool enough to read despite Cassie's antics.

"Good morning to you too." She made her way to the cabinets and pulled out a bowl and a box of cereal. As she was grabbing the milk from the fridge, the sound of her mother and Cassandra's shouting match got closer.

"Oh fucking please, Mom. Like you would even know I'm gone. If it's not in a bottle you don't even care." April shook her head, finding it hard to disagree with her younger sister.

"Dammit Cassandra, watch your mouth." Their mother responded as the front door opened, and slammed shut, signaling Cassandra had left the building. She heard the sound of her mother heading back up the stairs as she poured a bowl of cereal and joined Rachel at the table.

"She's getting worse every day, ain't she?" April looked over to Rachel, who had put her book down and was looking at her. Rachel's comment was correct, as April thought back over the last few months.

She was pretty sure that every day she was here, and not at Isolde's place or with Jessica, that Cassandra and their mom had gotten into it. On top of her getting into enough trouble at school that expulsion was on the table this past year.

"You can say that again. Woke me up from a nice and relaxing sleep." Her comment forced a long laugh from Rachel. She looked over at her sister, who was shaking her head while she laughed.

Her curly brown hair, much longer than April's own, and much lighter, bounced as her head moved. April felt a hint of jealousy at her body, which was athletic and fit, unlike her chunky self, as Cassandra often insulted her with.

"Really? You're telling me you slept through the worst of it? Lucky." April sighed, nodding. Her sister's words should have come as a shock, but somehow, she knew Rachel was understating the truth.

"Let's just say, you might wanna be careful if you go into the downstairs bathroom. She threw something at Mom earlier, and hit the mirror." This time Rachel's words did shock her.

As bad as Cassandra was, she couldn't think of a time when the girl had resorted to that level of violence against another person, let alone their mom. As she finished another bite of cereal, she watched as Rachel was getting up from the table.

"Thanks for the heads up, Rach. You heading out too?" She watched as Rachel rinsed off her plate, and began heading towards the living room.

"Yeah, gonna do mom a solid and clean up Cassie's temper tantrum, and then head over to Lisa's. You?" April finished the last bite of cereal and got up from the table to rinse out her own bowl.

"That's good. I'm thinking of swinging by that old Diner on Thirteenth Street. Isolde just started working down there." Rachel's eyebrow rose before she spoke.

"Oh, is that so? You mean the Family Diner?" April nodded, finishing up her used dish and returning the milk to the fridge. "Well, small world. That's where me and Lisa get lunch now and then. Guess we'll end up running into you little lovebirds later"

April rolled her eyes, as Rachel disappeared into the living room. "Ha ha, very funny, Rach." She yelled after her sister. She sighed as she returned the cereal to the cabinet. As she began the trip back to her room, the memories of the strange dream she was having before her rude awakening came back to her. The latest in a string of similar dreams over the last few months.

This one had taken place in an old park the two of them had discovered some years ago, hidden between a group of abandoned buildings. But what really puzzled her was not where it took place, but what had happened in it. She had been walking with Isolde, a common enough thing.

What wasn't so common, was the fact that the two of them had been holding hands. And, that it hadn't been uncomfortable, or even awkward. She pushed the memories out as she went upstairs to shower and get ready for the short ride down to the diner.

"ORDER-UP". MR. BURKE'S voice called out, before the subsequent ding of the small bell. She knew, out of everything about this job that was going to suck, that bell was going to take top billing.

She made her way behind the counter, and loaded the dishes onto her tray. She balanced the tray as she made her way to the table that had ordered it.

"One cheeseburger, hold the mayo, extra pickles, with a side of baked macaroni and cheese. " She read back the order as she approached, and began unloading the food onto the table. The elderly man thanked her, and she was off again.

The equally as irritating smaller bell, this one hanging over the door, sounded as she gritted her teeth. *Like seriously, how many customers does this place get in a day.* She took a moment to gather her composure, and turned to face the newcomer. Her face lit up.

"April?" She shook her head to regain her composure. "I mean, Welcome to the Family Diner. We're here to turn your hunger into pure satisfaction, one scrumptious bite at a time. May I show you to a booth?" The terrible line, something Daisy was ever so proud of, caused her best friend to burst out laughing.

"Sure, lead on." Isolde shook her head once more, any joy at seeing April fading away as she led her friend to an open booth. As April took a seat, she leaned in and whispered in her ear.

"Like girl, cool to see you but please tell me you are actually here to order. Much as I'd love to, I can't afford to goof off right now." April gave her a big smile, and nodded as she took the menu from its stand and began to look it over.

"Yeah, mom gave me some money to get something to eat, so I figured I'd come check this place out, and, ya know, poke fun at you." Isolde held back the frown she felt coming on. Great, Jessica's rubbing off on her. She pushed the annoyance from her mind, not wanting to get distracted.

"Oh, and umm, Rachel and her friends apparently eat here often, so I'll probably find some way to join them here and there."

Isolde nodded her head, and failed to hold back the small chuckle as she withdrew her notepad and pen. The idea of her best friend popping up more often both excited and worried her, knowing how much trouble the two of them could get into if she wasn't careful.

"Well then, what can I get you this fine, beautiful afternoon, ma'am?" April set the menu down and gave Isolde the side-eye. Her confusion was evident as she mouthed the word "ma'am?"

Isolde stifled another chuckle as she explained that it was just another "part of the job" She took down aprils order, a chicken salad with lite italian dressing, a large unsweetened tea, and a small side of in-house potato chips.

She made her way back behind the counter, as Daisy made her exit from the employee room, and began to watch her. She tore the ticket from the notepad, and stuck it in the slider, and dinged the small bell. "Order-in."

She turned to look around the lobby, and took a deep breath, at the short reprieve of no new customers. She heard Daisy walking towards her and turned to face her boss.

"Color me impressed darlin. You are doing a wonderful job so far. Dare I say better than that no'good'fer'nothin layabout that you done replaced. Keep it up girl, and you'll go far." She nodded, as Daisy made her way into the kitchen after patting her on the back.

She leaned against the counter, taking a breather, before glancing at the clock, noting that it was one-twenty five. News that put a smile on her face, as if she understood Daisy during her initiation, she had a fifteen minute break set for one-thirty.

While she waited on April's food, she made her way to the employee computer and checked, confirming her suspicion. She hung around for a few minutes, and clocked in her break, just as she heard that infernal bell, and Mr. Burke's "Order up."

She made her way out and around to pick up the order, letting Daisy know that she had started her break, before grabbing April's meal. Daisy gave her a polite nod, and took the apron from her, as she made her way to April's booth.

"Well, well, well, guess you just have the best timing ever. Just went on break for the next fifteen. She laid April's food out and slid in the booth across from her.

"Really? Sweet deal. So, then. How's the work life going so far?" April asked as Isolde settled in and gave her friend a rundown of her day so far.

As the two spoke, she noticed a Sheriff cruiser pull into the lot, and a young deputy got out. She watched as he let someone out of the back seat. The boy looked similar enough to the deputy, both being short and stocky, with blond close-cropped hair as to be related.

She watched as Daisy gave them that corny greeting, before checking her phone. Eight minutes left, as she sighed, and ate another of April's potato chips.

"Hey, stop that. I gotta maintain my lovely figure somehow, after all." April patted her stomach, prompting both girls to laugh.

She stopped laughing as she noticed the teen who came in with the deputy walking towards them. The look on his face gave away his intentions, as she braced herself for some kind of pick-up line.

"Sup, hunnies. How's it going? Looking for some company while we eat?" Isolde looked at April, as both girls rolled their eyes. She checked her phone. Six minutes left. She hoped this guy would take a hint, not relishing the idea of clocking back in and leaving April to fend for herself with him.

"Like, thanks but no thanks, dude, we aren't interested." April just nodded her head. "So like, could you please leave us alone?" The boy was undeterred and he was staring at April. *That pig, he's totally scoping her chest out.* She restrained herself from doing any of the dozen thoughts running through her mind, not wanting to get in trouble on her first day.

"Like, hey, eyes up here dude." She lifted her hand and snapped her fingers, before pointing her middle and index fingers outwards, and moved them from her own eyes to just in front of April's. The boy just laughed, causing her to grit her teeth.

Knowing how some guys could be, she figured job or nor job, someone had to teach him how to treat a woman with some respect. She was balling her fist, and was just about to get herself fired, when salvation came.

"Now sonny, I do believe I heard the young ladies here tell you they wasn't interested. Now you go on and shoo off, can't have you bugging my guests." Her eyes narrowed a bit as she looked at Isolde sitting across from April.

"Or employees." Daisy gave Isolde a questioning look as she checked her phone. Three minutes left, time to head back and clock back in. The deputy shouted something at the teen, who took off back to the other side of the diner.

April looked at Daisy, relief plain as day on her face. "Thank you, ma'am, he was bothering us." The older woman gave April a smile, and nodded her head. Isolde got up from the table and began to make her way back to the employee room.

"Like, time to go clock-back in. Enjoy the rest of your lunch girly, and I'll catch ya later." Daisy followed her back to the computer, returning the apron to her after she clocked back in. "

Gonna make it a habit of socializing on yer breaks darlin?" Isolde laughed, and shook her head. Daisy hadn't outright forbidden it, but gave the strong impression she wasn't fond of workers mingling with the diners on duty.

"Like, no, just a pleasant surprise, that girl is my best friend. Came in to get some lunch and give her support." Daisy smiled, and the two women made their way back into the diner and got back to work.

"HEYA SIS." APRIL TURNED around in the booth, to see Rachel, alongside another girl she didn't recognize, entering the diner. Lisa, judging from their earlier conversation.

"Hey, Stopping by for lunch?" She asked her sister, before she was led to a nearby booth by Isolde. April couldn't help but smile, realizing just how much effort Isolde was putting into this new job.

"You know it, best damn baked chicken salad in town." Rachel looked down at April's mostly finished salad as she walked past, and laughed. "Not that I need to be telling you huh? Great minds really do think alike." April couldn't resist a smile and a "Yup," as Rachel moved on to find her seat.

April sat around for several more minutes as she finished her tea, and turned around to look for Isolde, who was already on her way over.

"Your total, ma'am." She said, handing April a bill. She handed it back to Isolde along with the $20 her mother had given her. "And keep the change, ma'am" She said, her tone of voice taking a turn for the sarcastic at the last word. She watched Isolde walking off towards the counter after rolling her eyes, and failing to hold back a smile.

April got up to make her exit, giving Isolde a wave goodbye, a gesture her friend returned. As she headed towards the door, she saw the boy from earlier, once again looking at her, while talking to the girl who had come in with Rachel. She turned her eyes away, a feeling of disgust rising in her, as she muttered to herself, "creep" before exiting.

As she made her way towards her bike, she pulled out her phone to text Jessica. "Hey girl. Just scoped out Isolde at her new job. Doing pretty good honestly, you'd almost think she's been at it all her life.

Btw, you are so right, that uniform is gag city LMAO. Anyway, HMU, maybe we can hang for a bit."

She mounted her bike, and began to pedal away when her phone notification sounded, prompting her to stop and check it. "FML. So want to, but Sarah is on her way, gonna bunk with us for a couple of weeks. TTYL, and duh, told you girls that thing was FUGLY."

April sent a smiley face and thumbs-up emoji in response, and took one last look back inside the diner through the large windows. Isolde was walking towards the other end of the lobby, a tray full of food balanced on her right arm. April gave a soft sigh as she watched her friend, before turning to pedal off, back towards home.

Chapter 4

FRIDAY MAY 29TH AFTERNOON

As she clocked out, Isolde could not hide her excitement. Her first full week of work was over, and it had gone so well. More than that, all of her fears about the job ended up being for nothing as she found herself liking the job a lot.

She checked her phone on her way towards the employee door. A text from Jessica confirmed they were here, and waiting for her. She waved goodbye to Daisy as she left through the employee door onto the back lot where her best friends were waiting.

"Bout time. You'd almost think you care more about some job than your own friends, girlie." Jessica's playful banter just lifted her spirits further, as she unlocked her bike.

"Like, not on your life. So, you girls ready to swim, swim, swim?" As Isolde mounted her bike, April gave a soft laugh while Jessica took off pedaling.

"You know it, Ducky." April began pedaling as well, so Isolde followed suit. "Man, it's going to feel so good, given this slog of a heatwave." April said as the trio began pedaling off, making good on the plans they had made the night before to go to the river.

Wiping the sweat from her brow, Isolde had to agree. The past three days had been scorchers, with yesterday being the worst at a blistering ninety-five degrees. She didn't even bother riding her bike in that hell, getting a ride to and from work with Mr Needen instead. Something she would have tried to do again if she didn't already have plans.

The trio pedaled on, the current eighty-six-degree weather not feeling much better than the last couple of days. Especially with her stuffy work uniform that she wished she'd changed before leaving.

Before long, they had reached the edge of town, and the quiet and slow river that made up a border along two-thirds of the town. As they came to a stop in a small clearing alongside the riverbank, Jessica was already stripping down.

April began removing her own tshirt and shorts, and Isolde found herself joining in, happy to be out of that uniform. Within minutes, all three girls had removed their outer layers revealing their swimsuits beneath.

Isolde couldn't help but laugh at Jessica's single-piece suit. Much like her pajamas, it was a banana-yellow color, with a large green teddy bear on the front. She couldn't help but think it looked like something they would have worn when they were kids.

"What's so funny about my swimsuit, candy cane?" Jessica didn't even try to hide the mirth in her voice as she quipped back. Isolde struck a pose, turning her back to her friends, with her arm lifted in a flourish. "Like, how dare you talk to your candy-cane queen in such a manner." She put on a deep voice as she spoke.

"Sigh, the peasants must always be jealous of their betters." Her forced voice cracking up as she spoke while turning to face her friends. "Like this sweet ass two-piece."

She gave a twirl as she finished speaking, prompting an eye-roll from April, and another wisecrack from Jessica.

"Sweet ass? I mean sure, it's a nice swimsuit, but umm," she looked around, her left hand over her eyes as she spoke, "where's the ass, again?"

Isolde put her own hand to her face and gave a mock gasp. She turned her back to Jessica and slapped her rear. "Right here, girl. It's like, totally cool. I know you're just jealous." Jessica laughed at the sight while April remained quiet.

"Nah, girlie. Who'd be jealous of that? Things hanging out of your bikini bottom and I still can't tell where it begins and your legs end." The two went on for a few more minutes tossing increasingly ridiculous jokes at one another, before Isolde realized something.

"Like, hey, greatest pair of asses in the world to April, " She and Jessica both looked at April, and she snapped fingers to get April's attention, "what's wrong girl?"

April was staring off across the river, at the woods, a sullen look on her rounded face. She turned to face them, and Isolde's mood sank, and her tone shifted hard. Something was seriously bothering the girl. She watched as April struggled with her words for a few moments.

"It's Cassie." April had turned away again, back towards the trees. "Got woke up again this morning to her lovely voice, screaming at Rachel." Isolde walked over and put her hand on her friend's back, and began rubbing it. A gesture that she saw was appreciated as a small smile crept across April's face.

"They were still going at it when I got out of the shower, so I went down to make some food. Ended up talking to Mom for a bit." Isolde felt bad, anytime April's mom came into the conversation she knew things were going bad for her friend.

"The sibling fight made its way downstairs, where Mom naturally joined in." Isolde could feel the tension in April's back. "Well, to shorten a long story, Cassie was pissed because mom didn't have a spare hundred so she could get some outfit she and her friend wanted."

Isolde found herself confused, as it wasn't any kind of secret that the Levae's weren't financially well off, so what could have prompted such a ridiculous request in the first place.

"So she flipped out, and shoved mom to the floor before she left the house." The tension in April's back worsened, as Isolde felt like she was rubbing a car tire. April had mentioned something about the girl smashing a mirror, but to actually attack her own mother was unreal.

"Damn girlie, did your mom at least smack her or something? Shit if I shoved my father, he'd have me flying back to Victoria City, and not exactly by plane if you know what I mean." April shook her head to answer Jessica's question.

Isolde expected where the story was going next, and sighed when she was correct. "Rachel took off after her, and Mom didn't say anything, she just grabbed a couple of beers and went and locked herself in her room."

"Well, that explains why you've been so quiet today for." Jessica shook her head, before her frown faded, replaced by a grin.

"Shit girl, you're worrying too much. Your mom's just blowing off some steam. Can't say I'd blame her for it either if the few times I've met your sister is any indication." Isolde felt the tell-tale shudders going through April's back before her friend began sobbing softly.

Once more, Isolde's mood took a hard shift. She turned to face Jessica, balling her hands up. "Like what? What the hell Jess, that's not cool, dammit. You know how her mom is with the alcohol. Why do you think Cassie is so bad in the first place?" Jessica was visibly shaken from her sudden verbal lashing and turned away from Isolde.

"Yeah, you're right." Jessica walked over to April, putting her arms around the girl in a big hug.. "Sorry girlie, really. You know I didn't mean anything, just like to speak before I think." Something Isolde had no trouble agreeing with.

"Anyway, the waters calling, let's go." She watched as April took their friend's hand, and held it for a moment, before nodding her head. At that, Jessica ran off and jumped in the river, creating a large splash and sending ripples all over the once-still water.

Her momentary flash of anger had now subsided, Isolde looked back towards April, who was drying her eyes. Her friend turned and gave her a warm smile before she too went for the river, opting to wade in and stand around near the shore.

Watching her two friends, Isolde made her way toward the water. As she broke off into a run, a fun idea came to mind. She was now determined to jump in the water right between them, getting them both with the splash, as her thoughts turned towards her reaction.

They all knew Jessica was a wiseass who didn't always think things through, so why had she snapped so hard at her? As she hit the water, she couldn't help for feel bad for Jessica over her out of character reaction, something she'd make sure to apologize for.

STANDING IN THE WATER was refreshing. The cool water, running past her with the gentlest of currents, almost took her mind off of her family drama. Just once, she wished she could wake up to a normal house, a fun younger sister she could talk to and enjoy being around.

A mother who at least acted like she cared. She felt her mood slipping once more as she thought of her Mom, of all the pain the woman had caused, not only to herself but to her sisters over the years. Her thoughts were broken by a sudden noise behind her.

She heard the sound of Isolde running behind her and turned just in time to watch her friend cannonball into the river, right in front of her. The resulting splash hit her, and despite its unexpected suddenness, it was still refreshing, albeit unwanted.

Jessica had a short coughing fit, having taken the brunt of the splash, before the girl said a single word, "bitch," to Isolde. April found herself laughing, before flinging her own insult to her best friend. "Jerk."

She couldn't help but smile as she watched Isolde floating there, just ignoring their jabs, staring up at the canopy of tree limbs above them. Jessica took off and was now swimming up the river, being sure to not venture too far from the shoreline.

Not wanting to be the only landlocked friend, April waded out a little further, kicking herself off the bank, letting herself float along. She had to kick her feet a little more than she anticipated, as the current was stronger this far out, but it was still mild enough to be a non-issue.

She closed her eyes, floating along, feeling completely at ease. Her thoughts turned back towards the past, to all the times the three of them had been at this very spot over the years.

Now that Isolde worked five days a week, these opportunities would be fewer, a fact she knew she had to get used to. Guess this is what they mean by growing up, she thought, as her thoughts were interrupted.

The sound of splashing water made her open her eyes, and look towards the sound, a slight panic hitting her. Her moment of concern passed, as she watched Isolde and Jessica, laughing and splashing each other. She let out the breath she had held as she realized nobody was drowning.

She found herself watching Isolde, studying her face, which was beaming with happiness. looking at her friend's permanent tan left her feeling annoyed that she had forgotten sunscreen, as even with the shade of the trees, she was going to burn.

Several moments later, she forced herself to look away, feeling a different kind of burn in her cheeks As Isolde caught her staring. She shook her head and turned away from her friends.

What was that, you goofball? The thought came to her, as she wondered why she had been staring so intently at Isolde. Something she found herself doing a lot of lately. On top of those weird dreams. She thought once more, questioning what was going on with herself.

It wasn't just her, as she'd been noticing odd behavior from Isolde as well. She thought back to just before they had all gotten into the water. Jessica's words had hurt, but she knew her friend didn't mean anything bad. Isolde knew it as well, often getting riled up into Jessica's little games like that.

So why had Isolde gotten so defensive of her, that she would lash out at Jessica? She thought it might be stress from work, but all week all Isolde could do was brag about how much fun the job was.

As her friends continued to play around, she floated along for a long time, thinking over the situation before her thoughts were broken. She opened her eyes to see Jessica swimming past, towards the shore. Moments later the girl emerged and began walking towards their pile of clothes and bikes.

Isolde followed close behind, yelling at April, "Like, last one outs the stinkball girl." April found herself smiling, and shook her head as she made her own way to the shore. By the time she made her exit, Isolde was already hiding behind a couple of large trees, changing out of her wet swimwear.

Isolde's long hair, which was thin and straight and hung all the way past her waist, was now soaked and clung to her skin. The dark purple she kept it dyed in, a drastic change from her natural red hair made it stand out all the more.

As Isolde was buttoning her bra, April found herself cringing at the idea of keeping all that hair maintained. Something Isolde didn't seem too concerned over judging by all her split ends. Isolde bent over to pick up her uniform, which she had lain on a log, giving April a view she wasn't expecting nor wanting as she quickly turned away.

Her cheeks flushed with that tell-tale blush as she once more realized she had been staring, though she felt lucky that this time, Isolde had not caught her.

Before she could begin walking towards their bikes and clothes, she felt someone pulling her arm, and turned to see Jessica, leading her away, towards the trees on the other side of the clearing. Jessica had a serious look on her face, leading April to swallow hard, and brace herself.

"Ok, level with me. Is everything alright with you two?" The question left her confused, with Jessica picking up on it before elaborating. "Well, for starters the way Isolde came at me earlier." April was as concerned with it as Jessica was, but wasn't sure why she was being asked about it.

"I mean I deserved it but it was still a shock. And then we get out of the water, and there you are, blushing redder than my bike. Blushing as you were, you know, staring at Isolde's buck naked non-existent ass. So please, make it make sense."

April closed her eyes feeling that all too familiar burn in her cheeks once more. Isolde hadn't seen her that time, but Jessica had. She didn't know what to say, how to explain her actions because she herself didn't understand why she had done so.

She didn't know why she had done so any of the times she caught herself doing it. Worse, and something she was for sure not going to bring up to Jessica, was how she was feeling inside while she watched.

She opened her eyes, looking at Jessica and shaking off the thoughts. She was still waiting on a response and looking impatient.

"I wish I had an answer, but I don't. I mean Isolde's reaction caught me just as off guard as it did you." Jessica was nodding her head, before giving an "and?" April took a deep breath.

Jessica wasn't going to let it go, and to be fair, why would she? She thought back to how upset Isolde had been when she caught that boy staring at her own chest that day in the diner. Now, April was the one doing the staring, seeing a lot more than he had or ever would. She shook her head, hard, trying to clear the mental image out.

"As for me watching her, I have no answer." This time, it was Jessica who shook her head. April felt terrible, she had enough drama at home to deal with, now her she was sparking it up with one of her closest friends. She found herself trying to come up with some excuse that Jessica might buy.

Her attempt was brought short by the sound of a phone ringing nearby. She followed Jessica's gaze, watching a much deeper frown cross her friend's face. The specific ringtone was a dead giveaway that all three of them knew.

As Jessica walked over to answer her father's call, she felt sorry for her friend, knowing that their fun in the sun was now over. She grabbed her own clothes and made for the darkened hiding spot Isolde had changed in, and slipped out of her own solid blue one-piece bathing suit.

She took a look back at her friends as she changed back into her t-shirt and shorts. Jessica was arguing with her father on the phone, and Isolde was standing beside her, her hand on Jessica's shoulder.

As she began walking towards them, she felt a slight twinge of something, at the sight. A dark feeling she had never felt about Isolde, one one that left her all the more confused. She pushed the brief snippet of jealousy out of her mind as she approached.

"Fine, fine. I'm on my way. Yeah, ok, bye." She watched Jessica shut the phone off, before dropping it back on her dry clothes. Her face was red, though unlike her own red face earlier, something told her Jessica wasn't blushing. The anger in her friend's voice confirmed her suspicion.

"Fucking hell. Dad was supposed to be out for another hour or two, but he came back early. And yeah, I'm busted." She watched Jessica pick up her clothes, and walk towards the makeshift changing room for her own turn. She turned back to Isolde who had a depressed look on her face.

"Like, man, I feel sorry for her. You too. You both have such hard parents to deal with." This time, it was April who began rubbing her friend's back. She didn't know why she did it, it was more of Isolde's thing but she rolled with it.

"Yeah, can't argue with you there. Anyway, it's no big deal, right? At least we have families, even if they are hard to deal with." She smiled softly at Isolde before realizing her mistake. "Or lacking that biological connection in the case of a certain totally amazing person I know." she added on, hoping she hadn't just upset another friend.

Isolde laughed instead of being upset, putting her hand over her lips. April felt the relief wash through her as Isolde tilted her head.

"Like, really? When were you planning on introducing us to this totally awesome person then?" Both girls laughed as April picked up her purse, rummaged through it for a compact, and opened it, pointing the small mirror at Isolde.

"There, I've introduced you. Isolde, meet totally awesome person." Both of them burst out in heavy laughter as Jessica rejoined them, confused. She explained the joke as the three gathered their purses, mounted their bikes and pedaled off.

Chapter 5

SUNDAY MAY 31ST MORNING

April sat on the edge of her bed. The fog of sleep still weighing heavy on her, before her senses began to return. She could hear crying from the hallway, as she sat there, waiting for her brain to catch up with the rest of her now awake body.

Shouting from the hallway snapped her to attention. *Ugh, do they ever quit?* She thought, pulling herself out of bed to the sound of her mother shouting something in the hall. As she was stretching, she heard another person shouting. She raised an eyebrow and began to make her way to the door.

That was Rachel's voice. Those two never fight. She thought, stepping out into the hallway. She covered her mouth to stifle a gasp as she saw her mother.

Rachel was standing there, looking down at their mother, who was sitting on the floor. Her make-up was smeared from heavy crying, and April saw what looked to be an excessive amount of the stuff around her right eye.

Realization dawned on her that her mother had a black eye. Both women had stopped their fight as April left her room. Their mom was looking at the floor, Rachel continued staring at their mother, a look on her face that scared April. Their mom eventually broke the silence.

"Don't worry it's not as bad as it looks. Just a workplace accident." April was left there, her mouth agape, trying to figure out how to respond as Rachel helped their mother up, and onwards to the bathroom. She looked back and spoke to April as their mom entered the bathroom.

"Cassies in the downstairs bathroom, and trust me, not one of her better moods." She thanked Rachel for the heads up as the door closed. The shower and tub were off-limits, so she decided to go downstairs to make some breakfast.

Several minutes later, she was at the flimsy kitchen table enjoying a bagel with strawberry jam. She had run the situation she just witnessed through her mind several times, but no matter how she approached it it didn't make sense.

Last night was the latest in a series of weird disappearances their mom had been having overnight the last several months. Sometimes she claimed she was visiting a friend, other times a late-night job.

As a new thought entered her mind, Cassandra entered the kitchen. She didn't pay any attention to the young girl as she tried to think back, before accepting that she had no idea what their mother actually did for a living these days.

The woman went through jobs like Cassandra went through temper tantrums, and it had been a while since she had been let go from the last one she had. If Rachel hadn't stepped in with her own job, none of them may even have a house to live in right now.

Her thoughts were interrupted by the sound of something being slammed nearby. She looked up from her half-eaten bagel to see the milk jug on the other side of the table. A moment later, Cassandra was setting a bowl down hard enough that April worried it would shatter.

"Morning sis." She offered, expecting some insult hurled her way. "Yeah, whatever." The reply took her by surprise. She had expected a quip about her weight, or a jab about her looks, or really anything, but wasn't displeased to be wrong.

"See Mom?" Her sister asked, pouring a bowl of cereal. April nodded. "Says it happened at work." Now pouring the milk, her sister let out a derisive laugh. "Tell me something, between all those donuts you shovel down, you ever find time to wonder just what it is mom actually does? You know, besides drink her stupid ass to sleep every other night?" That was more like her sister. April shook her head.

"To be honest, I was actually just thinking about that before you walked in. Because she's gone for hours at a time, but there's no real consistency to her schedule." A fact that she was now thinking much harder about. Any actual job would have some kind of consistency, wouldn't it? The thought was something she figured on looking up sometime. "Oh, and it's a bagel, not a donut." Her comment prompted a snort from her sister.

"Whatever, like there's a difference anyway." She watched as Cassie returned the milk to the fridge, and contemplated trying to explain the difference between a bagel and a doughnut. But she pushed the idea aside realizing it would just push her sister into another tantrum, and she didn't feel like having a bowl of cereal lobbed at her.

"See ya, Cassie." She said as her sister was leaving the room no longer interested in their little chat it seemed, throwing her hand up and back in an aggressive wave as she left.

Once more alone with her thoughts, she took another bite of the bagel, savoring the way the jam added just enough sweetness to the otherwise bland food to make an enjoyable snack. She sat there for several more minutes, enjoying and finishing the bagel, before rinsing her plate and heading upstairs to gather a change of clothes to shower.

ISOLDE SAT AT HER DESK, bored despite the phone call with Jessica she was engaged in. "Like yup, yup, yup. The dude tripped and threw his coffee as he went down, and it went all over Daisy.

Was so funny, right up until she pointed me over to the mop." She giggled as she was describing one of the few notable incidents that had happened at work, a subject Jessica had been curious about.

"Man, I bet she was pissed. Can't imagine a coffee stain would do much to compliment those candy-cane skirts." Both girls broke out laughing, as Isolde thought back to that day, and the large stain Daisy had on the rest of that shift.

"Oh you know it. The only thing bigger than her frown that day was the stain." Isolde shook her head, chuckling at the imagery. That nagging sense of boredom creeping back in, as she once again caught her thoughts drifting.

"Man, sounds like a fun place to be." Jessica's voice took on a note of sadness as she spoke. "Not that Dad would ever even consider letting me work that far from home. Still, would love to see the candy canes in their natural habitat." Isolde had to shake her head as Jessica's tone of voice rose with her wisecrack.

"Like you should totally swing by sometime, You know, when you aren't grounded." Her jab prompted a groan from Jessica. "My break is usually around one-thirty."

"Yeah, might have to take you up on that. Though, just so we're clear on the whole grounded thing? Worth it." Isolde couldn't hold back the biggest grin as she thought back to their time at the river. Just how much fun it was, something she had forgotten until that day. Her reminiscing was cut short as she heard someone in the background on Jessica's end shouting.

"Ugh, Dad's back. Gotta get gone before he finds out I violated my phone probation. Later girlie." Isolde hung up the phone after her own goodbye, plugged it into a charger, and went and laid back on her bed. She lay there, staring up at the white ceiling, boredom growing stronger every minute.

Trying to keep her mind occupied, she thought back to her first week of work. She was proud of herself, as she hadn't gotten any orders wrong, or messed anything up. She had taken to the job like a fish takes to water, as Daisy had told her.

She then thought about the call with Jessica, wondering if she would actually be able to come by sometime. The idea of it was something she hoped would happen. *Get that girl out of the house and away from her father for a bit, be good for her.*

Her thoughts then turned to April, and how three of the days she worked, her friend had swung by. Twice she made it in time to catch Isolde on break, but the third day Isolde had gone on break earlier than anticipated and thus missed her friend that day.

Man, if both of them showed up one day on break. The thought brought a sense of joy to her, making her appreciate the job all the more. Something she never thought she'd find herself thinking. *Plus, there's all that money I'll be getting.* The thought of being able to buy all the snack cakes she wanted tantalized her, before her thoughts turned back to April.

She lay there, thinking. Despite the fact that Isolde had moved in here eleven years ago, becoming best friends the same day she had arrived, she never really got to know her friend's family. April was over here almost constantly over the years, but Isolde had only been inside April's house what? A dozen, maybe two, times at most over the years? She had had actual conversations with April's sisters far fewer times even.

She had met both of her sisters here and there, and seen their mom a few times, but she struggled to think of any occasion she had spent any real time with any of them besides Rachel, who had hung out with her and April a few times over the years. Before she got her own first job that was.

Thinking of Rachel's early workforce debut put her mind back on the subject of money, and another odd thought about April. On her first day, April said her mother gave her some money, so that ruled out Rachel. Yet as far as April ever mentioned, her mother wasn't employed. Hard to get a job when you're always piss drunk and blacked-out. The thought stung, as while it was far from inaccurate, it wasn't right to think of her best friend's only parent like that.

Thinking back on the subject of money, it wasn't a secret to any of them that the Levae's weren't well off. What was more of a secret, even Jessica hadn't been told, was just how close they were to financial ruin. If Rachel weren't pulling overtime and double shifts, her best friend might not even have a home. The thought pushed her to her feet, and onwards downstairs.

She spotted the exact person she was looking for, Mrs. Needen, in the kitchen. She grabbed a cola from the fridge and sat down at the table.

"Morning, sweetie." She answered the woman's greeting with one of her own. Opening the can, it's loud and satisfying snap as the seal broke followed by the short and sweet hiss was forever going to be one of her favorite sounds. She took a big gulp, savoring the sweet and acidic bite, before turning to her foster mother.

"Like, I was doing some thinking and all, and wanted to ask you something. It's umm, kind of weird though." Mrs. Needen turned from the counter to face Isolde. "Of course sweetie, weird questions are usually the fun ones to answer."

She took another drink of the soda, thinking of how to phrase her question. The awkwardness of asking someone else about her best friend's family was hard to ignore.

"So umm, I was thinking about my first week of work and all." A smile swept across Mrs. Needens face, as Isolde decided to open with something easy, her job.

"Oh, is that so. Everything is going well I presume?" Isolde couldn't resist a chuckle. *That's an understatement and a half,* she thought.

"Yup, yup, yup, that's one of the things I was thinking about. Proud of myself for how well I did and all." She stopped for another drink as Mrs. Needen congratulated her. "And like, one of the things I noticed, and don't get me wrong I was happy to see her, but it was weird that April showed up so often."

Mrs. Needen furrowed her brow at the comment. "And that got me thinking. I know, like, everything about April. And I know a lot of things about her family." She sighed as she said the last part, knowing that both women knew all too well what she was speaking of.

"But, but, but, I like, realized something. Aside from what April talks about, I don't really know anything about her family." That awkwardness came back on strong as she spoke. "I mean I've met Jessica's dad more times than I've met most of April's family combined."

Mrs. Needens smile left her face, a more neutral expression taking its place. "So I figured since you've been their neighbor for so long, if there was anything you could tell me about them?" She figured her foster parent's had to have interacted with their neighbors at some points over the years, particularly before she moved in here. Before April's dad passed, she thought with a twinge of pain.

"In particular, like what does her Mom even do anyway? April's never really spoken about it much." Now she watched the neutral expression leave and be replaced by a frown. Something about the subject was bothering the woman.

"Sweetie, honestly, we don't know them very well either, your father and I." Isolde had to stifle the sigh of disappointment. "Ever since Mr. Levae had his right tragic accident, Mrs. Levae pretty much shut herself off from the world. As for work? Well, I don't rightly know how she keeps her house afloat." Mrs. Needen sighed before turning to the oven.

Not at all what she was hoping to hear, as it wasn't anything new. Thinking back, she had seen the women coming and going on a fairly regular basis a few times here and there, but that stopped not too long ago. Near the end of the school year, the woman had seemed to vanish from the face of the Earth. Isolde was about to question her own parent further when the oven timer dinged.

"Perfect timing sweetie, just came up with a new cookie recipe. Orange chocolate chip." All other thoughts left Isoldes mind at the words cookie and new recipe. If there was one single pleasure on this Earth she would trade nothing for, it was being her foster mother's guinea pig for new cookie recipes.

FINISHING HER SHOWER, April got dressed and left the small and cramped downstairs bathroom. She noticed her mother heading towards the kitchen and decided to try speaking to her.

"Hey, Mom. What's up?" she said, strolling into the kitchen after her mother. The fact that her mother was up and about, looking to be in a good mood was something April didn't know how to process.

"Nothing much, hunnie. Cassandra is at a friend's house, and Rachel is pulling another all-nighter." She watched as her mother poured a glass of coffee from the basic little coffee pot. As her mother turned to face her, she noticed the excessive makeup job her mother wore, which did a very impressive job of covering up the black eye.

"Oh, cool. So what about you? You're dressed too well for a night at home." Her mother's outfit certainly suggested that she was planning on going out. Besides the excessive make-up, her mother had on her knee-high black boots, a long black skirt, and a dark gray long-sleeve shirt that worked to compliment her short, faded black hair. April also noticed the woman had her jewelry on, something very rare to see, a simple gold chain necklace and two faux-diamond studs in each ear.

Her mother gave a soft laugh. "Yeah, work tonight. Afraid you'll be home alone again hunnie, gonna be out most of the night." April's mother walked over, and wrapped her arms around her chest. She returned the embrace before her mother pulled away and leaned in and kissed her forehead. "Love you hunnie. See you later."

April had to choke back the nausea from the smell of alcohol on her mother's breath. "Oh, love you too Mom. If that's the case, I'm going to see if the Needens will let me stay over tonight and all." Her mother gave her a smile and told her to make sure she locks the place up if she does, and left the house. April sat down at the table and sighed.

The alcohol on her mother's breath was fresh. No way she was going to some job. Once more she found herself wondering what her mother was truly up to these days. Pushing the thought out, as she realized she had little way of finding out on her own. The thought of being alone in the house took over, unsettling her.

She'd never found too many things to be afraid of. She loved the dark, bugs didn't bother her, and even spiders failed to phase her much. She was the dedicated spider killer of the house after all, both of her sisters had a panic attack any time one of the little bugs made itself known.

But one of the few things she did fear was being alone in an empty house. She made her way upstairs, grabbed a change of clothes and some essentials, and stuffed them in her backpack. She made sure she had her keys, before heading out, locking up behind her.

A few minutes later, she was knocking on the Needens' door, and a moment after that, Isolde answered. She had to fight to hold back the smile that tried taking over her face at the sight of her friend, a curious thing given her current mood.

"Like, what's up girl?" Isolde's smile faded as her eyes fell onto April's backpack. She felt awful for showing up unannounced, and lowering what looked to be a good mood Isolde was in.

"Umm, Cass and Rach are out, and." April hesitated, not sure if she wanted to burden Isolde with her own concerns just yet. "Well Mom is finally out of the house for once." She gave a short laugh before adding on "and you know how I feel about being alone all night".

Nodding her head, Isolde let her in, and she followed the girl to the kitchen. Mrs. Needen was busy at work in the kitchen once more.

"Hi, Mrs. Needen." she greeted the woman before the smell of fresh baked cookies hit her. *That would explain Isolde's good mood, alright.* The thought alleviated some of her guilt at coming over.

"Hello there sweetie, what brings you over today?" She took a seat at the table, alongside Isolde, and told the women what was up, again omitting the more personal details.

"So, I know Isolde has work in the morning but I was wondering if it'd be alright if I stayed over. Not a fan of being alone all night in an empty house and all." Mrs. Needen gave her a big, warm smile as April already knew the woman's answer.

"Of course, sweetie, just don't go keeping her up late or anything, wouldn't rightly be appreciative if you made her late for work." April couldn't help but notice the giant grin on Isolde's face as Mrs. Nedeen brought over a batch of cookies. Nothing was getting through to that girl right now except these treats.

April took one herself, enjoying the heat in her hand that radiated from it, as they clearly just came from the oven. It looked like a plain old chocolate chip cookie, but there was a fruity smell to it. She took a bite and fell in love with it. It tasted like a chocolate chip cookie, but there was something else, an almost fruity, no, citrus note to it. She sat there, enjoying the cookies with her neighbors as the stress she felt melted away.

THE DISTANT PAST

The Warrior ran, clutching the small artifacts to her chest, praying she did not drop one. The sounds of her pursuer were getting closer. Taking notice of the fallen tree ahead of her, she scanned for a new path.

The sound of underbrush rustling was now closer than ever, so she chose to just go over the thing. Clutching the artifacts closer, she used her free arm to balance herself as she leapt up on top of the stump, and then with the grace of a feline, on top of the tree itself.

The sound of her pursuer shifted, growing more distant. The hope that it was moving off was a luxury she could not afford as she slid down the other side and began her escape in earnest. As if to confirm her suspicions, she saw the brush moving several dozen paces off to her side, and redoubled her efforts.

Far off in the distance, she could see through the thick vines the first of the huts of her village. Her legs hurt worse than they ever had before, and her lungs felt like the heat of a fire burned in her chest as she struggled to push herself on, a feat she was all the more certain she'd fail at.

Closer now to the village, she could make out the farthest hut, belonging to one of the village hunters. Salvation if she could just get close enough for her shouts to carry. As the thought brought a new sense of strength to her aching legs, all hope fled from her as her foot caught a vine and she felt herself going down.

She twisted at the last second, opting to fall on her back. Not only face her now certain death with some dignity as her pursuer was sure to be on top of her in seconds. But also to protect the artifacts from being crushed beneath her.

Catching what little breath she could, the Warrior watched helplessly as the brush several paces ahead parted. The first thing she saw were the large yellow eyes. They glared at her with a deep hunger, the black slits narrowed as they fell upon her.

The animal stepped further from the brush, its black fur fading into the dim jungle light and obscuring its true size. Without her blade, she knew she had no chance against this predator. Even with it her odds were slim, as she watched in horror as the animal crouched down low, before pouncing.

Her thoughts turned to her mission, to her failure as the animal soared through the air, time itself seemed to slow to a crawl. A noise to her side provided no distraction from the beast, now almost upon her. The movement of something coming from beside her did.

Shifting her eyes, the Warrior felt her fears lessen. A spear, two jagged and sharpened pieces of bone tied to a sturdy branch was moving towards the animal. She felt her heartbeat race as the spear made contact, both blades plunging into the animal just beneath its muscular neck.

Time seemed to return to its usual pace as the Warrior watched a young man, one of the tribe's hunters, lunging into the animal and driving it to the ground at the end of the spear. The animal, one of the jungle cats, was writhing on the ground as the hunter rushed up close with a small blade drawn.

The Warrior turned her head, not wanting to watch as the Hunter did what was necessary, opting instead to scramble to her feet. Her mission saved, she looked to the hunter, who just gave her a nod as she rushed back to the village.

Chapter 6

MONDAY JUNE 1ST MORNING

April rolled over on the small futon. "Hey girl, you awake?" She called out in a soft voice. Before realization set it. *Oh yeah, Isolde's probably at work by now.* The thought prompted her to check what time it was. *Yup, definitely at work.* She thought, seeing it was a little after ten in the morning.

She dropped her phone beside her and rolled over on her back. She let out a long deep sigh. She was still tired, having not slept well the night before.

Her thoughts drifted back to the night before, how she and Isolde spent hours talking. She let out a soft laugh, thinking about it. No matter how much time the two of them spent talking, there was always something else to discuss. A trait her friendship with Jessica didn't share, as the two had run out of topics on far more than a few occasions.

Rising to her feet, she let out a long yawn, alongside a stretch that felt like it might yank her arms out of their sockets. Looking down at her purse, she frowned, lamenting that she hadn't gotten any money from her mother to go visit the Diner. Without which, she had no excuse to go see Isolde today.

Who would have thought a job was in the picture for either of us, over summer no less? The thought felt heavy in her mind. Her thoughts remained on Isolde as she gathered her fresh clothes from her backpack and left the room.

Several minutes later, she was standing in the small shower of the upstairs bathroom, letting the hot water run down her skin. She couldn't hold back a grin at the thought of her taking a shower in her best friend's house while said friend was at work. *Like we are roommates, or something.* The or something of the thought lingered for a while

Once again, she felt a feeling deep inside, that she couldn't place. Something akin to sorrow, or longing that made no sense to her. As she washed herself, she began to realize just how much she missed her friend. A thought she had to laugh at herself for, having just spent the night with the girl. Yet all the same, she missed her friend right now.

No, not just right now. She thought, rinsing off. She thought back over the last few months. Ever since Cassie had started getting worse, and their mom fell back off the wagon, she caught herself missing Isolde often. Right now, in particular, she missed her friend dearly, despite knowing she would be back home and April would see her again later.

She shut the shower off, and dried off, thinking of how big an impact Isolde had on her over the years. Of how much she realized she leaned on her friend, a fact that put a frown on her face. She stood looking in the mirror at herself. Isolde was always there for her, always willing to drop almost anything to help her with her moods, her problems. *Why are you such a burden?* The thought hit her like a thrown sack of potatoes, as she turned away from the mirror.

She forced herself to think of something else, as she dressed. Not wanting to go back home yet, she thought of some other things she could do. Making her way back to the room, she had discarded several ideas.

She didn't like going for a bike ride alone, so that was out. She had no money, so no going to the Diner nor any kind of shopping. Gathering her stuff, she decided to text Jessica, despite knowing her friend was still grounded from sneaking out to go to the river with her and Isolde. Her idea, and another friend paying for her choices. She shook her head to clear the thoughts as she grabbed her phone.

Her fingers flew across the screen with the practiced precision of someone who had spent an unhealthy amount of time texting her friends. Her text asking Jessica what was up, and letting her know how bored she was, was sent, and she went back to getting ready.

Several minutes later, she was downstairs, where Mrs. Needen was once more in the kitchen. The older woman gave her a smile as she entered the room. The smell of something savory baking enticed her, despite not having much of an appetite at the moment.

"Morning, Mrs. Needen. Something smells good in here, trying out another new recipe?" She walked over to the sink and poured herself a glass of water. Mrs. Needen gave a soft laugh, at Aprils question.

"Morning to you too sweetie. But no, nothing new this time, just a good old-fashioned roast. Going to be an all-day affair, I'm afraid." The older woman opened the oven door to check on the roast, letting out a large waft of its heavenly scent. Maybe she had more of an appetite than she realized as she caught herself inhaling the meaty fragrance, tinged with the sweet smell of onions.

"There's a leftover pork chop, and some taters in the fridge, if you're hungry, sweetie." Mrs. Needen offered, picking up on her appetite's sudden re-emergence. She thanked her neighbor, and fetched the food from the fridge, unwrapped the foil, and began microwaving it.

"So, I was wondering something." She began, not sure what had prompted the strange thought she now held as she waited on the microwave. "About Isolde's job. Is it going to be a permanent thing or just a summer job?"

Mrs. Needen was tilting her head, looking at April as the Microwave dinged. She remained quiet for a few moments as April walked back to the fridge.

"Well, sweetie, I'm not really sure. While I'm fully supportive and rightly glad she has it, it was more of my husband's idea. I reckon it's up to her if she wants to figure out how to keep it during school months."

The words sunk her spirits as she poured some BBQ sauce over the porkchop, before making her way to the table to enjoy her unusual breakfast. The idea of Isolde holding the job even throughout the school year meant her weekends would be tied up. *Even less time to spend with her.* She thought, taking a bite. As she savored the forkful of mashed potatoes over BBQ pork chop, that feeling of missing her best friend came back

"Oh, I see. Wonder what she's planning on doing." As if her mood this morning wasn't already depressed enough, here she was focusing on something that was months away and making it worse. "Guess I'm going to have to ask her some time I guess."

Mrs. Needen watched her for a moment, as she downed another large bite. "Reckon you aren't used to this new change, are ya, sweetie?" The question couldn't be closer to the truth if the woman had outright asked if she missed Isolde wholesale, so she nodded.

"Yeah, in a way. I mean, I remember a few years ago, when Rachel got her first job, how it cut our time together short." She thought back to the now several jobs her sister had held since then, and how much their relationship had shrunk in the same time.

"But I guess with Isolde it's just, I don't know, different somehow. Weird, I know." Mrs. Needen walked towards her, and she felt the warmth of the woman's hand on her shoulder. She looked into the woman's face, noticing the strange look she wore. *Is that sadness?* She thought

"Sweetie," Mrs. Needen began, as April for sure picked up on something she didn't recognize in the woman's tone. "Sisters and best friends have different kinds of relationships. And the one you and Isolde have, well," A small smile crept across the woman's face, "well let's just say it's a very special one. So I'm not surprised you are having trouble adjusting."

As Mrs. Needen walked back to the counter and to chopping vegetables, she finished her meal in silence. What had she meant by that, that she and Isolde had a special relationship? Her thoughts were interrupted by the notification on her phone.

"Geez girlie, bored AF as well. Good news though, Dad's working late tonight so if you want, we can hang a bit." The text lit her face up with a big smile, pushing her thoughts of Isolde out as she fired back a text, setting up a place to meet. She thanked her neighbor for the breakfast as she headed upstairs to finish getting ready.

"ORDER-UP." ISOLDE didn't even notice the loud ding of the bell, a sound a week ago she was sure she'd hate. She loaded the order up, and made her way to the table to deliver it. She hadn't even finished laying out the dishes as another set of customers entered. She finished up with the table and greeted the newcomers.

After giving that still very much corny greeting, she was showing the young couple to a booth. She jotted the order, a salad with a baked potato and a BBQ sandwich, two sodas, down and passed it off to the kitchen with an "order-in," and another ding of the bell.

Free to take a breather, she looked around the busy diner. One week in, and she had the job down-pat. Being the end of the lunchtime rush, it was chaotic. She was rushing to and from, taking and delivering orders, refilling drinks, and clearing tables. But what stuck out the most, was how much she actually enjoyed it.

Her breather over at the sign of one of the tables being finished, she made her way over with their check. As she stood there waiting for their card to go process the payment, her thoughts turned to her own paycheck.

A bittersweet thought as she made her way to the register. She was happy to have money of her own, earned by her own sweat and tears, her own effort. She finished running the card, and made her way back to the table. However, the fact she only gets paid every other week annoyed her as she still had several days to go before that first check.

She felt the buzzing of her phone in the pocket of her uniform, an alarm she had been setting, signaling it was time for her break. She let Clara, the other waitress on duty know, and went to clock-in her break, before heading out back.

She turned over an old red milk crate, and used it as a seat, to get some relaxation in before going back on shift. Her thoughts turned back to her upcoming paycheck, and just what she would get with it. *Like, snack cakes. All the snack cakes.* She thought, looking down at the loose gravel covering the back lot.

She sat there wondering what it would be like to look into her new bank account, currently sitting on a few cents leftover from the twenty dollar transfer Mr. Needen had made when they opened the account and see that first check.

As she pictured walking home to dump a dozen boxes of every flavor of cake she could find on her desk, she started noticing a peculiar smell. She passed it off, thinking it was someone nearby using some bad charcoal for a cookout.

Thinking about other things she could get, she thought of the idea of getting her own mini-fridge, which she could keep stocked with all the soda she would ever need. *Keep some bottles of tea or water or something in there for April,* she thought, as her thoughts turned to her friend.

She found herself smiling, and not knowing why as she thought of April, likely still sitting at the house as she hadn't showed up today. She thought of all the times over the last several months the girl was over at the house. Over the years they had been friends, April had spent a lot of time at the Needens, a lot of time with her.

She shifted her weight on the milk crate, the weird smell getting much stronger as she looked around hoping to see its source. Not finding anything out of the ordinary, she continued her train of thoughts, now focusing on just how often April had been over in the last several months.

Isolde found herself smiling even harder at the thoughts, before wondering why it made her so happy that April had been spending so much more time with her. Her thoughts were broken by the sound of a distant firetruck siren.

She checked her phone, three minutes left, time to clock back in. As she reached for the employee door, the siren was deafening. A wave of acrid black smoke smacked her in the face as she opened the door causing her her to choke as she realized she'd found the source of the smell.

Coughing, she slammed the door while looking around, not sure what to do. The firetruck and main entrance were around front, so she took off, running faster than she had in a long time.

The flashing lights of the firetruck made themselves known, painting the front of the diner in an aggressive red hue as she made her way around to the front, panic gripping her as she looked around at the scene of chaos.

She watched as people, including the young couple whose order she had taken just before break, were streaming out of the building. Looking around and feeling relieved she found Daisy speaking with her husband.

Making her way to them, Daisy gave her a warm look, despite the frustration written across her face. Mr. Burke walked off to talk to a young man in cook's attire, as she reached her employer.

"Oh, Isolde, glad to see you're alright. Wouldn't do my poor old heart at all if you done got yourself choked up on that awful smoke." Daisy's concern touched her. She was still unsure what to make of her boss as the woman seemed to flip between warm and pleasant, and cold and bitchy at any given moment.

"Like, yeah. I went out back for my break, and got a face full of that smoke when I was trying to head back in." The slight smile Daisy had faded at the question Isolde asked, "like, what happened anyway?"

Daisy gave a heavy sigh, and looked over to the young man her husband was chewing out. "That no good fer nothin new cook my husband was training done went and buggered the whole damn kitchen. Poor boy up and started a grease fire then tried to hose it off with water."

Isolde vaguely recalled hearing something about not using water on certain types of fires, and guessed that a grease fire was among them.

"Now don't worry hun, these fine young firefighters got it right taken care of in no time at all." The words, and Daisy's shift back into her more pleasant mood, warmed Isoldes heart. She was just starting to really like this job, and would hate to have to be forced out of it so soon because of an accident burning the place down.

"I'm glad that it wasn't worse, like that would have sucked." Her words got a chuckle from Daisy. The thought that she hadn't clocked off of break hit her so she asked Daisy about it.

"Oh, now don't you go worrying your purple head about that missy. I'll take care of it all once we get this all sorted out. Anyway, I'll be closing up today, so you get on home safely, child."

The news felt bittersweet, as while she was glad to be off work, she was saddened by the loss of hours, and the effect on her paycheck it would have. Something she quickly learned would only be worse.

"Oh yes, before you go, I'm going to ask you come in as usual in the morning and wear something old that you don't much mind getting dirty. Only gonna keep you a half shift or so, so we can get the kitchen cleaned up something proper."

Isolde nodded, and said her goodbyes, before returning to the back lot for her bike. She pulled her phone out, sending a text to April, letting her friend know the turn of events and that she was headed home early.

As she finished unlocking her bike, she heard the notification go off and checked her phone, her mood once more turning positive as she read the text.

"OMG girl, no way. Jess snuck out again, and we're hanging over by the abandoned grocery store near her house. Get over here." She returned a text of her own, letting April know she was on her way, and set off for the short ride.

APRIL COULDN'T HIDE the pure joy on her face as she read Isolde's text. Her mood shifted in an instant from the dour and depressed to one of joy. "Hey, Jess, guess what? Isolde's off early, cause of a fire or something. She's on her way." Her giddiness had caught her friend off guard.

"Ok, that's an interesting turn of events. But damn, girlie, what's gotten into you?" Jessica's question rubbed her in a way she didn't like as she looked at her friend. "I mean, you spent the night with her. She would have, fires notwithstanding, gotten off in a few hours." Jessica had a point, she was acting a bit too over-excited.

"And this whole time we've been hanging, you've been a bit distracted, or something. So spill it girl, and no excuses or getting out of an answer, like you did when I caught you staring at her naked ass."

The burn in her cheeks made her turn away from Jessica. She had hoped that incident had been forgotten, but was mistaken. She thought back to her conversation with Mrs. Needen, and decided to just be upfront with her friend.

"Yeah, ok. Still have no idea why I was staring that day, so don't bother asking." The burn in her cheeks having subsided, she turned back to Jessica, who had a grin on her face while shaking her head.

"But yeah, there's something bothering me. I mean, you obviously know how bad things are at home." Jessica's grin faded, as April continued. "I've actually done some thinking on my own lately. And truth be told, I've come to realize how much I rely on you two for support, and especially how much I lean on Isolde."

Jessica's grin returned with a vengeance as she gave a snort, prompting April to frown. She could tell another wisecrack was coming and braced for it.

"Is that so, well damn, the way you were staring at her, I'm sure leaning on her is the least of your intentions for our candy cane flavored friend." Jessica let out a long laugh at her own joke, and April couldn't help but give into the good spirits and joined her. Leave it to Jess to take things in such a perverted way. As the thought entered her mind, she couldn't help but wonder just why it excited her so much.

After a few moments of laughter, her mood darkened once more, as she turned away from Jessica. She took a deep breath, while staring at a rock on the shoulder of the road. She felt Jessica's hand on her shoulder, and turned to face her friend. Leaning on her friends was one thing but it was far from the only thing she was dealing with.

"Joking aside," she stopped to let out a long sigh, turning to face Jessica. "I'm really not handling Isolde having a job very well." She felt her friend's hand rubbing her shoulder, and reached up and placed her own hand over it.

"I mean, I'm so used to having a place to go, you know, when schools out and all. Somewhere to escape the drama when Cassie starts up. Or when Mom." She let her voice trail off, not sure if she wanted to bring up her concerns over her mother's suspicious activities just yet. "When she gets drunk again." She made a hasty excuse, hoping Jessica didn't press her further.

"Girlie, I'm saying this as a friend, and none of my usual sarcasm here," Jessica was shaking her head, her voice as serious as April had ever heard it. "But you need to start working on yourself. I know, trust me, you know how my Dad is, so I know at least a little about how bad family drama can be."

She felt the knot in her gut tighten at Jessica's words, bracing herself for a harsh truth. "But there's only so much me and Isolde can do to help. I'm more than happy to be there for you, anytime, anyplace, anywho. Sure Isolde is as well. But." She felt Jessica squeezing her shoulder.

"But it's time to start standing up for yourself, against yourself. You let that family drama dictate your life, and frankly, it hurts to see it, girlie. That's one thing I know our purple headed glutton feels the same about."

April couldn't stop the chuckle from escaping, nor the slight grin from creasing her lips. As far as brutal honesty can go, that felt pretty tame. Despite being true. Wasn't the first time someone other than herself had told her she's too much of a burden, leaning too hard on other people. Rachel had given her that talk a few times. Cassie as well, though less out of concern and more out of a new way to insult her.

"Oh, and speaking of the bean-pole, there she comes." She shook her thoughts away and followed Jessica's gaze, and saw Isolde, decked out in that gaudy uniform, pedaling hard up the street. April's heart felt fuller as Isolde pulled up on the pair of friends.

Jessica was walking up to their friend, as April stood there, letting the joy of seeing Isolde again was away the longing, the feelings of missing the girl she'd held all morning.

"So, you hate your job so much you tried your hand at arson, is that it girl?" April and Isolde both rolled their eyes at Jessica's comment. Despite the unfortunate circumstances, April couldn't help but notice Isolde was in a good mood, based on the giant grin she sported.

"Like come on Jess, I'm a bit too old, and way too cute, and you know, not a raging monster for you to be confusing me with her sister." She pointed at April while speaking, and April couldn't hold back the laugh, as that absolutely felt like something Cassie would do. Something Rachel would probably do as well, now that she thought of it.

Once again, she stood silently as her two closest friends tossed irreverent jabs and quips back and forth. She felt at peace, in a way she hadn't felt in a while watching her friends.

"I mean, assuming your dad ever lets his precious out of his sight long enough for you to even get a job, then yeah, I'll accept that you aren't jealous." Isolde had a mocking tone in her voice, having once more taken Jessica's bait and getting into another back and forth with the girl.

"Oh just you wait, I got something cooking on that burner. It's going to be so fun seeing the look on you girlies face when." Jessica hesitated, clearly holding something back. "I get my own job and ended up making more than you ever could." April couldn't help but notice the shift in Jessica's face as she made up an obvious excuse.

Seeming to also pick up on it, Isolde looked like she was about to say something else when she pointed across the street. Both Jessica and April turned to look. April gasped, confusion overtaking her, as she saw her mother getting into a car, on the far end of the street.

"Like, isn't that your mom, April?" She squinted to get a better look, and was certain. The outfit she had worn yesterday was a dead giveaway, as if the familial recognition wasn't enough.

She watched the car speed off, not sure what to think. What was her mother doing this far from home, a trip that on foot would take almost an hour from their house, and their mother had no license, one too many DUIs saw to that.

"Yeah, it was. What the hell, Mom." Was all she could mutter, the jovial mood of their group now diminished. She decided that she was going to get to the bottom of this before long, as the trio got back to joking around.

Chapter 7

FRIDAY, JUNE 5TH AFTERNOON

As Isolde cleared the table she was working on, her mind raced with the possibilities her first paycheck brought. Making her way to the kitchen, she unloaded the dishes she carried, giving the young boy on dish-duty a smile. She found herself in a great mood as her phone began vibrating in her pocket.

Without skipping a beat, she reached down and silenced it as she made her way to the employee room and began clocking out. Clara was already waiting, and Isolde passed the work apron on to her colleague and began to make her way out back.

The bright afternoon sun blinded her as she left the building, forcing her to rub her eyes. She made a mental note to pick up some sunglasses first thing.

"You're not supposed to look at the sun, you know." As her vision was returning, she looked up to see April waiting by her bike, this time riding her sister's pink and black road bike. Isolde's smile threatened to tear her face apart as it spread.

"Like, hey girl, what are you doing here?" As she asked, she pulled her phone out, and loaded up the app for their local bank, and began to sign in. Her excitement to see if her first check had been deposited was cut at the tone of April's voice.

"Oh you know, the same-old same-old. Cassie's getting more violent, she actually hit Mom, like full-on punched her." April was sighing after she spoke and looking at the ground.

Isolde just shook her head, wondering if Mrs. Levae was ever going to actually do something about her out of control child, especially before she turned her violence on her sisters. On April. *Then I'll have to do something about the girl.* The thought shocked Isolde, with just how defensive she found herself once more getting over April.

"So I booked it, no way was I hanging around that drama. Bit embarrassed to say I've kinda been hanging around for over an hour out here." She heard the soft chuckle her friend gave as the slow app on her phone finally finished, and she scrolled down.

A smile flashed across Isolde's face, before fading into a frown, at which April asked "what's wrong?" She shut the phone off, thinking about Mr. Needen's short lecture on taxes and other nonsense. The man had warned her to not overestimate how much she was going to make, and she realized once more the man was correct.

"Like nothing, just surprised how little I actually made." She took a good look at her friend, as any frustration she still felt melted away. As she looked at the girl, a small smile crept across April's face. Something about that smile made Isolde feel happy, a kind of joy she wasn't used to feeling.

"Like come on, what we need is some good old fashioned processed junk food. My treat." She watched the smile creep further across her friend's face, before unlocking and mounting her bike.

Twenty minutes later, the pair were locking their bikes to the bike rack outside of the grocery store, before heading in. As the girls wandered the aisles, she couldn't help but notice April stopping to look at, or read every other piece of junk food.

"Trouble deciding, huh? I know what that's like, having to decide which snack cakes I want when the Needens go shopping is a bitch." April gave a soft laugh as she was reading a package of chocolate covered marshmallow cookies. Isolde knew her friend didn't get too many treats like those cookies and took them, shoving them in her basket with a "my treat, remember?"

They continued making their way through the store, checking out each new section of foods, and engaging in casual conversation. Isolde found herself thinking back once more, on just how much time the two of them had been spending together.

Passing an aisle of various chips, Isolde grabbed a bag of party mix, thinking about how much she still enjoyed spending time with her friend. As April declined the offer for her own bag, Isolde found herself thinking about just how close the two had been getting lately.

She knew her friend counted on her to be there for her, and it was something she took pride in doing. Pride, and something else. There was something else, some other feeling tied to it, just beneath the surface, scratching at her mind.

They ended up at the frozen section, and Isolde stopped, staring at the rows of ice-cream in all shapes, flavors, and sizes. The train of thoughts fled her mind as she looked over the myriad of options.

As she was reading the flavors, puzzled by some of the names, most notably rocky-road, she heard April laughing at her. She turned to her friend, amazed at the look of genuine amusement on her face, a rare sight.

Don't tell me, the queen of junk food hasn't ever had ice-cream?" She turned back to the rows of frozen treats. The Needen's were lactose intolerant, only ever buying basic milk to use for cooking so there was a lot of dairy products she had either never or rarely had.

"Like nope. You know how the Needen's are with dairy, so we just never had any around the house." She turned her attention back to one of the sections, looking over the treats as one flavor caught her eye.

She opened the freezer door, and picked up a small single serving of mint-chocolate chip, and watched as April settled on a similar size of that rocky-road flavor. They continued their banter, making their way through the store, stopping to pick up a small box of plastic spoons and a pair of sunglasses before checking out, and leaving the store.

They unlocked their bikes, and began making their way around the back of the store, to sit in some shade, and enjoy their frozen snacks. April took a big bite of the chocolate looking treat, as Isolde was amazed at her friend's bravery. If the chill in her hand from holding the container was any indication of the treat's temperature she was amazed at how easily April was eating it.

She popped the lid off of her own container, and stared at its soft green hue, and noticed several large chocolate chips poking out. The top was beginning to melt, though she could feel the frigid chill in her hands letting her know the rest was very much frozen.

She took a spoon, and scooped up a small bite, her taste buds exploding with flavor as she savored it. Her tongue was going numb from the cold as she savored it. Thinking back, she found herself amazed that she had never had any other, non-dairy frozen treats before.

"Ok, like, this stuff really is cold. But man, it's so damn good." She took another, much larger bite, savoring it for a longer moment before grabbing her head. She felt April's hand on her shoulder, small comfort to the blistering pain in her head as she forced herself to swallow the frigid bite.

"Slow down there. As you just found out firsthand, brain-freeze is a bitch." Isolde shook her head as the pain subsided. "Like holy hell, you ain't joking, what the hell." She rubbed her forehead as April laughed. Isolde looked at the ice-cream in her hand, and watched April down another bite with no problem.

"So, like, how do you do it, and not get brain froze?" She watched as April took another large bite, before explaining that it's all about not letting it sit in your mouth too long, and definitely not letting it sit on the roof of your mouth.

Several minutes, and no less than five more bouts of brain-freeze later, the girls had finished their ice-cream treats, and were pushing their bikes along the sidewalk engaging in small talk. Movement up ahead, on the other end of the block caught her eye. She squinted, before recognizing the girl in the lead of the small group that just turned the corner.

"Hey, girl, ain't that your sister up ahead?" April looked to where Isolde was pointing, acknowledging that it was indeed her sister. They sped up to meet with the other group.

"Hey Rach, what's going on?" Isolde stood around as the sisters talked about a few things. The other girl with them also stood silently, as did the boy who was behind Rachel. A boy she recognized.

As the sisters engaged in some small talk, Isolde felt her blood boiling. That same boy who had bothered them on her first day of work was once again staring at April's ample chest. Once more she found herself feeling incredibly defensive of April.

"Like watch where you keep those eyes, buddy." She shouted, moving herself between her friend and the lech. The anger in her was taking over at the thought of someone staring at her best friend. Once more, Isolde felt that other, deeper emotion poking its way through her subconscious as she glared at the boy.

"Brandon, what's wrong with you?" Rachel also chastised the boy, after Isolde pointed out what she caught him doing. She watched as he turned and walked to the other side of Rachel's friend.

"Eh, don't mind him. He's just walking with us on the way to Alice's house. He just moved in some months ago and the two are dating." Rachel explained as she returned to speaking with April.

Isolde wasn't too familiar with Rachel's group of friends, certainly not enough to picture who Alice was. But she for sure knew that she wasn't too keen to meet up with anyone that willingly dated a pig like this Brandon.

Isolde looked at April, wondering where this strong defensive feeling was coming from. The girl was laughing at something Rachel had said, as Isolde found her eyes locked on her best friend. Her face was rather plain, no freckles like Jessica nor any hint of a tan like her own skin. Despite this, Isolde couldn't help but notice just how attractive her friend was.

How attractive April was? The thought hit differently. She had never found herself thinking about either of her friends as attractive, as she studied April's face. Yet, try as she might to deny it, there was an undeniable attractiveness to her friend. She wondered if that was what kept drawing this Brandon's eyes, as she looked down at April's shirt.

She recognized the shirt as one April wore often, but for the first time she took notice of just how low cut it was. And how much cleavage it showed, as Isolde realized what it was that Brandon was looking at.

Like that's all he sees? Tits? Not how beautiful she is? The thought about Brandon being a perv disgusted her. As the part about April being beautiful intrigued her. Did she really just think of April as beautiful? She pushed the thoughts out as she focused on the group conversation once more.

As the two groups conversed, she couldn't help but notice how different Rachel, and the girl with them, Lisa as she had discovered, were from her own group of friends. They seemed more mature somehow, certainly far less liberal with the cursing.

More than that though, she couldn't place it, but something about Rachel's mannerisms rubbed her the wrong way. Something just seemed, somehow fake about the girl, like she was putting on a facade.

"Yeah, tell me about it. Like I said, Isolde here was the one who spotted Mom." The mention of her name brought her out of her thoughts, as she turned to face April. No sooner than she had, she found herself boiling over once more, and stomped over to Brandon.

"The fuck did I say, you asshole?" She planted both palms on the boy, shoving him to the grass on the side of the sidewalk. The look on his face as he was once more eyeing up April lingered in her mind.

She felt April pulling her back, as Lisa got in front of Brandon, preventing her from swinging her now balled up fist into his smug nose. Something she desperately wanted to do, as the anger had completely overtaken her.

"What the hell's wrong with you, fucking psycho?" He said, wiping the freshly mown grass clippings from his white t-shirt, and blue jeans. She smiled internally at the few pieces clinging to his hair. Her rage subsiding a little as she felt April's hand on her. *Like there's that damn feeling again.* She thought as it was once more scratching at the surface, this time feeling a lot more familiar.

"The fuck is wrong with me is you won't stop staring at my best friend's tits." She spat the words at him, prompting several moment's of back and forth amongst the group. The bickering ended when Rachel, who had been whispering with April, turned to him.

"How about you just go on, and get out of here, Brandon." Isolde watched a sick grin cover his face as her rage began building again. She was contemplating pulling herself out of April's grasp to slug him.

"Shit, like what's it to you, anyway? Who cares if a guy takes a look, free country and all." No longer willing to let her friend hold her back, she pulled away, taking a step forward, her fist balled. She was stopped as Rachel put her hand out, before taking her own step towards the boy.

Isolde couldn't hide the smile this time, as Rachel shoved him down once more, this time on the sidewalk. "Who cares? I care alright. I care about you perving on my sister. Get the hell out of her and I might not tell Alice about this." Whatever the misgivings she felt about Rachel earlier were, she couldn't help but feel respect for the girl. Anyone willing to stand up for their sister like that had to have some good in them.

Her rage subsided as Brandon took off, a sour look on his face as he flipped them all the bird. She turned back to the group just in time to get ambushed by April, giving her a big hug. Rachel gave them a coy smile, and a thumbs up as she returned the hug.

Returning the hug, Isolde wondered about the odd smile, as she once more felt that feeling deep within. Now however, she felt like she knew what it was, a suspicion that left her stomach knotted.

She broke off the hug, which had lasted a fairly long time as Rachel was still grinning that coy little grin. The two groups said their goodbyes, and she and April were once more headed home.

Chapter 8

SATURDAY JUNE 6TH EVENING

Isolde found herself laughing at Jessica's fitting mockery of her father. She watched the girl on her phone giving an animated and overly dramatic reenactment of her latest scolding.

"Like, girl," she had to take a few moments for the fit of laughter to pass before continuing, "you are so going to get in a world of trouble one of these days." She watched Jessica flick her hair in a mock fashion.

"Why, I thought you girls knew me." Jessica gave the phoniest pout Isolde had ever seen. "I mean, my name is Jessica Trouble Mariana, after all." Both girls broke out in all new fits of laughter.

"Yeah, yeah, yeah Ms Trouble. So have you given any thought to my question?" She had texted Jessica earlier, asking her for some ideas on something the three of them could do to celebrate her first check.

"Well, there's not much in this bum of a town. I mean we could go see a movie, that new horror movie looks pretty good." The idea interested her, before she remembered. "Like, yeah, it does but April hates horror movies, Ms. I thought You Girls Knew Me." Her moment of laughter was brought short by the look that crept over Jessica's face.

"Yeah, I forgot that. Speaking of April," Isolde didn't like the tone of her voice, "there's something I've been going back and forth on bringing up to you." She steeled herself for Jessica's news. Serious was a rare state for her smartass friend.

"Ok, so I've been struggling over whether to tell you or not because she was pretty embarrassed and all." Isolde felt a grimace coming on. While April often blushed, Isolde had only very rarely seen anything close to embarrassment in the girl.

"You remember the other day, down at the river?" Isolde nodded, thinking back to how fun it was, until it was cut short by Mr. Mariana's call. *Dude really needs to chill, chill, chill.* She thought, as Jessica continued.

"Well, when you were changing, I kind of caught her, like, staring at you." Jessica fumbled over getting the words out. *Staring at me? Like, what?* She couldn't shake the confusion.

"Like, when I was getting ready to go swimming and taking my uniform off?" She asked, not sure what Jessica meant. Her friend looked down, and off screen of the camera, blushing.

"Umm, no. I mean." She waited a few moments as Jessica struggled over her words. "Umm, she was hardcore, in a damn trance watching your naked ass changing over by the trees." Jessica finally blurted out. The news left her feeling odd. It left her feeling that deep and warm and ever so odd feeling that she was not going to dwell on anymore.

"Like, seriously? Huh. That is odd, and I can see why you didn't bring it up. Though that leads me to having to ask why you did bring it up." She watched as the blushing left Jessica, as her voice returned to a more serious tone.

"Well, between that, and your own outburst at me," Isolde felt bad, and offered another apology, which Jessica accepted before continuing. "I've been paying more attention to her of late. In particular, how weird she's been acting, especially around you."

Isolde got up from her desk, and began pacing around her room. This was certainly not how she expected this conversation to go. April, watching her change? That wasn't too unusual, the girls had changed in front of each other more times than she could count. But that she was staring? Blushing? That was weird, and she didn't know how to process it.

"Like, yeah, to be honest, I've noticed it too. Not the weirdness towards me or anything, but just how distracted and down she's been." She had turned back to the camera on her phone, and to Jessica. She was glad to know someone else had picked up on April's mood of late.

"Yeah. The other day, the same day you tried to burn your job down, " Jessica laughed at her quip, but Isolde wasn't in a joyful mood. "I confronted her about it all. Still got no answer on her staring, but she did admit something."

Once more the tone in Jessica's voice left her feeling a bad way. So she asked her friend to go on.

"Well, she told me that she had been thinking and realized how much she leans on us. Which I mean, we both knew after all." Isolde nodded. It wasn't a secret to anyone that April had a lot on her plate, much more than she or Jessica. Nor that it was a burden both girls were happy to help with.

"But more than that, she confided in me that she's having a very hard time coping with you having a job." Isolde sat down on the edge of her bed, having not expected the weight of Jessica's words." Both girls sat in quiet contemplation for several minutes.

So is that why she's spending so much time over here lately? She discarded the thought, as April's activities extended back months, well before not only her job but even her own birthday.

"Like, yeah, I guess that makes sense. She must be so used to having an escape over here that my absence must be getting to her while I'm at work." Isolde broke the silence that hung over the room like an oppressive blanket.

She couldn't help but feel terrible. Here she was finding so much joy in this new job while her best friend suffered in silence as her main escape was now so much more limited.

"You know, despite it all, and this is the main reason I brought this up, but there's something else bothering her. I could tell she was holding something back that day, and every time I've brought it up since she dismisses it out of hand." Isolde couldn't help but wonder what was bothering their friend so much that she would hide it. She stood up to shake the thoughts away as her mind once more thought back to that feeling, wondering if it had some part in this mess.

Isolde once more set to pacing, and once more confirmed to Jessica that she too had noticed April acting shifty whenever the conversation had turned to her mother over the last week. She returned to her desk, as the two girls began trying to piece out what was bothering their friend.

THE SOUND OF THE PAINTING that hung on the wall crashing to the floor woke April from her nap. She hadn't even wiped the sleep from her eyes before she heard the tell-tale sounds of Cassie and their mom going at it.

Sighing, she sat up before she gave a large yawn, and pleasant stretch before grabbing her phone. She fired off a quick text to Isolde, asking if she minded her coming over. The sound of their mother shouting something reminding her how little she wished to be at home as she prepared to get dressed.

She was pulling her shoes on as her notification sounded, the text from Isolde telling her to come on over lifted her spirits. She gathered her things and set out, stopping at the bottom of the stairs as a book flew past, barely missing her.

"Cassandra Levae! You go apologize to your sister for that." She could hear the anger in her mother's voice. Now officially a part of the drama, she made her way into the living room. Just as Cassie turned to her, glowering.

"What? Apologize for what? If she wasn't such a fucking fatass she wouldn't have almost gotten hit." Once more, her sister's words stung deep. She watched as their mother walked up to the girl, putting her hand on Cassies shoulder, hard.

"You apologize to your sister, right this instant." April was taken aback by the tone in their mother's voice. She rarely took this much of a direct approach. *Rarely acted this much like a mother.* The thought stung in its own way.

"No. Maybe she should apologize for eating all the cereal. Fucking cow doesn't need it after all, just look at her." Despite the painful barb, she felt a pang of guilt, as she had finished the cereal earlier this morning before Cassie woke up.

"Cassandra, if you don't apologize this moment." Her mother's words were cut short, as Cassie reared up and shoved their mother to the ground. "Or fucking what, Mom? What are you going to do? Go drink yourself stupid again? Go fuck around with some loser for another black-eye?" The tears of rage streaming down Cassies face were unlike anything she had witnessed from the girl.

"What the hell do you even care? All my life, the only memories I have of you? Are with a fucking bottle. At least, you know, when you are actually around and not sneaking off at all fucking hours, drunk as shit."

April had no time to react before Cassie was stomping her way past, shoving her to the side as she passed to leave the house.

April caught her balance, just in time to see Rachel exiting the bathroom, and proceeding to help their mom up. April watched as their mother walked into the kitchen, and returned a moment later with a bottle of wine, heading for her room.

"Going to your little girlfriends again? Don't worry, I'll track down Cassie." She didn't even mind Rachels corny jab about her friendship this time. Cassies words weighed too heavily on her. She had never seen so much pain on her sister's face before. Pain she was sure was showing on her own face as she began walking towards the door.

As she left, she saw her sisters in the front yard, arguing. She made her way to them, shock hitting her as Cassie turned to her and apologized. At least, in her own way.

"Look, I mean, you are a fatass, but I'm sorry I went so hard on you." She walked over and put a hand on Cassie's shoulder, giving her sisters a weak smile. "It's just, you know how she is. I bet she's in there drinking herself stupid before she runs off again tonight. And where does she even go anyway?"

Cassie's question hung with her. She tried to think back to any time she had met one of her mother's friends. But she couldn't think of any, or much of any kind of social life their mother had had. The look on Rachel's face said that she knew something she wasn't telling, so April questioned her.

"Well, I don't know where she goes. I can tell you girls it's not a friends house she's going to, like she claims. I mean, she's not exactly a social butterfly." Rachels words rung true, with Cassie chiming in "more like she's a total fucking loser."

Rachel put her hand on Cassies other shoulder, and gave her sister a smile. "Cassie, trust me, I know how much it hurts, the way she is. But, and I'm not making any excuses for her, but there is a reason for it." Rachel's words had piqued her curiosity, a shared sentiment based on the look on Cassie's face.

'You were too young to have met him in any meaningful way, but you know how dad died when you were a baby, right? Well, the reason Mom is the way she is, it's because she's never been able to get over his death." April felt her mouth fall open, a small gasp escaping.

"She's been torturing herself over it for the last twelve years." She watched as tears streamed down Cassie's face. Whether they were tears of rage, or sorrow, she couldn't tell, as the girl just gave a soft "whatever" before going back inside.

Rachel hung around looking at April. The look on her face suggesting that the girl was torn with indecision.

"There's more to it, isn't there? She asked her sister, worried about what else she knew about their mother. Rachel sighed, and led her to the porch where they both took a seat on the stairs.

"Yeah. Please don't say anything to Cassie, or Mom or those goofy friends of yours, ok?" April nodded, now actually scared of what Rachel was about to divulge.

"The crash that killed dad? Almost killed me?" Despite being too young herself to remember much of the event, it had been a constant shadow over their household ever since. She nodded as Rachel continued.

"Well, the reason she's never been able to get over his death, why she drinks until she passes out? It's because she did it. The crash was her fault" April took a moment as the words began to sink in, confused as she had always been told their father was driving that day.

"Wait, how? Dad was driving wasn't he?" The way Rachel looked down at the ground was enough for April to realize that had long since been a lie.

"Nope. Mom was driving. We were all on the way home from a Christmas party, that much is true. The problem is, Mom didn't exactly count her drinks, if you catch my drift." April felt like the world itself just fell on her chest. *Mom was driving drunk that night?*

"Honestly, I've wanted to say something to you, maybe even to Cassie for so long. It's been hell since I learned it all." Rachel was crying, something April knew meant the girl was in real pain. Something she was sure she'd have plenty of once her shock wore off.

"How? How did you find out?" She stammered the words out. Rachel wiped her eyes with a sleeve before putting her other hand on April's.

"Alice. Her mom is a cop after all. The things you find out when one of your besties has that kind of access and all." Rachel reached over and gave April a hug, before rising to her feet. "Going to go in, make sure Cassie hasn't done something stupid. Well, stupider than usual. See ya."

April made her way to Isolde's house in solitude, thinking over Rachel's words. And how she seemed to know something about where their mom was going, but chose to keep to herself. But most of all, trying to piece her feelings together about this latest family revelation.

ISOLDE'S LATEST BOUT of laughter was interrupted by a notification popping up on her phone, dampening the audio of the video call for a moment. She read the text from April, and fired off her own reply inviting the girl over.

"Like, that was April. Shit was hitting the fan, so she's on her way over." She informed Jessica, who was talking to her sister, Sarah off-screen. Her friend gave a nod, as Isolde sat waiting for the other conversation to finish. Several minutes passed, as Sarah left and Jessica returned her focus to the conversation.

"Hey, sorry about that, girlie. She had some family news to share and." Jessica's explanation was cut short by the loud knocking on Isolde's door. She got up, and unlocked the door. The joy of the conversation she'd been having with Jessica left, as she looked April over with a sigh.

"Wow, girlie, you ok over there?" April ignored Jessica's question, and just walked over and fell down hard on the bed. She had been crying pretty hard, and looked like someone had just died in her life. Isolde felt a shudder running through her gut as it twisted itself up into a knot, as she sat down beside April.

"Like what's wrong girl? You said there was drama in your text but this." Her voice trailed off, leaving Jessica to pick her train of thought back up. "I don't think we've ever seen you looking this down, girlie.

Isolde wrapped her arms around April, who still hadn't said anything. "Is she ok? Ask her if something happened, or something. I think she's in shock." Isolde was barely paying attention to Jessica, despite feeling the same concern. More than that, she felt something else, a pain, deep inside. Something she hadn't ever felt before.

Seeing April in this state hurt worse than anything she had ever experienced in her life. She squeezed her best friend tighter. The world could literally be ending outside her door, and she wouldn't care so long as she could be here for her friend.

Several moments of hugging passed, before April spoke. "Umm, I'm ok. Thanks, you two." She gave Jessica a small smile through the camera, and turned to Isolde. The smile on her face seemed to grow three sizes as she did, and Isolde felt something, some kind of giddiness as her best friend looked at her, despite the emotions running heavy. *You know what it is.* The thought came sharp, challenging her as she pushed it aside.

"So, umm, shit got bad at home." She proceeded to give them a play-by-play of the events she witnessed not too long ago. Isolde looked over at the phone screen, at Jessica, who was being quiet. *Damn, even Jess is speechless.* The thought weighed on her.

A thought that was broken when Jessica did speak. "You know, I don't mean anything bad or nothing." She gave Isolde a sharp look, making her look down at the floor. "But Cassandra does have a point. I mean, your mom really needs to start acting her fucking age."

The edge in Jessica's voice took Isolde by surprise. Isolde found herself troubled by how much she agreed with Jessica, and how much she didn't want to say it out loud. The look on April's face suggested she had more to say, so Isolde told her to go on.

"No offense taken Jess. And I agree, actually. I've been doing a lot of thinking, ever since we saw Mom out by that abandoned store the other day." She felt April tense up, and began rubbing her back, to which she received a very warm smile in thanks.

"I've gone back, thinking over and over. Just to realize, I don't really know all that much about my own mother. So you can guess from the way I walked in here how I felt over something else Rachel told me."

Isolde found herself no longer rubbing Aprils back, nor able to keep her jaw from hanging open as April gave them a recap of Rachel's revelation. She turned to the phone at the sound of Jessica laughing. It was a hollow, mirthless laugh, more of a symptom of shock than anything.

Once more Isolde found herself hugging April, wishing desperately she could do something, anything to put a proper smile on her beautiful face.

"So, girlie, if you only just found that out, then why have you been so shifty about your mom lately?" Isolde felt relieved that Jessica approached that elephant in the room, and began rubbing April's back again.

"Umm, yeah. About that. Truth is, what she's doing, where she's going? It's been bugging the hell out of me." Once more Isolde found herself sitting in awe as April relayed her thoughts and concerns, going back to how their mother had come home from, and said with air-quotes, work, with a black eye. All the way up to Rachel's shifty behavior minutes before April arrived.

Isolde found it was her turn to give a humorless laugh. "Like, wow. I'm so, so, so sorry April. I mean, that's like, deep. I mean, are you sure there's something even going on? Maybe she was visiting a friend?" Her question rang hollow in her own head as she asked it. That was not exactly the kind of place for casually meeting friends, prompting her to wonder why her own friends had been there.

"Ugh. That's what she said she was doing that day. But, nah, not buying it." Isolde scrunched her face up, and looked at April out of the side of her eye. Seeming to have taken notice of Isolde's confusion, April explained that neither she, nor her sisters had ever seen their mom mention, or spend any time with any friends. That the fact that her mother was still pining for her late husband had prevented her from ever making any.

"Like, shit. Man, I wish there was something we could do for you girl." Her back-rubbing was once more interrupted by Jessica piping up.

"Did someone say wish? Better break out that lamp, girlie. Cause I'm your magic genie tonight." Isolde couldn't help but laugh. While Jessica's weird sense of humor did grate on her at times, at others it was the perfect thing for the moment. She noticed April's look of confusion, and was eager to hear whatever plan Jessica was cooking up.

"Well, and this is assuming the Needens are ok with it being a work night for Isolde. But I mean, we live like two streets over from where your mom was. Maybe you two spend the night tomorrow, and we go on a stakeout. Have your sister text you when your mom leaves and if she goes back there, we can see what's up."

Isolde felt a grin pulling her face apart. Jessica always came up with oddball plans, but this one was odd enough that it might just work. She gave April another hug, and went back to the desk, moving the camera into a better position for all three girls to see each other, as they began ironing out this plan.

Chapter 9

THE DISTANT PAST.

The Warrior knelt before the First Father. Her heart raced as the man looked over the artifacts she had retrieved. Her anxiety escalated as she felt the gaze of the man's mate, the First Mother.

"Your services have been performed most adequately, young warrior." The large, hairy man, his skin among the darkest in the tribe, made his way out of the hut with the artifacts. She didn't look up, anticipating the First Mother to address her. Instead, she felt the woman's hand on her shoulder.

"Come now, I should think we are past these formalities." The Warrior raised her head, her heart slowed its rapid beat as she looked at the older woman's face. She had the lightest skin in the village. Her long hair, black with a reddish hue, flowed down the length of her back, and down over her large and supple breasts. Looking at the woman's face, she couldn't help but think that despite the woman being old enough to have mothered her, she was still stunningly beautiful.

As she looked into the woman's dark brown eyes, she felt herself being guided by the woman, guided into an embrace. "Relax, my Warrior. My Mate will be gone the rest of the evening." The Warrior turned back to look at the entrance of the hut. " A good chance the entirety of the morrow as well. Come."

She wasted no time accepting the offer, locking her lips with the older woman, as the two embraced. The kiss was deep, passionate, and the two held it for as long as either dared. The Warrior was the first to break the kiss off, not taking her eyes off of her illicit lover.

Once more, she felt the woman's hand on her shoulder, being led to the pile of furs the woman and her mate used as bedding. Her heart once more began to race, as the woman sat on the bed, pulling the Warrior down, as the two collapsed into a heavy embrace, where they resumed their deep kiss.

Once more breaking the kiss off, she found herself laying there, holding the older woman close. Their shared embrace lasted for what may have been a full moon for how little she cared. The warmth she felt, the peace, the love she had in her heart was so strong, that she would even risk a confrontation with the First Father to keep this cuddling going.

Once more, she found herself drawn into a deep kiss by the First Mother. The Warrior felt what seemed to be a fire burning inside her, her passions had never reached this level before as she hungrily returned the First Mother's kiss.

Once more, the kissing came to an end, as the woman looked deep into the Warrior's eyes. "Tonight, you share my bed, Warrior. Tonight, we share our bodies, and our love."

The Warrior felt herself drawn in by the older woman. As the two lovers laid there holding and hugging, kissing and feeling, she felt at peace. A joy, an ecstasy she had never experienced before, as the two began to show their love in the most passionate ways.

MONDAY JUNE 8TH EARLY AM

Isolde woke with a start. *Like what the fuck was that?* The thought felt like an understatement. Years of dreaming of the jungle warrior had never ended up like that. She rubbed her arm, not so much to wake the thing up, having slept on it in her nap, but more out of not knowing how to feel. The feelings, the raw passion the Warrior had felt lingered heavily on her mind.

Her thoughts returned to the present, as Jessica slapped her with another wisecrack. "Someone was dreaming good. I don't know what you were dreaming of over there, but I'd appreciate it if you didn't give me any details, ok sleeping beauty?"

She felt the same burn in her cheeks that April must be feeling, if the redness in the girls face was any indication. Isolde rolled her eyes, and stretched, pushing the last bit of sleep from her system. She noticed both friends had their shoes on already, clearly ready to go.

A knock on the door startled her, her thoughts having drifted back to the dream. She watched April get up to open the door, as she began pulling her own shoes on. Jessica's Sister, Sarah was on the other side.

Last night had been the first time she or April had met the woman, who was one year younger than Jessica at sixteen. She had an almost reddish blonde hair that hung straight past her shoulders, and was even more freckled than her sister.

While Jessica chose to live with their father for the sake of her friendships, her sister lived with their mom several hundred miles away, in a place called Victoria City.

April returned to the group as Sarah wandered off, and relayed her message. Jessica's dad was asleep, so as soon as they got the text from Rachel, it was go time. A text that came much sooner than Isolde had expected, as she was still lacing her shoes up.

"Go time. Mom just got picked up out front of the house." Isolde felt a pang of fear for her friend. She was torn, as the trio snuck their way out of the house. Torn between wanting to see her friend get the answers she craved, and between her desire for this to be one big waste of time. A waste of time that would, at least for the moment, spare her best friend from any more painful family revelations.

Within minutes, the trio had made their way to the same street, and were taking up hiding spots inside the half collapsed building that at one time, long before any of them had been born, was a grocery store. Isolde sat next to Jessica, with April on the other end of what used to be the main window, as they waited.

She whispered a little with Jessica, but overall the trio remained as quiet as they could be. There really wasn't a bad part of town, so to speak, but Jessica did live in what would be the closest to one. The trio ducked again, as another car drove by.

She looked at her phone, a large yawn prompting a giggle from Jessica. It was one-fifteen in the morning, and she had to get up at seven. So she knew the group didn't have much more time for their stakeout, but the next car to come proved they didn't need it.

APRIL'S HEART THREATENED to crack her ribcage with its hammering. She held her breath as the latest car, a black SUV slowed to a stop right across the street. As the vehicle took off, her spirits sank. There was her mother, the same gaudy outfit on. April looked over to her friends, who just gave sympathetic looks.

They remained in painfully awkward positions, taking the slightest peaks out, as April's fears began to get the better of her. She knew her own mother would chew her out, before forgetting it all an hour later, should they get caught.

The Needens would be disappointed in Isolde, but she would get off with some small punishment that wouldn't have much impact on the girl. She looked over to Jessica, who was cautiously poking her head around the corner of the pile of rubble that had once been a wall.

If they were to get caught, knowing how Jessica's father gets, she'd be on the first bus to Victoria City, and that would be the end of their friendship, at least in its current form. Her dour thoughts were broken by the sound of another car approaching.

She poked her own head around the corner of the remaining windowsill as a red sedan pulled up. Her attention was drawn to the driver's side door, which had three large gashes across it. Squinting, she deduced that it was some kind of decal. Taking one more look at the other to make sure they weren't watching her, she pulled her phone out, setting it in the corner of the windowsill, and began recording.

As they watched, her mother was leaning over the passenger side window, talking with the male driver. She couldn't make out what was being said from this distance, but her mother's actions were unmistakable. *Did. Did she just flash him?* April realized she'd have to rewatch what she recorded, assuming the phone picked anything up at all to confirm. But she was certain that her mother had.

Watching her get in the car, and lean over onto the driver's lap, her head disappearing from sight as the car sped off confirmed what she had been fearing. A fact that Jessica was the first to put a voice to.

"Holy hell, April? Your mom's a hooker?" Her words held none of the usual snark or sarcasm they knew and loved Jessica for. She looked off, up at the sky and the handful of stars poking through the overcast sky. She retrieved her phone, and made her way to the others.

"Yeah, looks like it." She whispered. More out of her own tumultuous feelings than any concern of getting discovered. She felt Isolde's arm around her, giving her a side hug that brought no real comfort as the trio headed out.

Several minutes later, the trio had made it back into Jessica's room. They had made the trip in silence, no one having spoken since her acknowledgment. Isolde was the first to break this new silence.

"Like, umm, so I get that this might not be the best time to ask but are you going to be ok? You want to talk to us about it?" She tried to give Isolde a smile but her efforts proved futile. Even a false smile was beyond her current mood.

"Thanks, but not right now." She could see the pain in her best friend's face. Looking over to Jessica, the girl seemed like she had something on her mind. Something she didn't seem too keen on keeping in her mind.

"Ok, I'm not trying to downplay how you feel girlie. But I'm curious why this is such a big deal? Ok sure, it's not the least disgusting job you could do but I mean, well I don't know what I mean." Jessica was visibly struggling to put that thought to words. Looking back to Isolde, she could see the same look of concern.

She looked at her hands, focusing on her pudgy fingers. She didn't even know how to feel. Jessica had a point, she'd never really thought ill of the so-called oldest profession. So why did she feel so much anger inside?

Her mind was flooded with the mental image, and the feelings that came with her mom coming home with that black-eye.

The tears were welling up in her eyes, and she could feel the soft shudders going through her chest as she tried to think of how to explain her feelings. The three girls looked between each other, with Jessica still looking confused.

April couldn't take it, she wanted to be anywhere but there. She got up, and after letting her friends know she was going to the bathroom, left the room. Several quiet moments later, she was sitting on the floor of the bathroom.

How could she even begin to explain to her friends what she felt right now. What her fears have been like lately? No matter how neglectful her mother was, she was still her mother. What if the next time she doesn't come home with a black eye? What if she just doesn't come home?

The tears flowed hot and fast as she sobbed on the bathroom floor. Anger, sorrow, and fear mingled in her heart as she sat there sobbing for several minutes. Her isolation was broken by the sound of someone knocking on the door, followed by a soft voice saying "It's Isolde, can I come in?" She got up to unlock the door for her friend.

As she did, she couldn't help but think, that if it had been anyone else she would have just ignored them. Even, no, especially Jessica. Isolde was just about the only person she wanted to be around in the whole world.

ISOLDE WATCHED APRIL leave the room before returning to facing Jessica. "Like, I think I get it. She's scared for her mom." She watched Jessica slowly nodding, understanding their friend's predicament.

She looked at the clock on Jessica's computer, it was a little before two in the morning, and she knew work was going to suck in the morning. But sleep was the last thing on her mind, as they sat waiting for April to return.

After sitting, getting up and pacing, and returning to her seat, she grew tired of waiting. Tired of waiting and concerned over April's prolonged absence. She let Jessica know she was going to check on April, and made her way to the bathroom, knocking and announcing her presence in a soft voice.

Moments later, she was sitting on the bathroom floor across from April, who had been crying heavily. She reached over, and wiped the tears from her friends eyes, not even thinking as she did. She saw her friend trying to put on a smile, and gave her a big shining example to imitate. Her plan worked as April's face finally cracked into a smile.

"What would I do without you, you fucking dork?" The tone of pain in April's voice felt like needles in her ears, in her heart. She decided to try and use some humor to lighten the mood. She rose to her feet, gave a small twirl followed by a curtsy.

"Yup, yup, yup. The queen of the dorks, at your service, m'lady." Her efforts were rewarded by a soft chuckle from April. *Well, like, it's a start.* She thought, returning to the floor. She placed her hand on April's shoulder, enjoying the warmth it radiated off in the chilly house, as the Marianas kept the AC on at seemingly all hours.

"So, like, I tried explaining it to Jess. You're scared something is going to happen to your mom, aren't you?" She thought back to her own childhood, months before she met the Needens, met April, when her own mother had passed. At just five years old, she couldn't really comprehend it, but she still recalls the pain she felt, all these years later. The idea of April going through that after already losing her father erased any humor left in Isolde.

April looked at her, just sitting there staring into Isolde's eyes for several moments. Finally, she placed her palm over Isolde's hand, still on her shoulder. Once more, Isolde found herself relishing the warmth of her friend's hand. But was it just the physical heat, or was there something else. The thought was interrupted by April.

"Thanks. Yeah I know she's not a good woman. And a pretty lousy mother, but she's the only mother I have. I, I don't know what would happen if something were to happen to her." Isolde had to fight her own tears at how bad she felt for April right now.

Isolde painfully sympathized with her friend. "What would happen to me? What would happen to Cassie, the poor girl is fucked up enough as it is. I'm terrified to even think of what it would do to her." Isolde could see the tears welling up in her friend's eyes once more, and reached her other arm over, hugging and holding her friend as she began sobbing into Isolde's chest.

"Like, I wish there was something I could do, girl. Some answers I could give to make this all better. But the only thing I can think of is to just tell you to talk to her. I mean, I don't know." Isolde felt her own eyes watering as she fought to force some coherence to her thoughts.

She felt April's arms wrap tighter around her, though the girl continued to not speak, only crying softly. She sat there, hugging and rubbing her best friends back for what may as well have been the rest of the week, for how little time mattered to her right now.

No, what mattered was being here for April. Was helping her through this. Was. Her thoughts were broken, as she started to realize something. Seeing April in this state hurt, that was a given. But there was something more. Something stronger, deeper. That damn feeling, once more. This time, however, it was strong enough to command her attention completely.

As the two girls sat there holding each other, Isolde thought back to the dream she'd had not all that long ago. Where that warrior was holding, hugging her queen or whatever the woman's role was.

She sat there, too afraid to even speak, not knowing what to even say or think, as realization dawned on her. Removing the pain from the equation, sitting here and holding April, she felt the same way that warrior felt in her dream as the two women cuddled so closely. The same feeling she'd been having about and around April for some time now.

The same warmth, the happiness, the peace and the... She squeezed her eyes shut, forcing the train of thought from her mind before giving a mental voice to the last word. She gave April a much firmer squeeze as she began wrestling with her own thoughts and emotions.

Chapter 10

WEDNESDAY JUNE 10TH Morning

Isolde shut her alarm off, looking over at April to see if she had woken and was grateful that she hadn't. Isolde lay there, watching her friend, very much still asleep. She couldn't help but notice the small smile on the girl's face as she slept, hoping she was having a pleasant dream. *Like, seriously she totally deserves it.* She caught herself smiling as well, and let out a long and deep sigh.

April had been here in her room Monday afternoon when she returned home from work and had not gone back home yet. A fact that left Isolde feeling torn. She was all too happy to do whatever she could for her closest friend, and did she ever need it right now. She let out a long and pleasurable stretch before rising to her feet.

She took one last look at her sleeping friend and started gathering her things. She was indeed happy to be there for the girl, but at the same time she hadn't had any time to think, to process what she felt the other night. The feelings she had while holding April. *I think I'm in...* She slapped herself on the cheek to stop the thought from finishing in her mind, leaving a stinging red mark.

She rushed down the hallway, and took a quick shower before throwing her work attire on and heading downstairs. Mrs. Needen was in the kitchen waiting on a pot of coffee to boil as Isolde grabbed a pack of cinnamon donuts and a soda. She heard the woman giving a loud tsk and turned to face her.

"Sweetie, when are you going to start eating a proper breakfast? All that sugar is right going to catch up to you one day, you mark my words." Her foster mother gave her a soft smile as she spoke.

She looked down at the package of processed junk food in her hand and realized the woman had a point. She slipped the treats in her purse, a snack for later and walked over to the cupboards and retrieved the canister of oatmeal and began preparing a small bowl, and placed a mug of water in the microwave.

Man, if April were to walk in on me right now, opting for oatmeal instead of snacks. The thought left her feeling a little better as the microwave dinged, signaling her water had boiled. She retrieved it, pouring it into her bowl, enjoying the warmth of the mug on her hands.

The same warmth she felt radiating from April, sitting on Jessica's frigid bathroom floor. The warmth she felt every time she hugged the girl. *Like every time I hug the girl that I'm in...* She slammed the microwave door, desperate to shift her thoughts elsewhere.

"Now Isolde, I'm rightly glad you've chosen a better breakfast, but that ain't no cause to go attacking the kitchenware sweetie." She closed her eyes, regretting her mistake as she turned to face Mrs. Needen to apologize.

"Well, apology accepted young lady. Now, are you fixin to tell me what's got you so shook?" Isolde grabbed a banana and made her way to the table to eat her breakfast. She sighed before taking the first bite. How exactly was she supposed to explain her feelings to the woman, when she didn't even fully understand them herself?

Like, how do you tell someone that you are. She dug the stubs of her fingernails deep into her palms, holding them there while focusing on the pain, until the thought passed. She felt Mrs. Needen's warm hand on her shoulder, and smiled weakly at the woman.

"Sweetie, something is clear as crystal bothering you. Would that something have anything to do with your extended houseguest perchance?" She chuckled, as she had wondered when April's extended stay would get noticed.

"Like, sort of yes, sort of no?" She finished her bland breakfast, and placed the bowl in the sink before finishing the conversation.

"I mean, I'm just stressed out. Some of it is for sure related to what April is dealing with."

She gave a quick rundown of April's concerns about her mother's disappearing acts of late, being sure to leave out any mention of her and her friend's little stakeout. She couldn't help but notice the woman's smile fade as she spoke. Looking at her phone she realized she had no time to spend probing, as she set off for work with a goodbye to the woman.

Two hours later, she had just finished cleaning the only dirty table in the diner. As she returned from dropping the dishes off, another customer entered the building. As she gave her required greeting she couldn't help but notice the woman's features.

She had hair nearly as long as Isolde's but which was a vibrant red. She had a pleasant, rounded face, and was plenty curvy. As she led the woman to a booth, she couldn't help but notice just how pale her skin was. So much so that it made the bleached white wall she sat beside look dark by comparison.

She forced a smile as the woman placed her order, yet another of those BBQ sandwiches and a sweet tea, and she went to fill it in. As she stood there waiting on the order, she had to stop herself from thinking about April once more.

She closed her eyes, leaning on the counter and letting her false smile fade. *You can't keep this up, girl. You need to face the facts.* Her thought was interrupted by the ding of the bell, and she turned to gather it up on her tray.

Moments later she was reading the order back to the woman, while placing the plate out on the table. She once more forced a smile, and began to turn away when she felt the woman's hand on her arm.

"Having a rough time, lil lady?" The woman looked around the empty dining area, before turning back to Isolde. "Now I don't expect Mrs. Daisy back there to mind if you humor me for a spell while I enjoy this lovely breakfast." The woman beckoned her to sit on the booth across from herself.

Not really feeling like declining, nor having much of anything else to do with this woman being the only current customer, she obliged. "Thank you kindly lil lady. Now, it wasn't that long ago when I was a feisty young thang like yourself." She watched the woman crack a large grin as she spoke.

"So I'd like to think I'm still pretty fluent in my teenage angst interpretations. So let me see if I've got this right." Isolde's curiosity peaked, as this woman intrigued her. The woman studied her face for a few moments.

"That's the boy trouble look, though I'm picking up something else. Family drama perhaps?" Isolde couldn't help but give a soft laugh. While she had the specifics wrong, she was pretty darn close, and let the woman know.

"Like, no boy trouble. And no family drama, either. At least not my own family. My best friend on the other hand." She let her voice trail off, and watched the woman enjoying her breakfast sandwich. Between bites, the two women had some conversation, where Isolde gave some of the less personal facts of what April was dealing with.

"Like yeah, and really I just wish I knew what to do, how to help her but I don't." She was looking down at the table, tracing the black grid line of the tablecloth with her eyes, when the woman spoke, a softness in her voice that hadn't been there prior.

"Well, lil lady, you weren't lying about it not being boy trouble." She looked up at the woman, who had a grin on her face, curious at her emphasis on the word boy. "You're in love with her, aintcha?"

Isolde let out a loud gasp. The words she'd gone to such pains, sometimes literal pain as the cuts on her palms from this morning reminded her, to avoid shook her. *Like is it that obvious?* She thought, as the door's bell chimed, and she looked up to see an elderly couple entering.

"Well, must thank you there," She followed the woman's gaze to her nametag, " Isolde, for humoring me this morning. You go on and get about your job." As Isolde nodded, and started to get up, she felt the woman's hand on her arm once more. "Can't much say I envy your predicament, lil lady, but take some free advice. Find you someone you trust to confide in and think about how best you should go and proceed, lest you go breaking that poor thang's heart." She gave the woman a nod and smile before greeting the newcomers.

APRIL FORCED HERSELF to get out of bed. She wasn't sure how long she had lain there since waking up, thinking about her emotions. She looked over at Isoldes empty bed, loneliness gripping her as she reached for her phone. She fired off a text to Jessica, hoping her friend was free to chat as the solitude was crushing her.

The last two days had been the worst emotional rollercoaster she had ever felt. After leaving Jessica's, and riding with Isolde to work, she had gone home. Her mother hadn't been there, and Rachel was at work, and she had been in no mood to talk to Cassie. So she had gathered some clothes and went over to Isolde's, the Needen's being all too willing to let her hang around til Isolde got home.

She walked around the room, stopping to look at everything in it, without actually looking at anything in particular. Both of her friends were happy to help her, through conversation, emotional support, and a lot of unwarranted wisecracks from Jessica.

Her thoughts turned to her mother, as she wondered what the woman was doing. She hadn't seen or spoken to her in two days, and only Rachel had texted her, to which she had just replied she was hanging out with Isolde for a while.

She jumped a little, startled by the notification on her phone, which she rushed over to check. She flipped through a few notifications from the phone itself, crying about needing some update and another moaning about running out of space. She found the latest, a text from Jessica and opened it.

"OMG girly FML With Sarah shopping. Sorry can't chat RN TTYL." She tossed the phone down with a deep sigh. It was a little after ten in the morning, so Isolde wouldn't be home for several long hours.

She paced around the room, debating with herself if she should try going home, but she dismissed the idea as she wasn't ready to take the advice Isolde had given her on the bathroom floor, and wasn't at all ready to confront her mother.

Her thoughts turned back to that encounter. Despite how angry, how hurt she was, Isolde was there for her, and hadn't left her side. She thought deep on just how much Isolde mattered to her, how she was still the only person she truly wanted to be around right now.

Her thoughts still on Isolde, shifted, and were now about how odd her behavior had been since that night. She sat down on the edge of the bed.

Isolde had seemed distracted the last two days, and very much on edge. April wondered if it had something to do with her family drama but didn't believe it had any relevance. Regardless of how Isolde had been acting, April was glad to have someone so supportive, so loving in her life.

So loving. The words bounced around in her mind. She thought back over the last couple of days, at Isolde's behavior towards her. As supportive as she had been, April couldn't help but pick up on something else, how frequently she had caught Isolde looking at her, only to snap her head away to look at whatever her eyes fell on.

As she continued the odd train of thoughts, she found herself moving through the house, and into the living room, where Mrs. Needen was sitting and reading a book. The woman looked up and gave her a smile as she entered the room.

"Rise and shine there, sweetie. You done got yourself some good rest I hope?" She nodded, and made her way to the couch across from the two recliners the Needens often sat in. She felt the woman's gaze on her, and looked up to see a curious look on the woman's face as she asked April what was wrong.

Before she even realized what she was doing, she was giving a detailed summary of how she felt, and what she had learned about her mother. She felt guilty as she didn't stop to omit the bit about them sneaking out the other night. She hoped she hadn't gotten her friend in any trouble, the last thing she needed was to throw a wrench in their relationship.

Relationship. The word stuck out in her mind as she was finishing her summary. Wasn't that what Mrs. Needen had said to her not too long ago, that she and Isolde had a special relationship?

Mrs. Needen gave her a soft smile, while sitting there watching her. *Watching,* like she had been so engrossed in watching Isolde change that day. Her thoughts turned back to that day at the river, How she felt watching her friend, both in the water and while she changed.

She focused her thoughts on what had happened before they entered the water. To how Isolde had snapped at Jessica, acting uncharacteristically defensive of April over Jessica's comment.

Something the girl had been doing more of lately, as she thought back to the incident with that boy, Brandon. Her thoughts were interrupted by Mrs. Needen.

"Well now, if that isn't a tale. Rightly none too pleased at you girls sneaking out in the night like that. Going to make sure Isolde knows it too." April gave another sigh, one more log on the fire to deal with, making it up to Isolde for getting her a scolding.

"Though it does pain me that you had to learn the truth about your mother. More so, I'm sorry it's something that was kept from you, most especially by myself." She looked up at Mrs. Needen, not sure she had heard the woman correctly. So she asked for clarification.

"Yes sweetie. I've known for some time. My husband is all over town for his job, and he's seen her on a few streets, peddling her, well, her wares shall we say." April gave a scornful laugh. She knew why the woman had kept it from her, in some attempt to spare her from such a painful truth. But some part of her resented that she hadn't been told. *Guess you can't always tell when someone is keeping something from you after all.*

As the two women sat engaged in small talk, April couldn't help but think about her latest thought. She wondered, could Isolde be keeping something from her? Once more her thoughts were interrupted by her neighbor.

"Now I can't rightly tell you the best course of action, but I can tell you this sweetie. No matter how bad things get over there," she noticed a coy grin come over the woman's face, "so long as you and Isolde are as close as can be, you've always got a place here."

April nodded and thanked the woman, curious about that smile. About what else the woman knew and wasn't sharing. Did she know what Isolde was dealing with? What had her so on edge, ever since the two of them sat hugging each other on that bathroom floor.

Hugging each other, something she and Isolde had been doing a lot of lately, she noticed.

They had always hugged, though it was usually more something Isolde started. The girl was a very hands on kind of friend, always with a hand on her shoulder, a hug, or a back rub. Something she could use right about now, as she thought about how wonderful the girl was at giving them.

She wondered how good she would be at giving one, having only done some small mockery of the act a few times. Would Isolde like it if she gave her friend one after she got home from work? Take her mind off of whatever was bothering her maybe?

Yeah, she was sure Isolde would love that. Love. Once more the thoughts bounced around in her mind, this time pushing her to think deep about her feelings. About how she felt that warmth, and a deep sense of happiness every time she and Isolde were together.

The feelings she had, the longing and missing Isolde she had experienced so much of lately. Once more as strong as ever as she sat there in the girl's own home, too afraid to return to hers.

The unexplained giddiness she felt every time Isolde showed up. The way she felt, before Jessica caught her staring at the girl that day. The excitement she felt and couldn't explain at Jessica's wisecrack on the subject.

She sat there as Mrs. Needen went back to her book. Her thoughts went back over the various trains of thought she'd had this morning, and she laid back on the couch, feeling the color leaving her cheeks as her mouth hung open, as she began to put it all together.

I think I'm in love with my best friend.

WEDNESDAY JUNE 10TH Afternoon

The work day had been slow and boring, something Isolde was thankful for as she finished clocking out. She gave Clara a weak smile as she headed out of the employee door to unlock her bike.

As she mounted it, she half stood, half sat on the bike as she took a deep breath, staring at a tree across the street and the small squirrel that was flitting around on one of its branches. April would for sure still be at the house. A thought that under any other circumstances would have had her pedaling hard to get home as soon as she could.

As she watched the small critter vanish up into the tree she let out a deep sigh, and began to pedal off, much slower than she ever had. April was the last person she wished to see, at least until she had a chance to wrangle her emotions, her feelings.

As she pedaled, lost in thought over what that woman had said so casually, she heard someone shouting her name and looked up, and down the street. Rachel was riding down the street, towards her on her pink and black bike.

She slowed down, letting Rachel catch up to her, thankful for the delay in getting home. Rachel gave her a smile as she pulled to a stop beside Isolde.

"Hey, glad I caught you. So uh, is everything all right with my sister?" Isolde felt the frown stretching over her face. *Like hell no she's not.* The thought dug her even further into the depths of her mood.

"No. No she's not at all, and going off what she's told us, you have a pretty good idea why." She watched the look of confusion spread across Rachel's face, before it was replaced by one of recognition. Rachel dismounted her bike, lowered the kickstand and leaned against an electric pole, sighing.

"She found out about Mom." Isolde nodded and gave a rundown of the night at Jessica's, leaving out her own emotional revelations. As she spoke, she also dismounted her bike, and stood there with her arms crossed, glaring at Rachel.

"Like, so you knew and didn't bother telling her? I mean that's pretty messed up don't you think?" She chastised the older girl, wondering how much of her anger was from Rachel's secret keeping, and how much was from her own.

Rachel gave a nod before speaking. "It is. I found out a few months ago, because Mom came out and told me point blank. She begged me not to say anything to my sisters, and honestly?" Isolde watched as a scowl crossed Rachel's face. "I didn't say anything to them because I didn't want them to worry about Mom like I have been. Wanted to avoid burdening them with the same shit April is now dealing with."

Isolde felt her own frown deepen. Whatever anger she felt at Rachel for keeping that secret from her sisters, from April was replaced by a much deeper rage at their mother. What kind of woman burdens one of her children with something so heavy, and begs them to not even speak of it to her sisters?

The thought weighed on her as she and Rachel walked their bikes for a while, talking. Before long, the two had mounted their bikes and were pedaling towards Isoldes house. Her mood flatlined, something she hadn't thought possible, as she dreaded the conversation the two of them were about to have with April.

Several minutes later, she was leading Rachel into the house, and sure enough April was sitting in the kitchen with Mrs. Needen. The smile that wrapped around April's face as she saw Isolde was almost enough to crack the icey cold feelings surrounding her heart. *Almost*, she thought, as she stepped aside to let Rachel in and lock the door behind her.

APRIL HAD SPENT THE afternoon downstairs, engaged in idle conversation with her neighbor. They sat now in the kitchen as the woman was preparing dinner, some kind of stew with a lot of meat and a side of freshly baked garlic bread.

The smell of the bread in the oven tantalized her as she once more looked at the clock. It was almost five in the afternoon, and Isolde was off work at four so where the hell was she?

She was thinking about going back upstairs to grab her phone to text Isolde when she heard the front door opening. She let out the breath she realized she was holding as she watched Isolde walking in, as a giant smile lit her face up at the sight of her best friend.

A smile that just as fast faded from her as she saw Rachel following Isolde in. Isolde had caught her gaze and was motioning her to follow as the pair headed upstairs. She let Mrs. Needen know and made her way upstairs as well, following Rachel into Isolde's room. She smirked a little realizing this was the first time Rachel had ever been in Isolde's room.

She took a seat on the futon as Rachel took the desk chair and Isolde sat on her bed. The look on each of the girls' faces was enough to let her know she was not in for fun and games.

"Hey sis, good to see you again." She returned her sister's pleasantries, still not sure if she was ready to even speak to the girl, but relented as she recognized that she was going to have to, whether she wanted it or not.

"Isolde filled me in on you girls' nocturnal adventures the other night, and what you learned about Mom."

April balled her fists and turned away from the others, the anger building within. She could tell from Rachel's tone of voice that she already knew what they had found out, and it only pissed her off all the more.

"Yeah, and you knew, didn't you? She challenged. Turning back to the other two she noticed that Isolde was looking down at the floor, and she seemed to be lost in her own world. Rachel on the other hand had a frown on, but one that seemed more born of sorrow than anger.

"Yeah. Like I told her, Mom outright told me a few months ago. It was right after I got my latest job, and began helping with groceries." So she's known for months. What else about their mother did she know and wasn't telling?

"Why didn't you tell me? Or Cassie? I mean come on, that's not exactly something you keep from your sisters, not something about our mother, not like that." She listened as Rachel gave her explanation. As her sister spoke, she caught Isolde looking over at her, only to turn her head back to the floor when April had noticed.

She felt a warm feeling inside when it had happened, still unsure how she should even feel, as she was still unsure of her own feelings for the girl just yet.

"Like what the fuck is her problem? She goes out and gets beat up, and lays that shit on one of her kids and makes her keep it from her sisters?" The raw anger in Isolde's voice took April aback. Not that it was something she could blame her friend for. "I mean your mom is a piece of shit, sorry not sorry."

She watched as Rachel nodded, and she thought about her own feelings over Isolde's words. She found herself conflicted, as the words did hurt, no matter how bad a parent was, hearing your best friend call them a piece of shit hurt. But on the other side, Isolde was absolutely correct.

"You have nothing to be sorry for Isolde." This time it was Rachel who spoke, breaking the silence that had fallen after Isolde's little outburst. "Truth be told, watching Cassie lately, the violence she's shown towards Mom? Part of me wishes it were me shoving her to the ground."

The revelation took April by surprise, as she found her jaw once more agape. Rachel had always been the most level-headed of her sisters, so hearing how much their mother's actions affected her, to the degree that she wanted to lash out herself was not something she expected.

The three of them sat around for a long while, engaged in varying topics, mostly related to her mother and family. Along the way, she had caught Isolde staring at her several more times, each time giving her that same warm feeling. Each time reinforcing her newfound belief. And each time, making her all the more worried, afraid of what would happen if Isolde didn't feel the same.

Chapter 11

WEDNESDAY JUNE 10TH Evening

April followed her sister inside. The first time she had set foot in the house since Monday morning. She watched as Rachel disappeared into their mother's room, before popping her head out a moment later beckoning her in.

She made her way inside to see her mother and sister sitting on the bed. Though she couldn't be sure, it seemed like her mother hadn't begun hitting the booze yet. A small miracle given how late in the evening it was.

"So what's with the family meeting girls?" Her mother asked, looking between them. April wasn't sure how to begin, and counted her blessings that Rachel took that initiative.

"She knows, Mom." April watched the look of rage flow across their mother's face as she turned to look at Rachel.

"Excuse me, what? I thought you promised you weren't going to say anything to your sisters. This isn't something they need to worry about." April snorted, a sick amusement at her mother's words. *Not something we need to worry about? The fact that our mother is coming home with black eyes given to her by total creeps isn't something we need to worry about?* The thought brought out a deep rage.

"Fuck you, Mom." Her words took both of the other women by surprise, Rachel in particular as she watched her sister mouthing out the words "what the hell?" She stood up, her fists balled and she slammed one of them against the wall hard enough to knock one of the pictures to the floor. The shattering glass of the frame didn't bother her as she continued.

"I don't care if you want to fuck every loser in town. Hell if you get paid for it, all the better." She had to take a moment to force herself to stop gritting her teeth in order to continue. "But do you have any idea, any kind of idea what it does to me? To Cassie? Hell even to Rachel over there to see you come home beaten?"

She watched her mother looking down at the floor. *Yeah, you should feel bad.* She thought, not at all ready to stop her own outburst. "You say it's not something we should have to worry about? Ok, then tell me something. What the fuck are we supposed to do when you don't come home at all the next time? What if some asshole decides a black eye isn't enough? What the hell would that do to us? To Cassie, Mom. What the hell do you think would happen to her if you got yourself beaten, or even raped out there on the streets? If you got murdered?"

The tears were flowing all around. Even Rachel, who almost never shed tears, was letting the rivers run free. Her own tears flew hot and fast. "Or do you even care? Do you even care about how bad you've fucked her up with your drinking? Your neglect?" She could feel the pain in her heart overtaking the rage.

"Oh, and just for your information, Rach didn't say anything to me until after the fact. Me and Isolde spent the night at Jessica's the other day, and we snuck out. I saw you with my own eyes getting into a car, and going down on the fucking driver. A red sedan with goofy ass clawmark decals."

"You're right." Her mother's words were soft, meak and she almost thought she had imagined it. "I failed you girls. Cassandra most of all. I just don't have many options for taking care of you girls." Her mother's attempt at an excuse, at justifying her choices left April with a feeling of disgust.

"If that's true, if this is your last resort or something, why don't you get yourself cleaned up? Get rid of the booze and get a real job, like Rachel or even Isolde has a damn job these days." The anger and pain in her heart were waging the equivalent of world war three in her heart as she spoke.

"April, hun, you've seen so many times how that works out for me. At least this way, this kind of work pays well enough that me and Rachel can keep the lights on, and food in the fridge." April wanted to fling some kind of counterargument, but she just felt defeated, as she turned to look at the wall, her back to her family. She found herself looking at the shattered picture frame, and a fresh round of tears began falling.

She bent over to pick the picture up. It was a picture of a blue kitten, drawn in crayon with the name Ocean written in a child's handwriting across the bottom. A picture she herself had drawn years ago, of the cat they had at the time. She was a beautiful old tabby, with deep blue fur. She had passed away several years ago, leading Rachel to get a replacement pet in the form of Buster.

She didn't even know her mother had kept this old thing, and looked around the walls to see several other drawings, report cards and more of hers, and both of her sisters framed on the wall.

How could someone who acted so indifferent, so callously neglectful, keep such treasured mementoes? Once more, she found herself at a loss in regards to her mother.

She turned back to the others, Rachel was holding their mother, who was still crying. April thought about what to say, as she wanted to try and bring the peace back, settling on a question. "Ok then, if this is what you are going to keep doing, then why not be more careful? Why go see men who hit you like that?"

She watched as her mother wiped her eyes, and looked up at her. "Most of my," her mother paused, clearly trying to work out how best to word her thought. "Most of my clients are one and dones, and most don't last more than a few minutes." Her mother looked back down at the floor, her hand rubbing the side of her face where she had had the black eye.

"But there's a new guy, moved in some months back. He's become a very frequent regular. Pays better than most other clients as well." April shook her head as she listened to her mother describing these men as clients.

"At first it was the basic stuff he wanted. Which was fine. But over time he started wanting more." She watched as her mother shifted around on the bed, rubbing her arms.

"More, specific things. He offered to pay more and at first it wasn't too bad, but he just kept raising the stakes so to speak. That black eye came from me turning him down. A reminder to know my place as he put it."

This time, it was Rachel, who had been sitting quietly on the bed to butt in. "If this pig is so bad, why do you keep seeing him? I don't give a damn how well he pays if he beats on you for refusing."

She watched as Rachel was rubbing their mother's shoulder. Her sister had a good point, no amount of money was worth that. She watched her mother sit in silence for a couple of minutes before answering.

"It's precisely because he is a pig. If I don't give in, he'll ruin me. Ruin us." It took April several moments of trying to figure out what her mother had meant, before Rachel cleared her confusion up.

"He's a pig? You mean, he's a cop? Wow." Rachel putting it into perspective weighed on her. Weighed on the whole room, as April watched her mother finally going for the bottle of wine beside her bed.

Rachel got up and left, looking disgusted, as April spent a few minutes in vain trying to convince her mother from drinking before she too left, realizing the family meeting was over.

ISOLDE SAT AT HER DESK, flipping her phone around in her hands. It had been a while since April and her sister had left and she had spent the time since thinking.

Thinking about how relieved she was when April finally decided to go home, giving her a chance to grapple with her emotions. Thinking about how many times she caught herself staring at her friend, feeling that same warm happiness despite her own inner turmoil. Thinking about how many times she had blushed when getting caught by April

But most of all, she was thinking of how to proceed. She was still refusing to say or even think the word, but she was certain beyond all doubt that it was what she felt for her friend. Not the kind she had always had, the same kind she had for Jessica, but something much deeper, much fiercer.

She looked at the three empty snack cake wrappers littering her desk as she reached over to grab the last one in the box. As she sat there enjoying the chocolate flavor of the outer layers, and the fudge creme filling she turned her phone on, and opened her message app on April's contact.

She had no idea how April felt about her, beyond the obvious feelings that come from such a close friendship. Would she be receptive should Isolde tell her the truth? Or would she shun her, driving a death wedge in their friendship.

The agony of indecision had reached its climax, and she flipped down to Jessica's contact, firing off a text letting her friend know she desperately needed someone to talk to.

She got up and paced around the room. As she walked she thought over the different ways she could bring it up. As well as the different ways Jessica might react.

Her musing was brought to an end as her phone notification sounded, and she rushed over to check Jessica's response.

"That so girlie? Surprised you texted me. Not that I'm complaining, bored AF over here LMAO. Anywho, what's got you so desperate to talk to someone? And why ain't you talking to April?"

She laid the phone down, squeezing her eyes shut. It was the moment of truth, and she still couldn't bring herself to even think the word in her mind, so how was she even going to tell Jessica? She wrangled with the thought for several moments before picking up the phone, and firing her reply off.

"Because I'm in love with her." She dropped the phone on the desk, sighing. She had to just blind type to get it out, but now it was out. *I'm in love with April.* She ran the thought through her mind several times, feeling better every time she thought it.

She still had no idea how April would take the news, nor how it would affect her friendship but at least someone else now knew. The phone began buzzing moments before she heard the ringtone, as she picked the phone up, bracing herself for the talk.

"Say that again girlie? You what?" The tone in Jessica's voice took her by surprise as she steeled her resolve.

"Like yeah. I've been dealing with these feelings ever since we all spent the night over there." She looked down at the desk, relieved to be talking to someone about this but scared at the same time.

She gave Jessica an overview of the way she had been feeling, the thoughts she had had, and her thought process leading her to this conversation. Her friend sat in silence for several minutes before speaking.

"Wow. Not really sure how to process this, you know? Guess I should have seen it coming with how close you two are." Isolde gave a chuckle, as in hindsight it does seem pretty obvious. "You know, now that I think of it, I'm pretty sure it's not a one sided thing either."

Jessica's words intrigued her, prompting her to think back, towards anything that might have given her that impression. Besides Jessica catching April staring at Isolde while changing, she couldn't think of much.

"Like really? Why do you think that?" She asked, anxious to hear Jessica's reasoning. If there was a chance that April felt the same way towards her? Her heart fluttered as she could feel the blush coming on.

"Well, the way she was staring at you that day for one. Hell, the way she's always looking at you. If I had a nickel for every time I've caught her giving you one of her longing stares, I'd be able to buy my own car by now."

Isolde couldn't hold back the smile. So April had been caught staring at her as well? Not very strong evidence, but also not nothing. The two continued the line of conversation for a little while, leaving both girls unsure, but suspecting of April's own feelings.

"Well, until I figure this out, please, please, please don't say anything to her?" She asked. She could hear Jessica's sigh over the phone, as her gut tied itself into a knot. Jessica wasn't much for sighing.

"I'll think about it girlie. No promises though. But I do have something to say myself." Isolde braced herself, the tone of Jessica's voice unsettling her. "I will be the first person to congratulate you two if you end up together, and I'll figure out some way to keep you both in my life if you don't. But if you two start any drama with each other over this?" Isolde swallowed hard several times as Jessica Spoke.

"Then I will not speak to either of you until you resolve it, whether in a good way or a not so good one. Deal?" Isolde leaned back in her chair, rubbing her forehead. She felt bad for dumping this on Jessica, and recognized the girl had a point, as there was a good chance of drama even if April felt the same. So she gave her reply before the two continued talking. "Deal."

Chapter 12

THURSDAY JUNE 11TH Afternoon

Isolde clocked out, and took her exit, finding herself surprised that both April and Jessica were waiting, bikes in hand. A moment of panic ran through her as she looked over to Jessica, scared she had told April, but the girl just shook her head.

"Like what's the occasion? Didn't expect either of you to show up." She didn't even have to force herself to sound natural, ever since her phone call the night before she was feeling like her old self. Her old self plus feelings for her best friend, she thought while the three of them took off.

"Oh, nowhere too special, just try and keep up." April said, giving her a coy smile. She wasn't sure where her friends were leading her, but she was happy to follow. Happy to have most of the weight she'd been carrying around off of her chest.

This was also a good opportunity for her to start paying closer attention to how April acted around her, to see if Jessica's suspicion held water. A suspicion she worried the girl was correct on.

The girls rode for a short while, before coming to a stop close to Jessica's house at a convenience store. Jessica looked over to Isolde, her hand out. "You, card or cash, now. We need some drinks. Isolde tilted her head to the side, sizing up her friend. She couldn't disagree with the idea of a drink however, so she reached in her purse and pulled out a ten dollar bill and handed it to Jessica with a "just get me whatever."

April wanted a bottle of water, and Jessica set off. As she reached the doors, she turned and looked at the pair, shouting with a wink, "Now don't you little lovebirds go disappearing on me or anything." Isolde felt her face burning, as she caught April's gaze for a moment before turning away. Her heart had skipped a beat.

For the brief moment she had made eye contact with April, she picked up on the girl's own blushing, but more than that she had that same coy smile on her face. April broke the silence, as Isolde picked up on something, some note in her tone of voice she didn't recognize.

"You can always count on Jess to be a showoff, huh? I mean, unless you want to go off and disappear on her or something?" Isolde couldn't hide the next round of blushing so she turned away from April. *What the hell girl. Man If Jessica told her already.*

The thought returned her emotions to some semblance of normal, so she turned back to April. *Still wearing that little smile, huh girl? Well two can play this game.*

"Like sure I'm game." She wanted to see just how far April would take this. "Would like to have that drink but I mean, it would be nice if we took off together," she felt the blush returning and hastily added "I mean like as a prank of Jess or something."

She caught April's gaze once more, wishing she could read the girl's face but she bore too neutral of an expression, beyond that damn smile that said everything and nothing at the same time. The pair waited in silence, with Isolde realizing that if April was up to something, she was going to have to let her friend make the moves.

Minutes later Jessica had returned, handing her her change, a dollar and some pennies as well as a bottle of cola. April got her bottle of water, something Jessica also had, but Isolde noticed she also had a bottle of diet cola and asked about it.

"Oh this? It's for Sarah. That's where we are heading. It's about time you two get to spend some time with my sis, and you, especially

April, get you out of that family drama for a bit." Isolde smiled at the idea. They hadn't gotten to spend much time with Sarah the other night, so she was looking forward to getting a chance to get to know her a bit.

She looked over at April once more, taking a drink of her water. *Yeah, can't really disagree with Jess about you either girl.* The thought hit her harder than she expected as the trio pedaled off.

Minutes later they had locked up their bikes and were heading into Jessica's house. She had let them know her father was at work so not to worry, a fact that they already knew given she was out of the house on her own.

Isolde followed her friends to the living room where Sarah was already waiting. Isolde took a seat on the loveseat as Jessica handed her sister the soda. She felt the seat falling a little inwards as April took the seat next to her.

Isolde looked around, noting that Sarah was in a recliner, Jessica was sitting on a kitchen chair, leaving this loveseat as the only other seating arrangement.

She caught Jessica's gaze, the look on her face telling Isolde all she needed to know. *Like that jerk is doing this on purpose.* She wasn't sure whether to be annoyed or thankful for Jessica's subtle help.

"So umm, hi again." Sarah's voice was soft, the girl was clearly a bit shy. April and Isolde gave their own pleasantries to the girl.

"Umm, so Jessica's told me a lot about you two. I'm sorry we haven't had much of a chance to meet. Dad's a bit too strict about letting us wander around outside though we all know how much a certain someone listens." The girl turned to glare at her sister, who just laughed.

"Well duh, I'm a big girl and I've got two other big girls," Jessica looked over to Isolde with a humorous glint in her eye, "well one big girl and a damn candy cane to watch out for me."

Sarah and April both laughed at the comment, while Isolde had just rolled her eyes, already sick of Jessica's joke, though if she knew her friend it would be far from the last time she'd hear it.

"So I don't see why I'm not allowed to go out when I want. Besides, you're the one living in the big city where all the shootings happen. If anyone needs to be overprotective it's mom."

Sarah's gaze fell to the floor as Isolde felt a bit sorry for the girl. Jessica wasn't wrong, Victoria City had been in the news any number of times over the years for one shootout or another.

"Yeah, uh, wasn't there a big gang fight there like a month or so ago?" April asked the group, to which Sarah replied. "Umm yeah. It's why Mom sent me out here to stay for a while, until things cooled off back home. She's coming in this weekend."

The news was bittersweet to Isolde as she felt bad for the girl living with such danger all around. But on the other hand, the possibility of finally meeting Jessica's mom excited her. She laid back in her seat, as April gave a stretch beside her.

"Yeah, hopefully you two girlies can meet her before she drags sis away again." Sarah gave her sister a small smile, and said something, but whatever it was didn't register to Isolde.

She was careful not to move her head as she shifted her eyes down to her hand, sitting on the edge of her cushion. April's hand was resting on top of hers, and she wasn't moving it.

AS JESSICA AND SARAH were talking about their mother coming in, April found herself thinking about her feelings. Thinking about how nice it was to be sitting so close to Isolde, and most of all, how the girl had given away so much at the gas station.

Half paying attention to her friends, she decided to test Isolde a little, and faked a yawn, and the accompanying stretch.

She noticed Isolde's hand laying on the seat beside her, and brought her own hand down on top of it softly as she finished her stretch. She stifled a chuckle as she watched Isolde's eyes move down to her hand though neither girl moved.

For a test, she couldn't help but notice just how nice this felt, and wished she could hold her friend's hand for real. The look on Isolde's face was a dead giveaway. She was enjoying this, maybe more than April herself was.

Once more she found herself having to accept that she truly did have some kind of feelings for her best friend, feelings it now seemed certain were reciprocated.

Her warm musings were interrupted by Sarah's question. "Oh, umm, so are like, you two together or something?" She faked a look down at her hand, and quickly removed it with a look of shock, or something she hoped looked like shock on her face.

"Oh, uh, no, umm." April muttered, as Isolde began blushing and Jessica burst out laughing. Sarah gave her a sympathetic look and a soft smile.

"Oh, umm it's ok if you are. We don't judge, do we sis?" Sarah looked over at Jessica who just nodded. "I mean, I have a girlfriend as well so yeah." April felt a pang of guilt over having confused the girl, though her words did bring some measure of comfort. At least she now knew Jessica would be ok if she and Isolde ever did anything, as she was now certain her friend had feelings.

Feelings that she too felt in return as she looked over at Isolde, still red from blushing and gave her friend a warm smile. She turned back to the others, with Jessica still giggling. "Oh, you do? That's cool. But no, me and Isolde are just good friends, that's all. Didn't realize my hand was on hers is all." Just good friends. The thought came with a sting all its own as she realized she was starting to really wish it weren't the case.

"Like yeah I don't know how much Jess has told you but me and April live beside each other, and we've been the best of friends since we were kids." If she weren't already sure of Isolde's feelings by now, the sadness in her friend's voice was all the giveaway she needed.

The group engaged in conversation, with April herself chiming in here and there. As the conversation flowed, she thought about her own feelings. How she was going to proceed, or even if she should. She thought back to her messed up family situation, wondering how her mother, and her sisters would handle the news if she came out as a lesbian in love with her best friend.

She focused on the word, as she had never really thought much on the topic of sexuality. Moreso, she couldn't recall ever having any crushes on boys over the years. Thinking harder on it, she realized she had always been disinterested at best, disgusted at worst when either of her friends or sisters were talking about boys or boyfriends. *What a way to figure something out about yourself,* she thought.

She looked over at Isolde, who was laughing at some joke Jessica had made. Like herself, Isolde had never shown much interest in boys as far as she could remember. What would it be like? The thought carried its weight as she had no frame of reference to even begin to judge.

While Jessica had an ex-boyfriend, a loser who turned out to be a cheater, she had never had any kind of intimate relationship. A fact Isolde could likewise lay claim to. She felt a pang of sorrow in her heart at the thoughts.

The idea of both her and Isolde's first relationship being with one another was bittersweet. Something that excited her, all the while terrifying and even to some degree depressing her, as she accepted that she needed more time to process things before proceeding.

"Earth to April, May I have your attention sometime this June please?" She had to groan at Jessica's monthly pun, as she pushed her thoughts aside and turned her attention to her friend.

"What's up?" she asked, noticing the coy smirk on her friend's face. She couldn't help but wonder just how much Jessica knew that she wasn't saying. Had Isolde already confided in her? Should she? Regardless, she should pay more attention to the conversation at hand.

"Well we asked you a question but you were off in lala land or something. Now, what would you like to eat, you know food?" Jessica made a mock showing of eating something from an imaginary bowl. "Isolde's ordering out for us and we need to know where we are ordering from."

April had to laugh, though not at Jessica's antics, but because she was so focused on her own thoughts that she missed the whole conversation. The fact it was about food meant she had to have been deep in thought. She once more pushed the thoughts aside, and rejoined the conversation as the four of them went back and forth over which of the fast food places they wanted.

Chapter 13

FRIDAY JUNE 11TH MORNING.

April yawned, and stretched before climbing out of bed. She listened for the sound of arguing, or doors slamming or whatever had woken her up this morning. She felt uneasy as she heard nothing. She headed out of the room, and down the stairs to investigate.

As she entered the living room she couldn't help but wonder where everyone was, before she heard the sounds of arguing coming from her mother's room and made her way in. She had to cover her mouth, stifling the gasp as she saw her mother before the woman turned away from her.

She was holding a bag of frozen vegetables to the side of her face, a large bruise was visible peeking out from behind the brand label. More worrying was her mother's lip, which was swollen and burst open, dried blood all around it. As well as that damned gray shirt, ripped to the point one of her breasts was clearly visible, and heavily bruised.

"Courtesy of her new regular. She just came back about twenty minutes ago. Don't think I need to tell you but Cassie took this very bad." Rachel explained. Their mother turned back to look at her, tears in her eyes. "Been trying to convince Mom to fucking do something about this, to hell if the guy's a cop or not, but we have more important matters at hand. Cassie took off and now she isn't answering our texts or calls."

Her Mom finally spoke up, her voice shaking, and not at all sounding like her normal self, likely from whatever damage her face had suffered. "She took one look at me and just left. None of her usual theatrics, she just ran off. Could you please go out and look for her?" April gave their mother a nod, her concern for her sister outweighing her anger and disappointment in their mother.

She rushed upstairs to dress, and hopped on her social media profile, finding Cassandra's page and began messaging some of the girl's friends to see if she was with any of them. She also sent a text to Isolde, asking her to let someone know if Cassandra came down that way.

As she was leaving the house, she texted Jessica, to see if she was free to help her look. She received a quick reply as she finished unlocking her bike, Jessica was more than happy to help.

She further checked the few replies she had from Cassie's friends, none of whom had seen her sister this morning, and one of them admitted she wasn't replying to her either. She felt the knots in her gut twisting up as she rode off to meet Jessica.

The two girls had spent more than an hour riding up and down almost the entire side of the town they lived in. She tried to keep a hold on her panic, knowing this wasn't the first time the girl had run off like this. But the circumstances that had led to it were nothing like any of the others, she thought as her panic grew.

"Hey isn't that her?" She followed Jessica's gaze, and her heartbeat finally began to slow. Cassandra was sitting on the steps of one of the abandoned buildings as the pair rode up to her. Her sister gave her one of her usual greetings.

"What do you want, fatso?" April followed suit with Jessica and dismounted her bike. She ignored her sister's barb as she texted Rachel, letting her know they had found their wayward sister. She let out a sigh of relief as she turned to her sister.

"We were looking for you. Mom told me you took off and weren't answering her calls and asked me to come find you." Her sister scoffed at April's words.

"She did, did she? Fucking bitch. You see her face? What kind of nerve does she have coming home like that? And just who the hell beats on their friends like that?"

April took a seat beside her sister, placing her arm around the girl. Despite the anger and insults, she couldn't help but agree with her sister. Jessica took a seat on the opposite side of Cassie.

"Yeah I saw alright. Rachel was chewing her out when I left. I can't believe she let herself get so messed up." She had to stop herself from revealing too much, as she knew she now had a heavy burden to bear. Whether to tell her sister the truth or not.

Cassandra let out a laugh, more anger than any joy or humor in her voice. "Like she's going to listen. How many times do I have to say it? She doesn't care about us." April couldn't help but tighten her grip around her sister. She could hear the same pain she felt inside in her sister's voice.

"Hey, Cassandra, right? Trust me, your Mom loves you. She's one hell of an idiot, and you go right ahead and call her every name you need to, but just trust me. No matter how stupid she gets, she will always love you." April felt a shudder run through Cassie at Jessica's words. She couldn't help but wonder how true those words were after the sight of her mother this morning.

"Like you'd know. Bet your parents are at home, happy to see you, asking about your day and how you've been. What would you know about how fucked up our lives are?" Even though she knew it was coming, April was still taken aback by just how unfiltered her sister could be.

"Girlie, you think you have a monopoly on fucked up families? Let me tell you. Look beside you, at your sister. Think about your other sister, at home chewing your Mom out." April shook her head, pretty sure she knew where Jessica was going as Cassie just stared at the steps.

"Now tell me, do you get worried that you might never see one of them again? That you'll wake up one day and read a text from your Mom that one of them, like April here, was shot to death? Or gang raped and beaten? Because that's the fear I live with every day."

April couldn't help but admire Jessica's knack for commanding attention, through humor or blunt force verbal trauma as Cassie stared at Jessica, looking shocked.

"My mom? Like yours, she's a damn idiot. She had a good thing, a great family. But she couldn't keep her damn legs closed and fucked around with half the neighborhood before Dad got wise and left her." It was April's turn to feel the shock. She had known that Jessica's parents were divorced but Jessica had never spoken of the reason why.

"Now, she and my younger sister Sarah live in a big city, Victoria to be precise. A city ravaged by gang violence. She's actually been living with me and Dad for the last few weeks because of a damn gang war on their street, one that killed two of her neighbors in the crossfire." April shook her head, watching Cassie struggling with the facts Jessica was speaking.

"So trust me girlie, I know what it's like to spend so much time worrying about someone you love. I'm fucking terrified of Sarah going back home. Like you, I want to scream, and throw shit and just let my feelings out, but I can't." April found herself taken aback. Jessica had never spoken of any of this in the years they had known one another.

"Then why don't you? Why not just do whatever the hell you want?" Cassie had a different tone of voice from normal, as it seemed Jessica was getting through to her.

"Simple. Unlike you, I am the big sister, so I have to set an example for Sarah. More than that, as April here can attest, I have to deal with my Dad." April had been wondering when this subject would come up, as Cassie scoffed.

"What about him? Don't try and say he doesn't care about you or something, too fucking obvious." April shook her head, if only Cassie knew the truth. A truth she was sure the girl was about to learn.

"Nope. He cares a lot about me. So much so, that he's the opposite of your Mom. Right now, he's at work. If he wasn't, I'd be getting screamed at, and grounded for another week just for being outside right now." Jessica sighed, looking down at the ground.

"I'm a smartass, I know I grate on people, the people I care most about." She looked up at April, a sad smile on her face. "And I say shit without thinking, and hurt people, all because of how much my Dad has messed me up, because of how abusive he gets with his overprotectiveness."

Cassie looked back down at the ground, tears in the young girl's eyes. "Wow. Here I thought April just had the most perfect of friends. Guess there's more people out there suffering with shit parent's then I thought?" She looked up at Jessica, a puzzled look in her eyes. "Wait, if your Dad is so bad, why stay with him? You have a choice right?"

Jessica let out a half sigh, half laugh as she pointed at April. "That's why. Her and Isolde, the best friends a girlie can have. Not sure if you know, but Victoria is about five hundred miles from here, so hanging out with my besties? Not really an option if I went back there."

"I see. I don't think I'd be able to make that choice either if it meant being so far from Melissa and Jake. But at least you'd be closer to your sister, right?" Jessica nodded and sighed as the topic turned to Sarah.

April watched the two girls speaking, as she found herself thinking about her own fears about her mother. She realized Isolde was the only one even remotely close to her who didn't have to worry about losing family every day. As much as she felt for her friend, and as deep as she was realizing her own feelings were, she couldn't help but resent her a little.

"Yeah, and she's leaving tomorrow. Back to the city, and me and Dad will be back to worrying about her every day. So chin up girlie. You aren't in this alone."

April felt like her heart might have just stopped beating. She watched Cassie break into a genuine smile, and laugh, one filled with humor and good spirits. Something she had never expected to see. And something she felt terrible about taking from her sister, as she had made the decision. Cassie deserved to know about their mother.

"Don't worry, I'm sure Sarah will be fine. She seems like a good person, who doesn't go out and do stupid shit, looking for trouble." What started as an attempt to reassure Jessica turned bitter as she thought of her mother. "Unlike a certain someone." Cassie looked back at the ground, after chiming in with "yeah, like mom."

"Yup. Like mom." She turned and faced Cassie, putting a hand on the girl's shoulder and turning her sister to have a face to face. "There's something I need to tell you about Mom. Rachel has known for a while, and me and Jessica, and Isolde found out not too long ago.

April felt like shit as she watched her sister's mood sink further and further as she explained what their mother was really doing.

Several minutes of conversation passed, as the trio got up to head back to the house. Cassie was quiet, but April could tell the girl was fuming inside. *Back to her normal self again it seems.*

As April started off the steps, Jessica pulled her to the side, telling Cassandra to head on, that they'd catch up.

"What's the matter?" She asked, watching the smile fade from Jessica's face as she spoke. "Well, I've been doing a lot of thinking. Especially after the way you and Isolde were acting at the house yesterday. This conversation? All these emotions flowing around just made up my mind for me." April was now curious what other revelation Jessica might have, though she figured she already knew where this was going.

"Thing is, she's actually confided something in me. Asked me not to say anything, but the way you two have been acting, I'd rather not get caught in the middle so here. Read this."

She took the phone that Jessica shoved at her and read the texts, the last one made her sit back down on the steps. "Because I'm in love with her." So her suspicions were correct. Isolde had feelings for her.

"It's pretty evident that you share those feelings, I mean it's one thing to stare at her changing, but that little stunt with holding her hand yesterday?" A big grin broke out on Jessica's face, though her tone of voice remained serious. "That was way too on the nose girlie."

A fact April found it hard to argue with, as it had been a poorly thought out test in the end. At least, assuming that you could count a test that gave you the results you sought as poorly planned.

"Now, I'm going to tell you the same thing I told her. I don't care if you two get together or not. If you do I'll be your numero uno supporter, and if not, well you'll have to deal with me still being friends with her should you two split."

April did not like the sound of Jessica's words. Of all the things she had thought of, losing Isolde as a friend was not among them. "So you two need to figure this out, I mean she's going to be off work in a few hours, so better get to it."

April shook her head. "You're right, I'm not going to even try to deny that I have feelings for her. But I'm not ready, not yet, to face them out in the open." Jessica's sigh made her feel even worse for what she was about to ask.

"So umm, I'm not asking you to do anything much or whatever, just, don't say anything to her? If she outright asks or something, feel free and I'll deal with it, just please don't bring it up?"

Jessica shook her head, leaving April concerned before a big grin crossed her friend's face. "Fine, I won't bring it up but if she does, the cat's coming out of that bag you two psychos are trying to smother it with."

It was April's turn to shake her head, as once more Jessica showed what a way she had with her weird sense of humor. "And if you two spark up any drama between yourselves? I'm not talking to either of you girlies until you work it out. Got it?"

April nodded her head, and the two set off back for the house, catching up with Cassandra not long after and walking the rest of the way, pushing their bikes.

FRIDAY JUNE 11TH AFTERNOON

Isolde waved goodbye to Daisy as she left work. It had been a long and busy day, and the whole time all she could think of was April's behavior the night before. She checked her phone, not at all surprised to see two texts from April.

Reading them did leave her feeling shocked, as she felt bad for being stuck on the clock and not being able to help locate her sister, and relief that it had all worked out.

She fired off a text letting April know how sorry she was that she didn't see them earlier, due to not being able to get on her phone on the clock.

She didn't have to wait long for the reply. "Don't sweat it, it's all good. Jess is here at the house, come on over." Isolde couldn't help but wonder what was up with Jessica being out this late, knowing her father wouldn't be out much longer.

She rushed home, and let Mr. Needen know she was going next door, before heading over. She knocked on the door, and was greeted by Rachel, who let her in and led her to the living room. Sweeping her eyes across the room she couldn't help but grin. April was there with both sisters, and Jessica. Like this must be the first time this has ever happened. She thought, joining the group.

Jessica and Rachel took turns filling her in on the events of the day, and just why they were all gathered. April's mother was sleeping in her room, knocked out by whatever pain pills she took.

"Like damn." Was all Isolde could muster after the girls had finished debriefing her. She took a seat on the couch beside Jessica, prompting a snort from the girl as she whispered in Isolde's ear, "what, too shy to sit beside your girlfriend?" Isolde gave Jessica a light elbowing in the ribs as an answer.

She looked around the room. Her gaze fell upon April, who quickly turned away. Cassie was the next to speak. "So, hair-dye, you got any ideas on how to deal with our Mom? You are supposed to be April's best friend after all, so act like it and help out here."

Isolde shook her head, wishing she had some answer for the girl, which prompted a snort from her. She couldn't help but be a little surprised how well the kid seemed to be taking things, given how angry April had been when she learned the truth.

"What she needs is rehab. Get her off the booze and we get her off the streets." Isolde turned to look at Rachel, yet another frown in the group. She had a point, April said she's doing this because of her alcoholism keeping her from getting a proper job.

"Like, so if this guy, this client is a cop, why not just turn him in? Catch them in the act or something? She offered, as the group began discussing the idea. She couldn't help but feel good, to be engaging in an actual conversation and not focusing on her feelings for a change.

"I can only do so much, sis. I don't like the way Mom is making her money but we need it. How much harder do you think it'd be getting a job with those kind of charges on her record?" Rachel made a pretty good point, Isolde thought.

"Well, yeah, of course she'd face some kind of charges. Not like she hasn't gotten one too many DUIs as it is. Any job that would care is already off the table because of them anyway." April countered Rachel's concern.

"Well are you losers going to sneak out again to try and catch her in the act? What if she doesn't go back to that street, how the hell are you going to find her?" Cassandra had a good counter argument herself.

"Like, yeah, I hadn't thought of that. Without some kind of proof it's not like they'd believe a bunch of teens, certainly not against a cop." She had to side with Cassandra. She watched April turn from the group, and wished she could find some way to comfort her friend.

"Well I don't care how we do it." April turned back to the group. "One way or another, I'm going to help Mom get the help she needs. If I have to stalk every street in this bum ass little town to do it I will."

The group continued to go back and forth on how best to handle the problem, as Isolde couldn't help but steal several more glances at April, catching the girl stealing her own several times in the process.

Chapter 14

SATURDAY JUNE 12TH Afternoon

The phone buzzed again. Isolde reached over and put the thing on do not disturb mode. *Like calm down girl, I'm trying to get ready here.* She had rushed through her shower, and was now rushing to get dressed as April was outside waiting on her.

She had no idea what was up, beyond something Jessica had planned, *at the last minute*, she thought feeling annoyed. She had finished dressing and was putting her hair in a ponytail before making her way to her room to gather her purse and shoes. On the way she read April's latest "hurry up" text with a sigh.

A few minutes later, after having told Mrs. Needen she'd be back later, she stepped outside to see April waiting, once more on Rachel's bike. After unlocking and mounting her own, she addressed April's impatience.

"Like, you know how much I hate being rushed girl so why all the texts?" The way she felt about her friend notwithstanding, she was more than a little pissed at the girl. The duo began to pedal off with April in the lead. "Oh and exactly where are we going anyway?"

April gave a laugh, before slowing her speed to answer. "Question one? Because Jess was blowing my phone up with her own impatience. So if I had to suffer, so did you. Question two, that lovely new home away from home you've found every weekday."

Isolde had to roll her eyes. Of course Jessica was rushing April, and of course she in turn passed it on. But going to the Diner was an odd choice, and far from the first, or even the fifth place she'd expect Jessica to want to meet.

"Oh, well then, she say why she wants to meet there? You know, now that I think of it, has she ever even been inside the place yet?" She picked up some speed to keep pace with April. The girl wasn't such an easy mark to outrace when she was on a proper bicycle.

"Nope. Just a whole lot of, paraphrasing here, hurry the hell ups." As they arrived at the diner, Isolde thought about locking her bike up in her usual spot out back but decided against it since she wasn't on the clock. Instead she followed April out front and locked their bikes together. *Daisy needs to get a bike rack installed, like yesterday.* She thought as they made their way to the door.

They made their way inside, Clara and some other woman Isolde didn't recognize where on duty, with Clara being their greeter. After the company greeting, April informed her they were here to meet someone as Isolde noticed Jessica waving at them. She was at a booth with Sarah, and a woman Isolde didn't recognize.

"Jess is over there. Thanks, Clara, we'll be joining them." The duo followed Clara to Jessica's booth, and she took a seat beside Jessica, with April sitting across from her beside the unknown woman.

"Man, you have got to be some of the slowest people I know." Jessica said, her upbeat tone of voice as usual at odds with her words. "Especially you, bean pole. Where the hell does all that sugar you eat go if it's not on your thighs or giving you the energy to actually get here on time?"

Both April and Sarah laughed as Jessica poked Isolde in the side as she spoke. The woman across from Jessica gave a disapproving look. "Now Jessica, you know what they say about stones and glass houses. You shouldn't call out other people for your own failings. After all, you did wait till the last minute to invite them."

This time Isolde had to laugh alongside April. Jessica just rolled her eyes and turned to face April, pointing at her.

"Mom, this is April. April, my Mom, Janet." She then turned to point at Isolde, and made introductions. "And of course you've both already met Sarah, but what the hey, Isolde and April, meet Sarah. Sarah, meet my besties."

Everyone at the table except Jessica and her mom either groaned or rolled their eyes at Jessica's redundancy. Isolde in particular felt bad for Clara as her coworker was still standing there waiting to take their orders. She leaned over to the girl, and whispered an apology for her friends.

She was the first to put in her order followed by both April and Sarah. Jessica and Janet took the longest time deciding, before they eventually had their orders in as Clara set off. Isolde couldn't help but give a weak smile as she watched the girl head off. As much as this job was growing on her, customers like their little group who took all day to order would always be a nuisance.

"So, these are the friends I've heard so much about?" Janet's question drew Isolde's attention back to the group. Janet was looking at her. "So, Jessica tells me you actually work here? Tell me about it, and yourself if you don't mind".

Isolde's weak smile took on a much stronger presence as she began telling first about her job, then moving on to telling Janet more about herself. As she spoke, she felt someone's foot rubbing against her so she leaned back to take a quick glance. April's foot was rubbing back and forth, up against her leg. April herself was looking off across the table at something past Sarah, a very unsubtle grin on her face.

Well, well, well, you want to play that game huh, girl? She thought, as she finished giving her life story, and Janet turned to April, her turn to give some of her own backstory exposition.

"Well, there's not really much to tell about." As April was speaking Isolde decided to play April's own game, and rubbed her own foot along April's leg. The move worked, startling the girl into interrupting what she was saying, and looking under the table.

Isolde had to work hard to stifle the laugh she felt coming on as Janet gave her a puzzled look. "Everything alright April? Please don't tell me they got mice or someone let a dog run loose in here or something."

Isolde felt Jessica elbow her in the ribs softly, and turned to see a big grin on the girl's face, to which Isolde decided to play dumb and gave a light shrug as April continued.

"Oh, nothing like that, just had a random itch come up." She looked Isolde right in the eyes as she spoke, reaching under the table to fake scratching her phantom itch. Her grin had now become a somewhat sinister smile.

Isolde jumped a little in her seat, as she felt a pinch on her own leg, this time drawing Janet's eyes to her. She reached down to rub the spot and her hand brushed up against April's. The brief time their hands were in contact felt like an eternity, as Isolde relished the feeling, despite her own self-hatred at her fears. *Like just go for it you dunce, there's no way she doesn't feel the same.* She returned her attention to the table as Janet spoke.

"Ok, is everything alright with you two?" She looked between the two girls, a frown on her face. April was looking down at the table, focusing hard on staring. *Like she's totally trying not to blush I bet.* She thought as Jessica piped up.

"Oh they're fine, just trying to hide how madly in love they really are." Jessica clasped her hands over her chest, tilting her head as she spoke, her voice raised in a mock fashion. April turned away, no longer able to contain the blush as Isolde, feeling a deep red of her own coming on, glared at Jessica.

Janet had a look on her face that suggested she was debating on whether or not to believe her daughter. An opportunity Isolde jumped at.

"Like no, no, no. Nothing like that, just had a cramp in my leg, probably from how hard I had to pedal because of a certain someone rushing us so hard." She continued glaring at Jessica as she kicked the girl in the leg. Hard. Luckily, Janet knew her own child enough to know how much of a wiseass she could be and seemed to buy it.

The group went back and forth for a while, telling one another things about themselves, as they waited for their food. As Jessica and April began a bit of their own minor bickering, Isolde noticed the other waitress, whom she didn't recognize speaking to Daisy. Her curiosity peaked as she saw Daisy pointing at their table. The girl caught Isolde's gaze and waved her over.

"Like, Jess, cool it with the smart mouth for a bit ok? Anyway I'll be right back, work stuff."

She excused herself from the group and made her way to her boss and unknown coworker. Daisy gave her a smile as she approached, the other woman looking a bit flustered.

"Hi Daisy." She greeted her boss, who returned the greeting." So what's up?" Daisy turned to the other girl, and made introductions. "Alicia, this is Isolde, and vice versa." Alicia offered her hand, which Isolde took. "Pleasure to meet you, Isolde." Isolde returned the girl's pleasantry as Daisy turned back to face her.

"Sorry fer interrupting your little get together child, but Ms. Alicia here is in a right pickle and we was wondering if you might be willing to help out?" Isolde nodded, and asked for more details.

"Well, I have her on the books to come in on the mornin shift tomorrow, but some personal stuff came up. She's been going round trying to find someone willing to trade shifts with, so we figured on asking you. Seeing as yer here and what not."

Isolde told them she was game, and Daisy explained what she was going to do. Isolde would come in and work a shift tomorrow, and Alicia would cover her shift on Wednesday, to which Isolde agreed.

"Thank you so much. You're a real lifesaver, Isolde." Alicia gave her a quick hug, which she returned before excusing herself to rejoin her group. On the way, her already good mood jumped up another level as she saw Clara walking away, having delivered their food.

"Trying to suck up to the boss for some kind of employee discount girlie?" Jessica said as Isolde sat back at the table. Isolde shook her head, laughing at the idea of even having an employee discount.

"Nope, nope, nope. Turns out, that other waitress, Alicia, needed someone to swap shifts with so I'll be working tomorrow, and off Wednesday." Jessica nodded with a "right on," as Isolde looked over to April, who had another big grin on her face.

"So you mean we can actually hang out on a weekday for once like the old days?" Isolde couldn't help but feel a bit guilty as she nodded her head. She too missed all the free time the girls had to spend over summer breaks of the past, no matter how much she was loving this job.

The group continued talking as Isolde set into her meal, eager to try this BBQ pulled pork sandwich. *Thing must be amazing since every other order I take has one on the ticket. Two on every other other ticket.* She thought as she took a big bite. Whatever doubts she may have had about Mr. Burke's cooking melted away the same way the pork melted on her tongue, the sweet, spicy and tangy BBQ sauce the perfect compliment. The perfect compliment to the tender meat, and the eclectic company she found herself in as they continued to eat and carry on the conversation.

Isolde found herself particularly curious as Janet and Sarah were describing life in a big city. Despite the crime levels, which had come up multiple times in the conversation, Isolde was still fascinated by how different a city was to their own small town.

Sarah was looking down as she and her mother were discussing their plans to head back to the city early in the morning, a good fourteen hour trip ahead of them.

"Umm, yeah. It's so quiet and peaceful here though. Haven't heard a single gunshot the whole time I've been here." Sarah gave a quiet laugh. Isolde wondered how many gunshots the girl heard back at the city and asked her.

"Oh, umm, at least a few times a month. More when I'm over at Maya's house, she's not exactly in the best part of the city." Her face brightened as she mentioned her girlfriend's name, as Jessica turned to her sister.

"Bet you'll forget all about hanging with your big sis once your back in your girlfriends arms, huh girlie?"

"Oh you have no idea. As much as I've enjoyed this vacation, I've missed her so much." Isolde couldn't hide the spark of pain, and a hint of jealousy as Sarah was talking about her girlfriend. She snuck a glance at April, who was smiling at Sarah, but looking at Isolde from the corner of her eye. "I love her so much, it's been so hard to be so far away for this long. Going to smother her in kisses when I get back, if she doesn't do it first."

Sarah's smile brightened with her soft laugh, as Isolde heard a woman coughing in the booth behind her. She turned to see a rather large, pale, and elderly woman. She was turned in her own booth and giving their group a very nasty look. Most specifically, at Janet.

"My word, what kind of a mother are you?" She was staring daggers into Janet. "You let such an innocent and sweet child be corrupted by those," her gaze turned towards Isolde, a look of pure disgust in her eyes as she looked over Isolde's dyed hair, "those sinful freaks."

Isolde wasn't sure whether to be insulted, or amused at the comment. Sure, purple wasn't a very common hair dye around town as she was probably the only one to sport it. But what the hell did that have to do with being sinful, or corrupting people?

She shook her head to clear the thoughts as the woman began shaking her own head, while looking at Sarah. "Child, let me give you some advice," the woman began, as Jessica sat up in the booth on her knees turning to the woman.

"No, you let me give you some advice bitch. First, skip the dessert." Jessica looked the woman over, the look on her face was enough to make Isolde's blood run cold. "While you're at it, maybe you should skip the whole damn meal. Second," Jessica leaned in close to the woman's face, raising her voice. "Don't you fucking dare speak to or about my mother or my sister, and damn sure about my best friend like that."

The woman stammered something under her breath as Jessica looked like she was about to hit the woman. Sarah was crushing herself into the seat, clearly trying to shrink away from the world as Isolde put her arm on Jessica, pulling the girl back a little.

"How dare you address your betters like this, child. I see that failure of a mother didn't stop with the one child." The smugness in the woman's voice made Isolde want to join in with Jessica, pummeling the old hag, but she knew that was not a good idea, not at work. She pulled Jessica back into the seat as the girl lobbed more insults at the woman.

Isolde looked around the diner as the argument heated up. Her breath caught in her throat as she saw April staring down at the floor, a look on her face that Isolde didn't recognize.

Something was bothering the girl, and for once, Isolde was certain it had nothing to do with her family. *No, it's this bitch behind us, like she's got April as shaken as Sarah over there.* The thought pushed any reason out of Isolde as she started to get out of the seat, more than welcoming the legal and any employment related issues she was about to incur.

Her attention was drawn to the sight of Daisy making her way towards the two booths, a frown on her face as she ground her heels into the tiles as she walked. Isolde slunk back down in the booth, opting to see how her boss handled the situation.

"Now someone want to rightly explain what all this racket is in my establishment?" Isolde turned to face the old woman as heard her giving a tsk, and the tone of her voice was filled with a sickening smugness as she began to speak.

"Are you the manager? Good, because I'd like to register a complaint." The woman's fake smile faded, and she was now glaring at Daisy. Knowing her boss, things were about to get ugly as Isolde found herself wishing they sold popcorn here.

"How dare you let such degeneracy, like that queer little sinner in here with us good and decent folk. Only place their kind belongs is burning in the pits of hell with the other wretches and sinners" Daisy let out a deep sigh, as Isolde looked up at her boss. She found herself trying to copy Sarah, wanting to shrink away into the booth herself at the look on Daisy's face. Like holy. If looks could kill Daisy would be sending that woman straight to this hell she loves bringin up. The thought both amused and terrified Isolde.

"Well, now, let me tell you something. I'm not the manager, I'm the right owner of this here diner. And let me tell you, we don't rightly tolerate that kind of language here, Ma'am." The old woman started to speak, but Daisy silenced her with a raised finger and a "shush."

"No thank you ma'am, I rightly don't reckon I gave you permission to speak, now did I?" *Respect plus fifty*. Isolde thought, finding herself loving the way Daisy was handling that woman. "No, instead how about you listen for a spell, learn you some manners in the process if we might be so lucky."

This here fine establishment is family owned, family ran, and family friendly." Once more the old woman tried getting a word in and was silenced as Daisy slammed her hand on the back of the booth, hard enough to shake the whole thing.

"Family means more'en blood, ma'am. In here, everyone, all these lovely lil ladies and handsome young gents? Their family as long as they're in my diner, I don't reckon one whit about their skin color, social class, or," Daisy gave Sarah a warm smile, "who they might like to lay and keep emselves warm at night with."

Isolde took another glance at April, who was still looking down, not looking to be paying any attention to the scene around them.

"Fraid I'm going to have to ask you leave, and don't come back. Your kind ain't family, ma'am. Oh, and do be sure to read the name of the establishment on your way out, and maybe educate that no good fer nothin mind of yours to what family means to yourself before you go insulting mine."

Isolde's respect for her boss shot through the roof as she watched the old woman try several times to get a word in, each time Daisy shutting her down.

"Lookee here now, you can call the Sheriff, fat lot of good it will do you if I have to get my husband to toss you out on yer britches. Sheriff Dean is more'en likely to lock you up for trespassing as he is to even say one word to my Larry. Now are you going to git, or do I need to holler for my man?"

The wind having been knocked from her sails, the woman got up and stomped out, shouting that she was never going to eat here again, and intended to get all her friends to leave a very bad review. Daisy just laughed at the woman, not even saying a word. Isolde found herself laughing as the woman stomped out of the building, slamming the door so hard Isolde thought it would shatter.

"Show's good and over folks, please get back to enjoying your lovely meals." Daisy addressed the handful of patrons, most of whom had been staring at the scene. She turned to face the group, Sarah in particular.

"Now I do rightly apologize for that horrid display you fine folks had to sit through. You just let your waitress know I'm giving you a big discount as compensation. As for you little lady, now you don't go an pay any mind whatsoever to the words of that bitter old coot. Don't rightly see nothing degenerate about you nor this fine woman who done raised you right."

Daisy gave a nod and a smile as she walked off. Isolde looked around the table, the mood of the gathering didn't seem to be salvageable, but she was determined to try.

"Like, Daisy is right, right, right. Don't pay any attention to people like that stupid old lady. She's just jealous you have an awesome girlfriend and she's stuck dining alone." It wasn't much of one, but her words did bring a smile to Sarah's face. One that turned into a laughter fueled grin as Jessica chimed in.

"Isolde hit the nail on the head. Hell, I feel sorry for all of her cats who were looking forward to her leftovers tonight. Poor things are going to starve tonight." Her tag team-up with Jessica did wonders for getting the mood back on track, as Janet gave some words of her own encouragement, before turning back to learning all she could about her daughter's friends.

Throughout the remaining conversation, Isolde couldn't help but notice April not touching what was left of her food, nor looking up much from the table. Her "Nothing, just not as hungry as I thought," answer to Isolde's probes to find out what was bothering her sunk her own spirit further.

Whatever was bothering April left Isolde feeling a deep pain. She reached under the table, grasping April's hand which was resting on her knee. April moved her eyes up to look at Isolde, a warm and soft smile as she squeezed Isolde's hand.

SATURDAY JUNE 12TH Late Night

April turned over on her side, still unable to sleep. The rest of the afternoon went well enough after the unfortunate interruption, but her mood had not recovered. She knew people like that old woman existed, hell they were everywhere. But to witness it in person was unreal.

She looked at her phone, eleven fifty. Glad I don't have to get up early like Isolde, she thought, as her thoughts turned to her friend. Turned to their little back and forth game of footsie and Jessica's not so subtle joke.

She felt a smile coming on as she thought about how smoothly Isolde had handled that particular comment. She always was a quick thinker. She thought about the other qualities she liked about Isolde, wondering which ones had made her fall for her friend in the first place.

Her thoughts lingered on the way Isolde had held her hand in secret, beneath the table. They hadn't held hands for more than a couple of minutes, but those were the most amazing yet painful minutes she could think of in her life. Being so close to what she wanted so bad and not having the guts to say fuck it and go for it stung in ways she couldn't even process at the moment.

Rolling over on her stomach, her arms crossed on her pillow as she laid her head on them she wondered what it would be like, to actually be out and in the open with her feelings. How Sarah must have handled it, and how different their worlds must be.

How much she wanted to just tell Isolde how she feels, and how scared she was of what her friend's response would be. A fear she knew was irrelevant, childish. Though neither of them had said a word to one another on the subject, she knew that Isolde had figured it out, both of them knew of the other's feelings. *So why are we both so scared to touch the subject?*

Thinking about the fear turned her thoughts towards her own family. She tried to think of any time one of them had ever had a conversation or even so much as acknowledged the same-sex topic.

Well, Rachel frequently made jokes about her and Isolde being lovebirds, but she had to wonder whether Rachel was just giving sisterly banter or if her views were closer to that old lady. Cassie would absolutely use it for a world of new insults, but would they be born from her wrathful nature? Or would they come from something deeper, some kind of bigotry? She moved her thoughts to her friends next.

Jessica had made it clear that she'd be supportive and accepting. OBviously, having a gay daughter meant their parent's wouldn't have an issue either. She couldn't help but wonder next, just how the Needen's would handle it, should Isolde come home one day and tell them she was dating her female best friend.

Her right arm began tingling so she lifted her head. Even in the dim light filtering in through the cracks of her door, she could see the red mark on her arm where her head had lain. She rolled back over, laying there for a while before getting up to pace around the room.

The Needens were some of, no they outright were the nicest people she had ever met. Her thoughts turned to the strange relationship the pair had with Isolde.

They were only supposed to take care of Isolde for a short term, but ended up unofficially adopting her. More than that, the two treated the girl like she was their own flesh and blood, making it clear they though of themselves as her parents despite Isolde never being that direct. No, she always referred to them as the Needens, or her foster parents. Despite this, April knew the girl loved them all the same. The idea that there was that kind of unconditional love in the world did a lot to lift her mood up.

But would that love remain if they learned Isolde was gay, or bi or whatever? She slipped her door open, and snuck her way to the kitchen for a glass of water. Rachel was sitting at the kitchen table, reading.

"Planning on another stakeout with your girlfriends or something? Might want to change outta those PJ's." Rachel said without looking up, a frown on her face. "She's out there, of course." The frown faded, as April sighed.

"No, just having trouble sleeping." Rachel looked up, and watched as she poured a glass of water. "Come on, have a seat." Rachel kicked the other chair out, and patted it. With nothing better to do she obliged her sister's request.

"So what's so bad that it's keeping the girl who sleeps through Cassie's tantrums up?" April choked a little, and her nose burned as she snorted up a bit of the water she had been drinking as she pictured herself sleeping peacefully while Cassie stomped around throwing things.

"It's nothing much." She lied through her teeth, not sure yet if she should be full-on honest. "Just been dealing with a problem with Isolde. Not sure how to tackle it yet." She took another drink, as Rachel smiled at her with her head tilted.

"Is that so? Well, I can't even begin to imagine whatever problems the two of you could be having." It was faint, but April was sure she was picking up on a hint of sarcasm in her sister's voice. "Well, without knowing what the problem is, and knowing you, I won't know until you solve it, all I can say is this."

Rachel reached over and placed her hand on April's, and gave a soft squeeze. "Talk to her. Just be honest and tell her how you feel. You know, about whatever is bothering you." She added a wink as she spoke, leaving April all the more curious at her sister's behavior. Had she already figured it out? Was that why she always teased me?

April said she'd think about it, finished her drink and left with a goodnight as she shook off the thoughts. Minutes later she was back in bed, still wide awake. Checking her phone revealed it was eleven after midnight. Sighing, she accepted the fact that all this thinking wasn't going to solve a thing. Rachel was right, she and Isolde needed to talk.

She fired off a quick text to Isolde, knowing she was for certain asleep. Tomorrow, when Isolde get's off of work, they would meet at that old park downtown and it would all come out.

Chapter 15

SUNDAY JUNE 13TH AFTERNOON

Isolde paced back and forth. She had arrived at the small, run-down and overgrown park several minutes ago. She wondered what April's motivation for meeting her here was. After all, this place was about as private as you could get this far into town. *Like you even have to wonder, girl.* She shook her head at the thought, knowing all too well it was accurate.

The area she found herself in was a lot that had once been planted and transformed into a small park. Brick buildings made up walls on three of its sides, and its fourth was a large fence that was completely overgrown. The excessive foliage covering the fence worked wonders in hiding the place from the street and her bike which was chained on the other side.

Years ago the pair had found a way into the small area through one of those abandoned buildings. So much time the two of them had spent here over the years. Their own little paradise away from the rest of town. A place even Jessica had only been to a couple of times.

A noise off to her side drew her attention, the small piece of wood being moved told her April was here. She stopped pacing, but her heart was still racing.

She watched with her breath held, as April climbed through the small hole in the wall, and replaced the board they used as a make-shift door.

"Hey you." April said as she turned to face Isolde. The girl's voice was too neutral for Isolde to glean any hints in regards to her mood.

Isolde's heart felt as if it might hammer its way from her chest as she looked at her friend.

She decided to make a poor attempt at a joke to lighten her mood. "Like, I'm pretty sure someone went and cast a shrinking spell on that hole. Not so easy getting through anymore, had to crawl on my pretty little hands and knees." Both girls chuckled, as April walked towards the stone bench on the far side of the park. She followed, and took a seat beside April, who looked straight into Isolde's eyes.

The look in her eyes confirmed what she had been sure about all morning after reading April's text. Jessica had indeed told her. Not that it mattered, there was no way the girl hadn't figured it out on her own otherwise. *Especially the way we held hands yesterday.* She sighed, torn between the excitement of finally bringing this topic to light, and the fear of how it would go.

"So, you've probably guessed but Jess told me." Isolde looked down to the overgrown grass. She stared off for several seconds, before speaking. *Here it is girl, the moment of truth. Don't be a chicken anymore.*

"Like, yeah. I guess she did." She swallowed hard. "So umm, what now?" She squeezed the stone seat hard enough to hurt her hands, but didn't let go. After taking her own time to stare off, April spoke.

"I really don't know. It was a shock when she showed me your texts, you can be sure of that. But I kinda already knew." She looked at April, who was turned sideways on the bench, and staring at the wall behind them. April's words had done little to untie the knots in her gut, or slow her racing heart.

"I mean, it's been obvious these past months that something had changed in you. It was little things you know? At first I thought it was that job, but over time, little things stuck out in my mind. The more I thought about them, the more obvious it became." April sighed, and got up from the bench.

"So I tested you in little ways, like putting my hand on yours at Jessica's, to see how you reacted and all." April looked over at the board covered hole.

A deep bolt of fear went through Isolde that April would leave, but instead she walked closer, placing her hand on Isolde's shoulder. She wanted desperately to grab it, and hold it, but managed to restrain herself.

After holding the position for a few moments, she walked a few feet away, and stopped, with her back to Isolde. "It was actually kind of a relief, you know? In some weird little way. Ever since Jessica told me, I've been wanting to have this conversation. At least, until yesterday."

Until yesterday? The words were a dagger that pierced her heart with the icey cold of death itself. She watched as April turned to face her, eyes wet from tears. "After that old woman? I was up most of the night thinking about this, and what to even do or say. And I still don't know what to do."

Isolde wanted more than anything to hug her friend. "I don't know, because." April raised her hand to her face, biting her index finger knuckle. Something she only did when she was in a bad place,emotionally.

"Because I think." April was visibly shaking by this point. She turned her back towards Isolde once more.

"Like, I know. Because you feel the same way about me." April turned back to face Isolde, a smile on her face.

"Yeah, I think so. I mean, aside from all of this drama with Mom, you are all I can think about anymore. Guess I was right though, there wasn't any chance you wouldn't have figured it out on your own."

Isolde returned April's smile as the girl continued. "I mean, it wasn't easy to admit it at first. So many things didn't make any sense to me. Like how much I found myself missing you when you aren't around? You can be right next door, and a text, or call away, and I still miss you, and it makes no sense." Isolde looked to the ground, gathering her own thoughts, before speaking.

"It makes sense to me because that's exactly how I feel about you." Isolde got to her feet, and began pacing around the bench with April watching her. "For some time now? I've felt this feeling, deep inside. Something strong, powerful and warm whenever you are around." She gave April another warm smile.

"And whenever you aren't? It's like theres a hole in my heart, or soul or whatever. At first I didn't know what it was, like, some part of me thought it might be but I tried to ignore it. It wasn't easy, but I did it, for so long, until..."

She balled up her fists, not out of anger but from apprehension over letting the truth out. "The other night, like, at Jessica's." Isolde stopped pacing and turned to face April.

"When we were going to stake-out your mom and I fell asleep?" April nodded, presumably recalling the painful night. "I had another of those weird jungle dreams." April gave a soft laugh, before she interrupted.

"Really? Because it didn't sound like one from the way you were moaning." Isolde turned away, the red hot flash running through her cheeks as she blushed from embarrassment.

"Umm, yeah, sorry about that." She took a moment to gather her composure before turning back around. "But it was, and that does explain Jessica's comment when I woke up." She gave April a summary of the dream, being explicit about the feelings the Warrior had felt, in particular during the cuddling before they took it further.

"Like it was so, so, so much warmth, and peace, and love she felt, more than I had ever felt in my life, it was just so strong." She turned back to April, recalling just how strong those feelings had been.

"Well, after we got back, when you and I were holding each other in the bathroom? It hurt so much to see you like that. But more than that, the way I held you, and the way you were holding onto me?" She recalled the moment vividly as she spoke, the emotions every bit as strong all this time later.

April looked down to the ground, a slight smile on her face. "Like, I felt those same emotions, that same warmth, and just so damn much love for you. Way more than the kind I've always had, or the love I have for Jess, or hell even the Needens."

She walked up to April and put her hand on the girl's shoulder. "Like, I," Isolde took a deep breath, "April, I love you." April held it for a few moments before she turned, and walked another few feet away. She stood there, looking at the fence on the other side of the park.

"That is the best and worst news I've ever gotten. Because I love you as well. Isolde," April turned back to face her with tears in her eyes. "I'm in love with you too. But I don't know what to do with that."

Isolde walked over and sat down on the bench. The gravity of the situation weighing on her. Both girls had finally addressed their mutual elephant in the room, and April was not having the easiest of times with it. Not that she could blame her friend as she too had no idea how to proceed.

"I don't either. But like, what would happen if we don't try things out? Could we remain friends somehow, knowing how we feel?" This time April began pacing.

"No, I don't think that we could. I mean it's been hell keeping this in the last few days, I can't imagine going forward knowing how we both feel without being able to act on it." April's tears were in free fall.

Isolde could feel her friend's frustration in her voice. A frustration she felt just as strong as she picked up the dropped conversation. "Like, if we stay friends, they'll just keep growing right? But. But maybe we don't stay just friends? It's like, new to me and I wouldn't know how to even start but, what if?" She let her voice trail off, too afraid to finish the question, leaving it to April to do so.

"What if we gave things a chance? I mean, I've for sure thought about it, but I don't know. Honestly, I had so much hope that you did feel the same way about me, but." Isolde tensed up at the word but. "I mean I wanted to and all. Until that woman at the diner yesterday. It got me thinking. What would our families think?"

It was April's turn to let her voice trail off. Isolde walked over a little closer to her friend. "Like, yeah, for sure it wouldn't be easy. But, think about it, we are already so close, how much harder could it be to just go all the way?" April shook her head and did some of her own pacing. After another long pause, she turned to face Isolde.

"How hard?" Her voice had an edge to it. "How hard could it be? Very fucking hard Isolde. Think about how other people would see us for starters. Do you think it would go over well at school? How would I, we, handle it if people started treating us the way that woman did?" Isolde had to bite her tongue to keep from snapping back at April.

"Think about what our families would say, how they would treat us. Do you really want that kind of drama?" No longer willing to hold her tongue, Isolde lashed out.

"Like, fuck them. Fuck our stupid families, that backwards ass school. Fuck all the damn drama, it can go straight to hell, ok?" Her eyes burned from the tears, and her hands were trembling. "April, please, answer me one question, and answer it truthfully."

She walked right up to April, staring into her eyes. "Do you love me?" April turned away from Isolde. "I," She started, but Isolde wasn't backing down. She grabbed April by the shoulders, and spun her around. "April, do you love me?" April tried to turn away again, but she was having none of it. Several minutes passed as they stared at each other, before April answered.

"No shit, did I stutter earlier or something? Yes, Isolde, I love you." April was staring straight into her eyes, and she could feel the girl trembling. "But does it really matter how we feel about each other? Does it even matter what we want?" By the time she got the question out, April was full on shaking.

Isolde didn't know what to say, because as much as she wanted to say anything else, she knew deep down April did have a point. The world was not kind to people who did what they were talking about as they witnessed firsthand. But it didn't matter to her.

"You're right April, like I hate, hate, hate to admit it, but you are right. It would be one of the hardest things we'd ever do, but." This time it was April who did the interrupting.

"But what Isolde?" April pushed Isolde's hands away with enough force to startle Isolde. "What if we did it anyway? What if we did. What if we went home and told our families we were in love. What then? What if one of our families took it badly? What if we ended up on the streets, Isolde?" She looked deep into April's dark brown eyes. She knew deep in her heart that while April was completely correct, that her fears rang true, she also knew she didn't care.

"Then we will be happy together on the fucking streets. I don't care where we are, or like, who hates us, so long as we are together." "But," April began, prompting Isolde to hit her with one last question.

"April, girl, answer me this one question, and I'll leave it alone if your answer is no. We will walk out of here, go home, and that will like, be that I guess. Our friendship will be over,and we like, would have to figure things out with Jess and all, but if that's what you want, just answer no."

April walked away, back towards the bench. She stood there, staring at it before turning back to Isolde. "Ok, what." Isolde walked up to April, once more staring into her eyes, tears in both girls' as Isolde asked her question.

"Like, good. Now, ignore everything else. The fears, the doubts, the what-ifs ok? and tell me the truth. Do you want to take that chance with me? Like do you want to try being together?" April never took her own eyes away from Isoldes.

"Yes. Oh god do I. But isolde, it's." Isolde had heard enough, not letting her finish, she leaned in and kissed her best friend. It was an awkward kiss, as neither girl had ever kissed anyone. She could feel April trying her best to return the kiss properly, before pulling away and breaking the kiss off.

Tears were now streaming down April's face as she turned and sprinted towards the small opening. She threw the piece of wood aside, and looked back at Isolde. "I'm sorry. I want this so much but, but I just can't. Not right now. Give me some time to think, please Isolde."

Isolde felt her own tears flowing, the pain in her hear too much to bear as April spoke. Not spoke, Isolde realized. But as she pleaded, no, as she begged Isolde for time.

She watched in horror as April ducked into the small opening, and was gone. She fell to her knees, the gravity of her mistake settling in. She realized she had pushed too hard, too fast, and had only succeeded in pushing April away. She broke down in the worst cry of her life.

APRIL TRIED TO FOCUS on the burning in her legs as she pedaled away from the park. Focus on the pain in her lungs as they begged for more air as she raced down one empty street after the next. She wanted to focus on anything but the pain in her heart.

What the hell were you thinking Isolde? Despite her best efforts the thought managed to force its way in. As it did, the tears began to flow once more, forcing her to come to a stop, at the risk of crashing due to her now limited vision.

She climbed off of the bike, letting it fall to the sidewalk as she sat down on the steps of some store, now closed for the day.

She pushed herself into the corner between the wall and the door, hugging her knees as she sobbed, thoughts and emotions rushing through her mind.

Her phone buzzed again, so she put it on do not disturb mode before dropping it on the ground beside her. She ran through the conversation over and over in her mind while trying to make sense of her feelings. Of her actions or her wants and desires as everything within was in conflict.

She was as honest with Isolde as she had ever been with anyone, when she told her that she wanted this. So why run away? She squeezed her legs, feeling her nails digging into the flesh as her thoughts turned to the kiss.

My first kiss. She thought, the feeling still lingering on her lips. *My first kiss was with my best friend. Was with the person I'm in love with. And I ran away.*

The moment Isolde's lips had made contact with her own she felt a flood of emotions, a mix of love, lust, peace and warmth and joy that she could only describe as something magical.

So why the hell did I flip out like that? She kept coming back to the question as something, some voice within finally gave her an answer in the form of its own question.

What if someone had seen us? She knew there was no chance of that, the buildings surrounding that park were long abandoned, and the foliage covering the locked fence blocked any view of what stood behind.

What if it was Mom? What if it was Rachel, or even the Needens? The voice came back. Despite the absurdities of any of them being there to see, she couldn't deny the fear she felt at each possibility.

What if Mom did see us, and acted the same way that crazy old lady acted? What if. She let her thoughts trail, too scared of even thinking of the possibility she might wind up kicked out. A reality so many other young girls and boys in her position faced, if the internet and media were to be believed.

After that encounter at the diner, she was certain they were accurate as she wondered what would have happened had she gone with Isolde's advance?

How would her mother, her sisters have reacted that evening when she told them? What if she didn't. What if they had kept it a secret instead. Only known amongst themselves and Jessica?

She sat there with a million what ifs running through her mind, ignoring the pain in her legs as a trickle of blood began to run down her legs, a sign of how hard she was gripping them. Nothing could compare to the pain in her heart.

Her deep and turbulent thoughts were interrupted by the sound of a car horn, making her jump. She finally took notice of the damage she had done to her legs as she wiped the blood off and turned to see who honked.

There was a faded red pickup parked right beside Rachel's bike, which she only now realized was left out in the opening on the sidewalk. Whatever drama her feelings for Isolde might cause, her sister would have killed her if she let her bike get stolen.

"You ok up there sugah? Prolly not the best place to leave such a nice bike laying around." April looked at the driver, a pale, somewhat thicker woman with beautiful beet-red hair.

She retrieved her phone as she got up, taking careful steps so as to not trip due to the free-falling tears still messing with her vision. She reached the bike before addressing the woman.

"No, no I'm not but thanks for asking." April said, her voice meak and cracking. The woman shook her head as April spoke.

"I can see that. You wreck that nice bike or something?" April wondered what the woman meant, before remembering the damage she had dug into her legs and looked down at the fresh trail of blood.

"Umm, no. Just having some problems with my gir... With my friend." Stopping herself from calling Isolde her girlfriend felt odd, as saying it in her mind felt so natural, so right.

"I see. Wouldn't happen to have much to do with a purple haired waitress by any chance?" The question snapped April to full attention. How did this woman know about Isolde?

As if to answer her thoughts, and probably a reaction to the look of alarm that now sat on April's face the woman added on.

"If you're wondering sugah, the other day I had the pleasure of a brief morning chat with a waitress over at that Family Diner. Poor thang was down in the dumps about dealing with friendship drama but her feelings where written all over her cute little face."

April wondered how much Isolde had told this woman, as she just gave an "oh" in response.

"On my way to a friends house, I spotted that purple haired lil thang pushing her bike down this way, crying as much as you are right now. Put two and two together is all, figuring you must be that friend."

April looked down the street, back the way she had come. She didn't see Isolde and didn't want to, not right now. *Time. I need time to gather my thoughts first.*

"You gonna be alright to get home? More'en willing to give you a lift if you want." April considered the woman's words, taking one last look back before agreeing. The sooner she got home, the less chance of another encounter with Isolde she'd have.

The woman got out and helped her get Rachel's bike in the back and the pair climbed in the cabin. She gave the woman directions to her house and they set off.

"Now, I know good and well that if a girl ain't wanting to talk, she ain't gonna talk. But if you'd like to, I'm all ears." April considered the offer, but thanked her and declined. She didn't want to involve a total stranger in this.

"Well alright sugah, you just make sure you find someone to talk to, ok? Stuff like this'll eat you right up if you don't air it out." The woman gave her a warm smile as the two sat in silence the rest of the way back home.

Several minutes later, the woman had helped her get the bike down and was driving off. April looked around and saw nothing unusual, and no sign of Isolde so she rushed through locking the bike up and headed inside.

As she made her way into the kitchen, she checked her phone, over a dozen texts and nearly as many missed calls from Isolde. She flipped through some settings, her finger hovering over the confirmation icon as she hesitated.

The act she was about to commit, which she intended to reverse when she'd had some time to straighten her emotions out, nevertheless hurt worse than anything else. The simple fact she was even thinking of blocking Isolde's number drew a fresh wave of tears as she hit the confirmation and shut the phone off.

"Oh my god, are you ok?" April looked up to see Rachel sitting at the table, and without thinking she just walked over and hugged her sister.

"Not even close to ok but thanks for asking Rach." She took a seat beside her sister and dried her eyes, explaining that she was dealing with a fight with Isolde and wouldn't be seeing her for awhile. *If ever again, the way I ran off on her,* she thought, another dagger in her heart.

No, I will. I don't know if we can fix this, but I at least owe her a face to face, when I'm ready. That thought gave her a little more confidence, though not much.

She felt Rachel rubbing her back and looked up at her. She had a somber look on her face, but what stood out most was the coy grin she wore.

"You two finally admitted your feelings for each other? Went that badly huh?" April let out a gasp, and not even thinking asked if Isolde, or even Jessica had told her.

"Nah, it's been totally obvious for a long time now. Don't think Mom or Cassie ever bothered to pick up on it though." Rachel said with a warm laugh.

"Umm, yeah I guess it must have been. It certainly was to me in hindsight." April gave a warm laugh of her own. Rachel asked her if she wanted to talk about it, and she jumped at the chance, following her sister to her room where she proceeded to give all the details.

Chapter 16

THURSDAY JUNE 17TH Afternoon

Isolde trudged across the yard, stealing several glances at April's house along the way. It was several days later and the pain had only continued to grow with each passing day. Yesterday had been the worst, a whole day off of work, one they had looked forward to enjoying.

She had sent several texts, and tried calling April so many times since their last conversation, and all had been ignored. Looking at the door to April's house, their big dog lounging on the porch, she cursed her own cowardice. The one thing she had not been able to bring herself to do was actually go next door in person.

What the hell were you thinking. She chastised herself, despite knowing full well she had not been thinking. Mrs. Needen had often told her that her impulsive nature would get her into trouble, but she never gave much thought into just how much trouble she could find herself in.

Stealing one last glance at the neighboring house, she finished her walk across the yard, locked up her bike and headed into the house. She made the short trek into the kitchen, heading straight for the fridge, where she liberated a can of cola. Mrs. Needen was over by the stove, and addressed Isolde as she was turning to leave.

"Hey Isolde, if you feel like waiting a couple of minutes, I've got a batch of chocolate coconut cookies about to come out of the oven."

Some primal part of her soul was screaming at Isolde to stick around and eat as many of those cookies as her foster mother would allow her, but the more rational part of her brain knew she didn't have the appetite.

"Like thanks, but I'm good." As she started back towards the hallway, she was startled by the sharpness with which Mrs. Needen spoke, her voice raised.

"Isolde Emily Serana, now you go right ahead and have a seat right there at that table while I get these cookies out." Isolde was stunned, Mrs. Needen had never used her full name like that before. Not wanting to upset the woman further, nor really feeling like having any argument in general, she did as instructed.

She sat there for a few minutes, listening to the older woman removing the cookies, and transferring them to a cooling rack, before joining Isolde at the table. She reached over and grabbed Isoldes hand, while she spoke.

"Sweetie, what's wrong? The past few days you've seemed, I don't know, distant. Withdrawn even. Your father and I are getting worried about you, and clearly for good reason." Isolde looked down at the table, swallowing hard several times. The concern in the woman's voice tore at Isolde's heart, as she realized how much she had made her worry.

"Never, not one time since you came to live with us have you turned down one of my cookies. Why I rightly couldn't count the times we had to get on to you for sneaking them off to your room." The woman was correct after all, Isolde thought back to all the times as a child she would spend hours working out her genius plans to get at the cookie jar, each time the Needens found a new hiding place for it.

But how could she think about cookies now? Jessica was making good on not speaking with her and April both, and she was pretty sure she lost April's friendship altogether. On top of that she had these feelings to deal with, and no idea how to even begin that journey.

She never lifted her eyes from the table, staring a hole into its center as Mrs. Needen continued the interrogation.

"So please, tell me what's wrong. It's not that job, is it? Did something happen at work?" Isolde almost broke out a grin at the idea it was something work related. Work was the only place, the only time she felt anything close to normal lately.

"I always told your father that Daisy woman was some kind of character." Isolde wished, harder than anything she ever wished for before, that her troubles were somehow related to her boss. Anything so mundane.

More than that she wished she could just lie to her foster mother, and say that her problems were indeed work related. But she knew better, she knew that not only would the truth come out at the worst moment, but that she would hurt the poor woman in the process.

She finally raised her eyes. "No, no, no. It's not work, God I wish it was, like, you have no idea how much I wish it was." She heard footsteps behind her, as Mr Needen walked into the room.

"Mmmhmmm, are those fresh baked cookies I smell?" He stopped when he saw the women sitting at the table, the sullen look on their faces.

"Oh, what's going on here? Anything I can help with?" Mrs. Needen turned towards her husband, a look Isolde had never seen before was on the woman's face.

"Living room hunny. I'll have dinner on soon enough." Mr Needen got the memo, and made his way out of the room, leaving the women alone once more. Isolde was grateful. If she had to have this conversation, she wanted it to just be between her and Mrs. Needen.

"Thank you." Isolde said, her voice cracking as she spoke. "I. I like, I don't know how to talk about this." She raised her eyes further, looking out of the small kitchen window,and towards the neighbors house. Towards April's house, she thought.

"Mrs. Needen, I." Her voice trailed off, as the other woman followed Isoldes gaze, a look of recognition forming on her face.

"Something happen between you and April sweetie? Wondered why she hadn't been over for a spell." Isolde wanted to laugh at how massive an understatement Mrs. Needen just said, but couldn't bring herself to.

"Now, sweetie, friends go through these spats all the time, I'm sure whatever it is will pass and you'll be back to gossiping and all till three in the morning again in no time."

Isolde felt the sting of fresh tears filling her eyes, as she turned her head from the window, looking towards the floor. She squeezed the older woman's hands, as she spoke, her voice shaking.

"I don't know. I." The thought that April might never come around, that Mrs. Needen was wrong was too much for her, and the waterworks began to flow.

"Mom, I fucked up. Like I really fucked up and I don't know what to do." She expected to be admonished for her language, but her foster mother just sat there, looking shocked.

"I do believe that's the first time you've rightly ever called me mom. Sweetie, go on over to my room. I'm going to tell your father to order out and I'll join you in a bit."

Isolde forced herself to her feet, abandoning the unopened soda, and began the walk towards the back of the house. Towards her foster mother's room. She had to wipe her eyes in order to clear her vision several times, as the tears never stopped flowing.

Before long, she found herself sitting on Mrs. Needens bed, and a few moments after that, she was joined by the woman. Isolde reached over and hugged the other woman, burying her head in the woman's chest as she sobbed.

She had no idea how long the two remained in that position, before she lifted her head. She once again used her shirt sleeve, now damp from all of her tears, to dry her eyes. She looked up at Mrs. Needen, who had also been crying.

"Like, I said, I fucked up. I mean, I messed up." She corrected herself due to the look on the woman's face. Her foster mother's features softened a bit as she spoke.

"Hush now child, you use whatever language you need to, ok?" Isolde nodded, glad to be able to speak freely with someone.

"These last two months, something. Something I can't really explain happened. Like you know how close me and April are, she's my best friend." A fresh wave of tears began to form in her eyes.

"But I think I ruined that. I. I don't." The tears began flowing. "I don't know how but I'm in love with her." She had expected Mrs. Needen to have some amount of shock, or surprise at the revelation but the woman just sat there smiling softly.

"Been wondering if you were ever planning on breaking that can of worms open sweetie." Isolde stared at the woman for several moments. Mrs. Needen was clearly more observant than she gave her credit for.

Isolde forced herself to regain her composure before continuing. "Like, what's worse is that she feels the same about me." A look of confusion covered Mrs. Needens face.

"Well sweetie, if that's true, then what's the problem?" Isolde gave a summary of the main events of her last conversation with April.

"And, like you always told me, my impulsiveness would get me in trouble. You were so, so, so, right. Because. Because I just kissed her. I don't know why I did it, but in the moment it just felt like the right thing to do." She thought back to the moment in question, as she had many times since.

What the hell is wrong with me? The same question she had asked herself hundreds of times since the big mistake. She felt Mrs. Needens arms around her, as the woman gave her a consoling hug.

"Sweetie, every part of me wants to tell you that it's going to be ok, that it'll all right work itself out. And hey, it very well may in the end." The words brought a small amount of comfort to Isolde.

"But I'd be a bad mother if I said that wholesale. No, I'm afraid I have to agree with you, you most certainly did, as you put it, fuck up." Isolde began sobbing even harder at the woman's words.

Harsh truths were always the hardest things to hear, and this one was the harshest she'd heard yet. Mrs. Needen began rubbing her shoulders, a move that brought her little comfort.

"Now sweetie, what I can tell you is to give it some time. And I do mean it, give it some time, the longer the better. And then you go over there, you knock on her door. None of that texting or bookface stuff you hear?" The blatant misnaming of the social media app would normally elicit a giggle from her, but Isolde's mood was too dark for any kind of humor to hit her.

"And when you do, you ask whoever answers, or ask April herself if she answers, if she's willing to talk to you. If she is, you right own your mistake sweetie, and you try and work things out."

Isolde looked up at the woman, wiping her eyes once more before speaking. "And like, if she doesn't?" The woman's face grew sullen, and she squeezed Isoldes shoulder.

"Then sweetie, you accept your losses, and begin the painful process of moving on." Isolde began crying all over again, sobbing hard into the woman's chest once more as the woman sat rocking her.

ISOLDE HAD SPENT A little while longer speaking with Mrs. Needen before returning to her room, where she now sat at her desk.

She scrolled through the dozen's of texts she had sent April, all of which remained unseen. She dropped the phone on the desk and buried her head in her arms.

She thought back to the first day she had met the Needens. A social worker had dropped her off, though she was too young to understand anything going on.

The Needen's had tried to explain to her how her life was to be, but she just threw her backpack at them and ran outside. She remembered vividly just how terrified she had been, and how much she had just wanted to see her dad again.

Eleven years on, and the pain of being abandoned had still not fully gone away. She had sat there on the edge of the yard, crying that day, when another little girl had tried several ways to get her attention, ultimately succeeding with a snack cake offering.

Isolde found herself laughing, a sad and joyless laugh as she recalled how the two had pretty much become instant best friends, going straight next door to spend hours playing with dolls.

Best friends for eleven years, we've been inseparable. She thought, unable and unwilling to hold back another wave of tears as the idea that it might truly be over hit her.

She once more dried her eyes and retrieved her phone. She closed out of April's contact and opened Jessica's. She began to type out a text, and stopped to gather her thoughts first.

Mrs. Needen had never steered her wrong before, so she saw no reason to mistrust the woman's advice. No matter how much she knew it was going to hurt if things did go badly.

She returned to typing her message out. She made the decision, she was going to give April until the following Friday after tomorrow, one week to get back in touch. If she didn't then Isolde was going to do as she was told, and knock on the door.

She let Jessica know this in the text, and she finished the text with the most painful bit. That if April chose not to talk to her, or things went badly in some other way, she was going to move on no matter how much it hurt.

She sent the text, and dropped the phone again. Jessica likely wouldn't reply as she'd been making good on her word, and wasn't speaking to her. Presumably the same held for April but she had no way to confirm that suspicion.

The phone's notification sounding startled her, and her heart skipped a beat. One of her friends had finally texted her.

She opened the message, and her heart sank even further. Jessica had replied, with nothing more than a thumbs up emoji. She laid the phone down and made her way into bed, not tired enough to sleep but likewise not wanting to be awake.

THE DISTANT PAST

The Warrior glanced around, the area just outside the hut was clear. Counting her blessings, she darted out of the doorway, and into the dense brush.

A significant amount of time had passed before she made it to her destination, a small clearing with a pond. It was one of her favorite places to relax, since as far as she knew, no one else knew about it.

As she was preparing to slip into the pond, that theory was proven false, as she heard the sounds of the brush nearby rustling. Jumping to action, she grabbed her blade as a young man walked out of the jungle, spear in hand. A hunter, more than that, one of First Father's most trusted.

"You make for poor prey, Warrior." The man stood there, his spear at the ready as he watched her. She kept her own eyes fixed on the man, his words giving away his intentions, an amateur mistake.

"Did you not think your actions would go unnoticed? That you could," the man's voiced cracked with rage, yet another amateur mistake, letting his emotions run wild. "That you could attempt to mate with the First Mother like that? That you would get away with it? No, no matter how weak you are as prey or how pitiful your efforts to conceal your getaway were." The man took a step forward, raising his spear into a battle ready stance.

"I am here to bring you to justice, a fate no better than the animals you mimic." The Warrior gripped her blade, entering her own battle stance.

His eyes remained on her, tracking her every move, her every breath. He may have made several amateur mistakes, but he's still one of the elite hunters. The thought brought little comfort to her, though it did provide her with an idea.

The man was clearly letting rage take control, so why not push that further. "Of course I will, get away with it, as you claimed." He gripped the wood of his spear tighter, her plan was working.

"First Father is weak. He plays with trinkets while a Warrior takes his bed, takes his mate. What do you think that reflects on you, pitiful hunter?" She felt wrong in so many ways speaking the words, speaking ill of her leader like this. But found no faults with the words all the same.

The hunter narrowed his eyes, a look of hatred in them. This was her chance, he will attack at the first sign of weakness, but his rage will blind him. One strike, she thought as she began to circle him, blade at the ready.

Chapter 17

TUESDAY JUNE 22ND AFTERNOON.

April found herself wandering the streets once more, unable to deal with her own emotional state and the ever increasing family drama at home.

She had spent the last several days running her wants, her fears and her decisions through her mind every way she could think to do. Yet she was no closer to finding an answer. *What a lovely little mess I've made.* She shook her head at the thought.

As she was turning to round a corner, her thoughts were interrupted by someone shouting at her. She turned and felt the pangs of fear run through her as she saw Brandon jogging up to her.

"What's a fine ass hunnie like you doing walking all alone?" He wasted no time with his sleaze tactics, as she began to turn away with a "get lost and leave me alone."

Not wanting to deal with this, she began to turn away, when he reached out and grabbed at her, catching her shirt. The sound of the fabric tearing as he pulled her back around sickened her.

"What's wrong? Your psycho dyke ass bitch ain't here to fight your battles so you wanna run away?" The smugness in his voice and the choice of words made her blood run cold.

How did he know? The thought was there and gone in a flash as she balled up a fist, before she swung it at him.

He leaned back and she swung wide as he laughed at her. "All that pussy licking's got you swinging like one, huh?"

Her vision flashed red as she reached out and shoved him as hard as she could. He had been expecting it as he braced himself and she wasn't able to topple him.

"You think you're tough, freak?" He turned and looked around the street as her fears began to manifest. She had no idea what he was capable of, and no desire to stick around and find out.

"Fine with me, let's have some fun." The way he said the word fun threw up several red flags as she decided to get away as fast as she could.

She was in the process of trying to back up, mid turn when she felt the impact. Her cheek exploded in a blinding flash of pain as she fell to the sidewalk. When her vision cleared enough to see clearly, she saw him rubbing his fist, a sick grin on his face.

Her fear had taken over, as she lay there paralyzed. She screamed internally at her legs to get up, to move, to do anything as he took another step towards her, his leg reared back as if to kick her.

She closed her eyes anticipating the blow, as her mind filled with the image of Isolde shoving the boy. She found herself wishing that Isolde was here right now. She would take everything back, do anything to make amends if her friend just rode around the corner right now.

The blow landed, thankfully nothing serious as she had managed to crawl into a more fetal position and his shoe hit her legs. One good thing about being fatso, as cassie likes to call me. She thought, thankful for the extra cushioning on her legs.

Once more, she focused her thoughts on Isolde. Once more realizing how much she leaned on the girl, how much of a pillar of support Isolde was. Another kick, this one much more painful, hit her lower legs, which had much less padding.

That was it. A pillar of support. That's what it was that made her fall for Isolde, one of the questions she had burning for so long, now had an answer. No matter how much she leaned on Isolde, the girl always pushed back just as hard, helping April stand strong. Stand strong in the wake of the storm that was her family life. Isolde had long been her refuge, her salvation. Her rock, that kept her grounded, as she anticipated another blow. A salvation she would do anything to see once more.

Her salvation did come from around the corner, as she heard what sounded like a gunshot followed by the engine of an out of shape vehicle firing up.

As she heard the vehicle coming up the street, she opened her eyes. She looked around, not seeing Brandon at first. Looking behind her, she saw Brandon running off, looking back at the coming truck with a look of fear.

She laid there as the beat up and faded red pickup made its way down the street, the same way Brandon had run off too, before her fears subsided enough for her to get up and run the entire way back home.

Her lungs were begging her to stop and she had to ignore the pain in both her legs and sides as she finally made it home. Pain from the stitches of overexertion, and from being kicked multiple times.

She looked over at the Needens' house, knowing Isolde would not be home from work yet. *Please hurry home Isolde, I need you.* The thought brought her a sense of comfort.

She was no longer willing to let her indecisiveness get in the way. She had no idea how or what the two of them were going to do about their feelings but that was a bridge to cross later. Right now, she just wanted, no she needed her friend. Her rock, her support, her love. She couldn't keep the thought from racing across her mind as she climbed up the stairs onto the porch.

She sat on the porch to gather her thoughts, and catch her breath as another darker thought reemerged. Brandon had used some very choice words, in so far as using a slur when speaking of Isolde.

She dismissed the idea of Jessica having said anything to him, as she wasn't sure the two even knew of one another's existence.

Her thoughts then turned to Isolde, which she dismissed even faster. No matter how much pain Isolde must be in because of how April was treating her, she would never let that information out.

Hell, she'd be more likely to break his nose than even try talking to him in the first place. The thought brought its own sense of warmth, which faded almost as fast as it came.

There was only one person who both knew of her and Isolde's feelings and was on speaking terms with, or at least talking to people around Brandon.

The pain of the thought of Rachel betraying her trust like that hurt worse than her face, as she reached up to touch it. A spark of pain erupted as she made contact forcing her to pull a compact from her purse. She looked at her face through the tiny mirror, which was a deep purple and swelling.

Now that she was focusing on her physical condition, the full weight of the pain began to sink in, and she noticed the taste of blood in her mouth.

She opened her lips, panicking as she saw her teeth were stained with a faint red, blood mixed with her saliva.

She looked around her mouth with the mirror, noticing the inside of cheek Brandon had hit had a decent sized cut. She felt a sense of relief that all of her teeth were still there, and felt each one to make sure none were loose.

She pulled her phone out, debating on texting Jessica, begging the girl to break off her self-imposed exile, but knew she had something more important to do first. She spent several moments looking it up and began to dial the non-emergency police number.

A good while later, she had told the woman who picked up about what had happened, and was now waiting for a deputy to arrive.

She remained on the steps to the porch, as Buster came over and laid beside her with his head on her lap. She found a lot of comfort in rubbing the dog's head as she waited. He was a lot more petting-friendly then her old tabby, that was for sure.

She remained there, petting the dog as she thought about how she was going to handle reconnecting with Isolde. Pulling her phone out, she set to unblocking the girl's number, before finally reading the mountain of texts the girl had sent.

Her heart broke as she did. Though the words were just text on a cracked phone screen, she could feel every drop of the pain Isolde must have been feeling as she sent each one. Pain she now felt all the more, as she cursed herself for letting her cowardice do this, come between them like this.

It could be worse, we could be homeless right now, kicked out and abandoned. She laughed at herself for the thought. Isolde was right, damnit. She had been right all along. She was always right it seemed. Who cares if they ended up on the street.

With Isolde's job they could for sure find somewhere to rent. Jessica's father would probably be ecstatic to host them for a while, as it would mean all the fewer instances of the girl sneaking out to meet them.

Once more she found herself cursing her own stupidity. *To think, all it took was getting the shit beat out of me for daring to stand up for myself to put my thoughts on the right track for once.*

Stand up for myself. Something she was now determined to start doing. Jessica's words came back to her, and she found herself agreeing. April was her own worst enemy, standing in the shadows of her friends. Her family. No more. It was time to take Jessica's advice, Time to stand up for herself, against herself.

The sound of a car coming down the road broke her from her thoughts. She got up to put Buster in the house as she noticed it was a police cruiser. She closed the door behind her and walked out into the yard to greet the officer.

The man introduced himself as Deputy Canfield and prepared to take her statement. He seemed nice enough, if a little disinterested as April couldn't help but think he looked familiar somehow.

She began to explain everything that had happened with her encounter with Brandon, as the officer's tone of voice changed at the mention of the boy's name and description.

"Oh, is that so? Brandon you said?" The officer closed his eyes, sighing as he shook his head. She didn't like the scowl he now wore, as something about mentioning Brandon upset the man.

"Now I don't know what kind of game you think you're playing here but I don't like having my time wasted. Maybe you should think long and hard about pushing this any further, if you know what's good for you." The accusatory tone and blatant threat shook her to her core.

What the hell? Does he know Brandon or something, is that what this is about? She was about to respond to the man when her heart fluttered, as she saw Isolde coming up the street.

THE COOL BREEZE FLOWING through her hair, brushing against her skin, did little to combat the stagnant humidity. Just the act of pedaling her bike took more energy then she felt she had ever had at one point in her life.

Whether the lack of energy came down to her ever depressing mood, or the lack of an appetite she'd had lately she wasn't sure. Regardless, it took everything she had to keep pedaling.

But on she pedaled, as she rounded the corner onto her street. A chill ran through her as she saw the scene ahead of her, her heart sinking as she rode.

There was a Sheriff cruiser parked in front of April's house. April herself was in front, talking to a young deputy. *Arguing more like.* The thought pushed her sore legs to pedal as hard as they could. As she raced home, she couldn't help but notice several of their neighbors were out on their porches, or by the street watching.

Reaching her yard, she jumped off the bike, pulling her phone from her pocket as she did. She wasted no time in pointing its camera at the scene as she heard April replying to something the man had said.

"But I'm not wasting anyone's time. Do you think I did this to myself or something?" April was pointing to her face but Isolde couldn't make out what she was talking about from this angle.

"Oh yeah, so you say. Tell me something, do you know how serious a thing it is, making false allegations against a minor is?" The look on the young man's face disgusted Isolde.

"You don't, do you? Maybe I should bring you in, see if you wanna stick to this lie. Maybe we'll get the truth out of you one way, or another." Isolde had no idea what the context behind this argument was, nor did she care.

She could tell from the look on the man's face that whatever his thinly veiled threat implied, things would not go well for April. The screen door of her house open and close as she took a step towards the duo.

"Like, back off dude, what the hell's your problem calling her a liar?" She shouted at him as she heard Mr. Needen hollering something into the house, followed shortly by the screen door opening and closing again.

The deputy, startled by her interruption, turned to face her. "I'd suggest you stay out of this unless you wanna get dragged downtown as well as this lying skank." His eyes fell on her phone, pointed at him, and his face went flush with anger.

"Oh you wanna play that game, do you?" He took a step towards her, as he placed his hand on his gun. A bolt of fear ran through her as he spoke.

"Well I don't play games. So maybe you should turn that thing off, and delete whatever it is you think you witnessed out here. Or I might just have to come up with an excuse to use this." He patted the handgun, as he took another step closer, now well into their yard. "And delete it myself."

She was afraid, but her anger made her take another step forward, challenging the man in her own way. A loud clacking sound came from the porch behind her, making her turn to look, and she saw Mr. Needen pointing his shotgun down at the ground a few feet ahead of the deputy. His finger was on the trigger, ready to shoot if the need arose.

Isolde found herself in a new level of shock and fear. She knew the man had a shotgun, for home protection he always claimed. But here he was all but aiming it at a cop. A cop who had just made a blatant threat towards her with his own gun.

"I'd suggest you think carefully about your next move, son." The look of anger on the man's face intensified as he began to grab his gun, when Mr Needen spoke again.

"Uh uh son, might wanna take a good look around you." Isolde did so as well. Across the street, old man Merkins was standing on the sidewalk, his own handgun visible in his hands, crossed against his chest. The elderly man was glaring at the deputy as he walked closer.

To her side, their other neighbor, Miss Tyler, was standing on her porch, a rifle in her hand though she wasn't aiming it or even holding it at the ready. The scene was surreal. The Needens had always been pretty close to all their neighbors, but this was something else. All their neighbors except the Levae's, she thought, glancing at April.

Like herself, April was standing motionless, likely in shock as well. She looked back towards the deputy, amazed and terrified that people were putting their lives and freedom on the line like this, pulling guns on a cop.

The deputy removed his hand and turned back to Mr Needen.

"Do you have any idea just how serious of a problem you've just caused for yourself? You're one stupid ass man." Mr Needen gave a harumph before speaking, the tone of his voice sent a chill down her spine.

"Serious, son, is an understatement." The young man started to speak but was silenced. "Shut yer face boy. Ain't none of us wants to hear it." Isolde couldn't help but smirk as the deputy stood there scowling.

"Now, I don't know how things work back wherever you done came from, but out here? Out here, you step onto a man's property, and threaten his daughter? Threaten his neighbor's daughter? Out here that gets you shot son. Badge or no."

As Mr Needen was speaking, another cruiser had pulled up. The sharp chirp as its driver blipped the siren drew all eyes to it. Fear gripped her, alongside the thoughts of just how much worse this might get.

Isolde watched as Sheriff Dean got out of the cruiser, and strolled over to the young deputy, making sure to look at everyone out watching along the way.

She wondered if the causal pace with which he strolled was from age, the man being in his late fifties, or from a general lack of concern.

She knew of him from all the posters and yard signs of his election campaign a couple of years back. But she had never met the man. A hint of amusement ran through her, at the thought of him being much shorter in person than he looked on those signs. Alot less hair too, as the thin scraggly black mess beneath his hat was patchy and pock-marked with gray.

The young deputy's face took on a sickeningly smug look as he turned to the Sheriff. "Sherriff, glad you made it." Dean spat on the side of the road, interrupting the young man. Isolde looked around, as everyone was focused on the scene. Mr. Needen had not lowered the shotgun.

"Can it Billy. I knew you was gonna be a right damn headache the moment your transfer crossed my desk." The Sheriff's words visibly knocked the young man down several pegs.

"Excuse me? You aren't planning on doing anything about this?" The man turned around and pointed at Mr. Needen. "Are you trying to tell me you let just anybody threaten an officer here? You think this is some kind of Mayberry or something? Arrest these people."

The old Sheriff looked around at each of her neighbors. "Sure, I could do that. Could bring a lot of good, decent folks up on a lot of heavy charges." His eyes stopped on Isolde, and her phone, once more aimed at the young deputy.

"Could rightly lock a lot of people up, couldn't we? But you know, that's an awful lot of paperwork. And my old hands ain't so good with the handwriting these days." She saw a smile break out on the Sheriff's face.

"Mor'en'that, though. I'd have to take a good long look at whatever the lil missy there has on that phone a hers." He nodded to her phone, drawing the young deputies eyes back to it.

"And call it a hunch, but somethin tells me, you'd probably rather I didn't have to do that, now wouldn't you Billy?" The Sheriff looked around the street before addressing the small crowd, his voice raised. "Aight now, you lot go on and git back to your lives, now."

She watched as the neighbors did as instructed, as the Sheriff led the young deputy back towards his cruiser. The two began talking but she couldn't make anything said out.

She looked over to where April had been standing, and her heart skipped a beat. April was walking towards her. Her eyes were bloodshot from crying, her make-up smeared down her face.

Isolde's breath caught in her throat as she saw the massive purple bruise on the right side of April's face. Isolde found her eyes drawn to her friend's gray t-shirt, which had a large tear on the right shoulder as she wondered what had happened.

Her gut twisted itself up as April approached, not saying anything and instead opting to just hug Isolde.

She returned the hug with as much force as she could get out of her tired arms. The pair stood there hugging for what felt like an eternity. April was sobbing into her shoulder, as she rubbed her friends back. The embrace was broken by the sound of Sheriff Dean clearing his throat, prompting the two girls to look over at him.

"Pardon the intrusion lil ladies, just wanted to let you know the up and up. Billy shouldn't be bothering you lot anymore, but just in case, let your folks know to keep an eye, and barrel out for him." He gave them a wink as he turned to look at April.

"As for you missy, unlike that cityboy, I do in fact take my work seriously. So if you'd like, we can go down to the station and I'd be mighty happy to take your statement, and see if we can get you any help." April looked back at Isolde, and she gave her friend a nod.

"Um, yeah, ok. Um, Mr. Dean?" The old man gave a deep chuckle at April's words. Isolde found herself questioning her friend, at just how normal her voice sounded despite the chaos of the last several minutes.

"Now now, call me Sherriff, or just Dean, or hells, even Michael ifin yer so inclined. Just hold the misters, please." The warmth of the man's words brought a smile to Isolde's face, likely the first real one she's had in almost a week.

"Ok, well umm, Sherriff. I was wondering, if maybe my friend here could come with me?" The sheriff looked between them, and shrugged.

"Sure, don't see why not. Come along then, and we'll have you lot back in time for supper. She followed April and the Sheriff to his cruiser, her emotions rushing like a turbulent river. So many questions ran through her mind as she wondered what had happened to April, and more so, what had prompted this change of heart.

A change she was ever so grateful for as the pair climbed in the back of the cruiser, a place Isolde would never have expected to find herself. *Least it's not cause I'm the one in trouble.* She thought, as she looked over at April, who was looking around the caged interior. *Least not cause we are in any trouble.* She corrected herself.

Chapter 18

ISOLDE ONCE AGAIN FOUND herself hugging April, probably the fifth or sixth time since the duo had arrived down at the station. She found herself speechless as April gave her statement to the old Sheriff, owing more to her own building rage towards Brandon than anything else.

"And that's when you showed up, and well, I think you know everything that happened afterwards, Sheriff." The older man leaned back in his chair, rubbing his temples. He typed something into the laptop on his desk.

"That I do lil lady. Thing I don't reckon is what would make that city boy act out in such a way. Know he found himself in a world of trouble back in Victoria, forced him right out of the city and into my hair."

Isolde had to ball her fists to keep her cool as she spoke, the subject of this officer too much to hold back. "Like, speaking of, what are you going to do about him? I have the whole thing recorded if you need it." She started poking around on her phone but the Sheriff just shook his head and waved her down.

"Fraid that recordings a mite bit useless lil lady." Isolde had to bite her lip, hard enough to cause physical pain to keep from lashing out at the dismissal.

"Now, Mr. Needen and his neighbors got my full line o'respect for sticking up for you younguns." Once more the Sheriff rubbed his temples. "But I'm fraid to tell ya, he done broke a right lot of laws in the process. Iffin I had to look at that recording, sure I could take

Billy down like that." The old Sheriff snapped his fingers, startling Isolde. She didn't expect such a firm snap from someone so old.

"Have to take your pops and some other fine upstanding folks in as well. No, fraid we gonna need something else to stick em."

Isolde shook her own head. The idea that that creep might get away with threatening her. Threatening April. She looked over to April, who was staring at the desk. A sharp pang of guilt ran through her. *Stupid work, stupid impulsiveness. I should have been there for you, with you girl.*

"Umm, the Sheriff had a point." April's voice was soft, and tore at Isolde's heart. "What made that officer threaten me, I mean us." Once more The Sheriff was shaking his head as April stared at the desk. In the oppressive quiet in the room, she heard her stomach growling, realizing she hadn't eaten since this morning.

She had intended to eat at work, but never got around to it, given how busy they were all day. *Like you just didn't want to bother in your self-misery.* The thought smacked her pretty hard.

Then getting home, seeing that whole drama unfold, that officer. *That officer.* The thought tugged at her. Why would he not only call April a liar, ignoring the obvious signs of physical assault she bore, but go so far as to threaten her? Almost like he was protecting someone.

Her eyes flew wide open, as she slammed her hands on the desk. "Right give a man a heart attack lil lady, what's gotten inta ya?" The Sheriff jumped back in the seat, April likewise had been visibly startled by Isolde's outburst.

"Like, that's it. He's protecting someone." She turned to April, who was looking at her with a quizzical look. "Girl, you remember my first day of work, the first time we met that creep Brandon?" April furrowed her brow, thinking for a few moments before nodding.

Isolde turned back to the Sheriff. "Well, on my first day of work, I was on break and April here was having lunch when the guy who attacked her, Brandon, came over to harass us." The Sheriff had an eyebrow raised as she spoke. "Well, I watched him walking in, hell I watched him get of a car before that. A cruiser, and he was with an officer."

A look of recognition fell on the old Sheriff as he reached over and began typing something on the laptop. She looked over to April, who had a slight smile on her face, the first she had since arriving.

"Well lookee here, the lil lady was onta something." The Sheriff turned the computer to let her and April take a look. It was some kind of personnel file for the station, for Officer Canfield. Scrolling down the file, the Sheriff stopped on a family photo.

Isolde didn't even try to hide the look on her face as she saw the man standing beside Brandon, in front of a red Sedan. Something about the car stuck out, besides the gaudy decals.

"This the git what attacked you lil lady?" The Sheriff was pointing at Brandon, and April turned her head away and nodded. Isolde once more felt that sharp pang of guilt.

She looked back at the picture, the same smug look on both men's faces. How could someone do such a thing to a woman, to her best friend? She looked back at April, unable to decipher the look on the girl's face as she reached over and gave her another hug.

She felt April's arms around her and held the position, as she heard the Sheriff making his way back. As much as it hurt to see April like this, she would never forget how it feels to hold her like this, to comfort her. Her thoughts flew back to the last time she had done so, on the bathroom floor at Jessica's.

The night she had first begun realizing her feelings for April, when the trio had snuck out and caught April's mom in the act of selling herself. *Selling herself?* Once more Isolde felt a thought tugging at her.

She took another look at the photo. More specifically, she looked once more at the car behind the men. Recognition hit her as she poked April to get the girl's attention. As April turned to look, Isolde pointed at the car.

"Like, isn't that the same car from that night?" Isolde's words left April looking a bit puzzled. "You know, the night we caught your mom being a prostitute?" As the words left her lips, Isolde's hands flew up to cover her mouth. She looked at April, who's facial expression hadn't changed.

"Like oh my god girl, I'm so sorry I didn't mean to blurt that part out." She looked over at the Sheriff who was looking at the car in question, his eyebrow once more raised. She looked back at April, who was now poking at something on her phone.

April laid her phone on the desk, as the three of them began watching. It was a dim video, taken at nighttime. But Isolde recognized the event in the video at once. She looked over at April, a big grin on her face as she was impressed at her friend's quick thinking that night.

After the video finished playing, Sheriff Dean leaned back in his chair. "Well, color me impressed lil lady. Ifin that there aint full on video of a right officer of the law breaking said law." The Sheriff clicked on the phone, replaying the video.

"Now, this here's enough to take ol Billy down, get him out of a badge at the very least, but." The older man gave April a soft and sympathetic look. "It'd mean we gotta bring in yer mom as well." Isolde felt her breath catch in her throat, internally screaming at herself and her stupid decision to blurt out without thinking.

"Normally wouldn't leave a decision like this in the hands of a civilian, least of all a lil lady like yourself, but, it's your choice." Isolde watched April with bated breath as the girl sat there thinking for several moments.

"Umm, truthfully? I don't really care anymore. If it takes a crooked cop off the streets, do it." Isolde finally let her breath out, taking another much deeper one.

"Like, are you sure? You know what that will mean for your mom right? For your sisters?" Isolde wondered if April's decision was made out of the shock her friend must still be in. April just shook her head, before giving Isolde a light smile.

"I know. Trust me, I've gone over it all so many times. Thought about turning her in myself so many times. But I know she won't stop on her own." April looked back down at the desk as she spoke.

Isolde sat there thinking as the Sheriff was typing away at something. "So like, this is a last resort kind of thing?" Not looking up, April just nodded. Isolde heard the sound of the laptop closing and looked up to see the Sheriff getting out of the chair.

"Well, iffin you lil ladies would follow me, gonna have ya wait a spell in the lobby while I go deal with some paperwork." Isolde put her hand on April's shoulder, and the pair rose to their feet and followed the Sheriff.

APRIL SAT IN THE UNCOMFORTABLE chair, staring down at the marble design tiles in the waiting room. She shifted her weight once more, as the hard plastic made her left leg fall asleep.

She could feel Isolde's gaze on her the whole time they were sitting out here, but respected her friend's patience in not trying to get her to speak before she was ready. She took a deep breath, still staring at the tiles.

"Thank you." She could almost hear the shock in Isolde at the words. She forced another weak smile as she turned to look at Isolde.

"Thank you for being here with me. And for bringing up that bit about us catching Mom." This time it was she who reached over and hugged Isolde.

The warmth of the hug, the feeling of love she felt both from and for her friend were almost enough to wash away the miserable way she felt.

"Like wait, wait, wait. You aren't mad at me for blurting that out?" Isolde was the one to break off the hug as she spoke. April couldn't help but give a soft laugh as she looked into Isolde's eyes. The main thing she thought about during her ordeal was how much she wished Isolde was there, and now here she was.

"Nope, I'm not made at all. I'm happy that you did it. Like I said, Mom isn't going to stop on her own." She saw the confused look on Isolde's face fade, replaced with a deep frown. "Knowing that the man who's been beating her, this so-called client, isn't above threatening us? I don't even want to think of what he would do to Mom if she did try and stop."

She turned her gaze back to the tiles beneath her, shifting once more on the seat. The pair sat in silence for another several minutes, before Isolde's patience seemed to finally wear out.

"So, like, I hope I don't push you away again by asking but." April turned to look at Isolde, this time the smile on her face was genuine as she looked her friend over. It was Isolde's turn to stare at the floor.

"But why am I talking to you again, after ignoring you for a week?" April couldn't help but feel a mixture of pain and sorrow, and a ton of guilt for her choices. Isolde didn't look at her, only nodding. April found herself enjoying this rare look at a completely speechless Isolde.

She reached over and put her arm on Isolde's shoulder. "Because, all I could think of was you." April couldn't resist the deep and warm laugh at the confused look on Isolde's face. She gave her friend a rundown of her own thoughts and feelings during Brandon's attack.

She stressed the fact of just how desperately she wished Isolde was there with her.

"Like wow, girl." She once more enjoyed Isolde's embrace as her friend enveloped her in another hug. April returned the hug, wishing the moment would never end. "I'm so, so, so sorry I wasn't there. And for, you know." She couldn't see Isolde's face but had a pretty good mental image of how guilty her friend must look. "For, like, just kissing you like that."

April broke off the hug a little, keeping her arms on Isolde as she looked around the room, making sure they were alone. Noting they were the only two in the small waiting lobby, she reached over and returned Isolde's long overdue kiss.

It was a quick and awkward kiss, but April savored the brief contact. She raised her hand to silence Isolde as her friend began to question the act. "Save it for later, when we have the big talk." Isolde just nodded, and resumed the hug.

If this bliss is what awaits me? Then I don't care how many people like that old lady are out there. April nestled her head into Isolde's shoulders, squeezing her friend even tighter.

"I ran the entire way home. Five and a half blocks, I didn't stop once." She thought about the run, how painful it had been as her legs still ached even hours later. More so, the spots where Brandon had kicked her stung. She hadn't looked but knew they were a deep purple and likely swollen. "I thought about you the whole run. Thought about you, and about us. About what I really want."

Isolde broke off the hug, and April caught her wiping her eyes. She was just about to speak when they heard the sound of someone clearing their throat. April turned to see a young female deputy.

"Sorry to break things up, but we need you to come along and fill out some paperwork." April sighed, told Isolde she'd be back as soon as she could and followed the deputy off.

Chapter 19

TUESDAY JUNE 22ND LATE Evening

Isolde watched as the officers who had dropped her and April off were questioning Mrs. Levae. She spotted Rachel making her way towards the pair, and tapped April on the arm.

"Hey, do either of you have any idea what this is all about?" Isolde looked over at April, noticing the vile look she was giving her sister before she stormed off and into the Needens' house. She sighed, not knowing what April's problem with her sister was and shrugged.

"Like, sorry, but April got attacked by that pervert friend of yours, Brandon." Rachel's eyes went wide and she covered her mouth, shocked at the news. "Turns out the guy who's been smashing your mom, literally and figuratively is the dude's older brother, a cop. Well, her profession kinda came out down at the station."

Isolde felt bad once more as she saw Cassandra arguing with one of the deputies as the other was placing the kid's mom into handcuffs. Rachel sighed before heading over to corral her sister. On the way she told Isolde to let April know she'd take care of cassie. Having had enough of the scene, she made her way inside.

She spent a few minutes filling Mrs. Needen in before grabbing a couple of colas and heading to her room. She handed one to April, who was sitting on the futon as Isolde took a seat at the desk. She popped the can open, relishing the sound of the seal breaking and its subsequent hiss. She turned the chair to face April, getting a repeat of the delicious sound as April opened her own soda.

She took a large drink, the sweet and acidic fizzy drink was just what she needed after the stressful day she'd had. Once more she found herself in an awkward silence, lasting far too long.

She was about to open her second oatmeal creme pie when April broke the deafening silence. "Guess things aren't going to be pretty at home for me when I go back." Isolde let out a small laugh and nodded her head, taking another drink.

"Yeah, like, I don't envy you at all when it comes to dealing with your sisters." She tilted her head, and waited until April finished taking a large drink. "Speaking of which, what was up with the cold shoulder to Rachel out there?"

She watched as April smashed the now empty can. Isolde took it from her and tossed it in the waste bin by the bed. April filled her in on the fact that she knew Isolde and Jessica wouldn't have told Brandon anything, leaving only Rachel.

"Like, damn." Isolde shook her head in disbelief. "Always thought Rachel was the normal one, you know? The good one of your sisters." April made a sound that was somewhere between a laugh and a sigh.

"Me too. The only one I had any kind of a proper relationship with in that house anyway. That's over now though, I'll go to my grave before I ever forgive her." April's words filled Isolde with a strange sense of foreboding. The idea that her best friend's relationship with her sister was forever destroyed hurt, though she wasn't sure why.

"Anyway, I think we might, umm, have more important things to discuss, you know?" Isolde watched as April fidgeted around on the futon as she spoke. Letting out a sigh, Isolde leaned back in her chair. The moment she had been waiting for all evening was upon them.

The pair went at it for over an hour, each time one of them began to address things their nerves took over. They enjoyed a short break during that time when Mrs. Needen brought them up some tuna salad sandwiches. She had forgotten how hungry she was, a fact which left Isolde making a trip downstairs for seconds before the two resumed their efforts.

The room now sat in an awkward silence as neither girl knew just how to have this conversation without pushing one of them into another week long exodus.

Isolde sat there tapping her foot, her impulsiveness threatening to burst forth. She had moved from the desk to the futon beside April. Seeing no other way to tackle the subject, she let go and gave in.

"I love you. I love you so much and like, I want to be with you." She let the words fumble from her mouth rapid-fire. She looked down at the floor, hoping that blunt honesty would make some progress in this painful stalemate.

She felt April's hand on her face, guiding Isolde to face her. As she laid eyes on April, her heart skipped a beat. April was moving in for another kiss, and just like in the station it was another short and somewhat awkward one.

"I love you too." April once more looked to the ground. "I, I was so scared. The other day, at the diner the way that crazy old lady went off on Jessica's sister and mom? I couldn't get it out of my mind." Isolde leaned over and hugged April, rubbing her back as she continued.

"Umm, what if Mom acted that way? What if she kicked me out because of it? Because of how much I want to be with you?" Isolde felt torn once more, between how happy April's words made her feel, and how much pain she now realized her friend must have been in.

April took a few moments before speaking further. "That's why I ran. That day? It's why I ignored your texts and calls, and shut you out." The pain of the events still lingered, but Isolde understood where her friend was coming from, better understood her own mistakes.

"Like, I should have been more open to listening to you. I'm sorry, April." She felt terrible for her actions, trying to force things that day. Still, the fact that they were back to talking, and had even had a couple of small kisses gave her more confidence than she felt she deserved to have.

She felt April's arm around her, as her friend pulled the two of them closer. "Thank you, that means a lot. Anyway, now I don't care what Mom thinks." She looked into April's eyes, expecting to see the waterworks, but instead saw only determination.

"I don't care what she thinks, or what anyone thinks. All I know is how much you mean to mean. How much, how much I want this. Want you." Once more she felt April's lips on hers, a kiss that lasted several moments this time.

It was a little less awkward the third time, and despite how short it was Isolde felt it may as well have lasted a lifetime. April was now staring into her eyes, and Isolde could almost physically feel the love radiating off of her friend.

A love she knew she must be giving off as strong or stronger as April said the words she had longed to hear. "I, umm. If you still want to, I want to be your girlfriend." Isolde felt like her heart might swell to bursting with the amount of joy it now held, as she accepted April's invitation.

"Like, yes, yes, yes, I still want it. I want it more than you can imagine, girl. I want it as much as I want to be yours as well." It was Isolde's turn to lean in and give the kiss. This time the pair held it for a long time, a deep and passionate embrace.

As the two shared their loving embrace, Isolde felt something within, something deep and raw and powerful. She broke the kiss off, looking into April's eyes. She wondered what it would be like to just find herself lost in those dark brown gems forever. Forcing her attention away she noticed the most raw, and genuine smile she might have ever seen on her friend's face.

Her friend. The thought had an odd ring to it now, prompting her to ask once more. "Like, this is for sure, sure, sure what you want? To be a couple?" April grasped her hands and gave them a squeeze. Isolde relished the warmth of April's hands.

"Yes. More than anything." Isolde leaned in and gave April another quick kiss. "Then like, I guess it's official. I just lost my best friend, and gained a girlfriend. So, who's telling Jess?"

April laughed as she picked up her phone, poked around a couple of times and held it out away from them. Recognizing her now girlfriend's intent, she leaned in for another quick kiss, as April took the picture, and sent it to Jessica.

As April powered her phone off, Isolde fired her own quick text to Jessica. "Well guess you just got a promotion to best friend status, cause me and April are official." She followed suit and powered her own phone off, not waiting for a reply as she rose to her feet.

She reached her hand out, helping April to her feet. The pair stood there, arms wrapped around one another, with April's head resting on Isolde's shoulder. That raw powerful feeling, that desire had returned, and as if reading her mind, April spoke up. "Umm, so I don't know how to, but I want to. You know."

She had no idea herself, but she didn't care. She pulled away from April, giving her a big smile, nodded and walked over to hit the lights before the pair climbed into Isolde's bed. It was the first time the pair had ever shared the same bed.

THE DISTANT PAST

It wasn't supposed to be like this. The Warrior thought as she circled the hunter. No one was to find out about her affair with the First Mother, least of all one of First Father's most trusted.

The hunter stood ready, watching her. *Waiting for an opening, any sign of weakness and I'm dead.* The thought pushed her to clear her mind. One strike, one blow and it's over.

She kept her eyes on the hunter's twin-tipped spear, a lethal weapon against the animals he would normally face. But impractical in close quarters, against a trained blade. She shifted the blade clumsily in her hand, hoping the hunter picked up on the move.

Her ploy had worked, as the hunter was lunging. He brought the spear down in a wide swipe, an amateurish, but effective move as the blade grazed her just beneath her left breast.

She ignored the pain and made her own move, thrusting the bone blade straight at the hunter's gut. A true strike, as she watched the hunter crumple to the ground. She had no time to waste, as she began rushing through the jungle.

She had been careless, letting that hunter track her, a mistake she couldn't afford to repeat, as she began doubling back, and taking alternative routes to throw any further potential hunters off. She had to reach the village, to reach the First Mother, but she had to be sure she arrived alone.

Several minutes passed, as the Warrior laid eyes on the village, on the hut belonging to the First Father. She took a deep breath, steeling her nerves before stepping out from the shadows of the trees around the small clearing.

The usual guards were not present, putting the Warrior on edge, as she walked through the doorway. She looked around, and let herself relax a little as she saw the older woman standing beside some kind of wooden structure, with a large clay dish on top of it.

"First Mother, I'm sorry, but I was discovered. First Father may know about us." She lowered her head, shame over her failure flooding her heart, battling the warmth, the love she felt for the older woman.

"Relax, my lover. My mate knows. He has known for some time, but his heart and mind are elsewhere." The Warrior let herself relax a little more, curious at the words. *If First Father knew, why had he let it continue?*

The woman placed a hand on the Warrior's shoulder, and she reached up to clasp it. "I'm afraid, my love, that my mate is about to make a grave mistake. A mistake, I'm going to need your help to stop before we all meet our ends." The look of fear on the woman's face was enough to convince the Warrior that whatever this mistake was, it was serious.

"First Mother, whatever you need. I offer my services, my own life if needed." She felt warmth from the woman's smile as she began filling the bowl with strange and odorous plants.

Chapter 20

WEDNESDAY JUNE 23RD Morning

APRIL REACHED OVER, and fumbled around for a moment before hitting the right part of the screen to silence Isolde's alarm. She let out a large yawn while rubbing the sleep from her eyes, before turning her gaze to Isolde.

She slid herself from the embrace the two had fallen asleep in, propped herself up on her elbow and gazed at Isolde's still very much asleep face. She felt a slight frown coming on as she noticed the uncomfortable look on Isolde's face, wondering how she could be having a bad dream after that wonderful night. Before the stress and drama of the prior afternoon came back to remind her of why and how.

April let out a soft sigh, one of contentment and regret in equal measures at the idea of having to wake Isolde, knowing the girl was going to be dead on her feet today at work due in no small part to how aggressive she had been with Isolde the night before. *Awkwardly aggressive, that is.* She felt the blush coming on strong as she shook Isolde softly.

"Fibe mer minites." Isolde half mumbled, half fumbled the words as she tried to swat April's hand away. April was torn between her own desire to join Isolde in going back to sleep, and not wanting to face the repercussions of making Isolde late for work as she once more found herself gazing at Isolde's face.

Her light frown found itself curling into a smile as she did. Despite seeing her face nearly everyday for the entire time she knew the girl, she had never stopped to appreciate just how beautiful her friend was. *My girlfriend.* She corrected her errant thought with a chuckle. Once more she reached over and shook Isolde, this time more aggressively.

"Time to get up babe." The words lit her smile up all the more as they left her mouth. If last night wasn't proof enough that this was real, the look on Isolde's face, as she lay there staring up at April, was all she needed.

"Morning baby." April soon felt herself being pulled down into a kiss. It lasted only a few moments but she relished it all the same, as Isolde broke it off. "Like damn, last night was awesome but," her words were interrupted by a violent yawn as she stretched. "Today is going to suck."

Isolde stretched out the word suck for emphasis as April removed the covers, a momentary flash of embarrassment at the fact they were both in the nude before her somewhat sleep-addled brain caught back up. A moment of embarrassment that faded fast as she felt her jaw dropping.

Her eyes fell just below Isolde's left breast at the dried blood smeared over what looked like some kind of animal claw marks. She realized her reaction must be showing on her face hard as Isolde scrambled to a sitting position, a look of terror on the girl's face.

"Like what's wrong baby?" April took a moment to regain her composure, before pointing at the wound on her friend. The actual wound looked to be smaller than she first took it for based on the smeared blood.

"How? What happened to you?" April couldn't help but worry that she had been too aggressive the night before. She watched as Isolde moved her breast aside to get a better look, as she ran her fingers over it, letting out a soft "ouch".

What worried April the most wasn't the wound, but the look of terror on Isolde's face, an expression she held for a few moments before she quickly shook her head and looked over at April with a softer look on her face.

"Like, damn girl, you need to be more careful next time, ok?" She leaned over and gave April another kiss before climbing out of bed. April followed suit, still wondering if she had done that damage.

Of course you did you klutz, how else could it have happened? Not like Isolde has fingernails after all. She thought as she gathered her fresh clothes for the day, while Isolde gathered her undergarments, her work uniform still in the small laundry room beside the bathroom they were now headed to.

As she stood around waiting for Isolde to retrieve her uniform she resolved to take the advice given, swearing she would be more careful in the future. Her eyes wandered to the end of the hall, the door opposite the bathroom, the unused master bedroom.

She had always wondered why the Needens chose the small guest room on the first floor to be their bedroom, opting to leave this one unused. She saw Isolde exiting the laundry room and followed her into the bathroom.

She took one last look at the master bedroom, as she felt the blush return. For the first time, she was glad they hadn't chosen that bedroom, or she'd have to die from the embarrassment if they'd heard her the night before.

THEIR QUICK SHOWER over, Isolde stood looking at herself in the mirror as April was dressing. Despite being uneventful, if you were to ignore the bevy of kisses the two shared in the hot water, she was happier than she could ever recall being in the shower.

It was the first time she could recall showering with someone other than her own mother, and even that was a very hazy memory she wasn't all too confident in.

As she was in the process of putting her bra on, her eyes once more fell on the wound she now had. The fear once more gripped her as she ran her finger over the now scabbed and cleaned wound.

She felt a shudder run through her as the wound sparked with pain at her touch, signifying that it was deeper than it looked. She felt relieved that despite its appearance, it didn't look serious enough to need hospital treatment.

She rummaged around in the cabinet beneath the sink for bandages. As she was applying one to the wound, her thoughts were on the latest dream. She clasped her hands together, once more feeling the fear the Warrior had felt, fighting for her life.

The sting that exploded from the wound as she pressed the bandage to it focused her thoughts. She found herself terrified, and steeled herself to keep it from showing on her face. There had to be some kind of explanation, some rational scientific reason that the wound the Warrior had received was now on her own body.

Her thoughts turned to Jessica, as she was more than eager to have the girl back in her life not that the drama between her and April was over. More specifically, the entire situation reminded her strongly of one of the girl's favorite movies. Like, I'm pretty sure there weren't any torched pedos running around that jungle. The thought gave little amusement as she struggled to comprehend how it happened.

Moreover, how she had felt the blow in her dream. How she had always felt whatever it was the Warrior felt, like the fear as she fought for her life, or the love and lust she'd had for that first mother chick. Something that was different from her normal dreams, where she never felt anything.

Her thoughts were broken as she felt April's hand on her shoulder. "Might wanna hurry up there, babe. Don't wanna be late or anything." The soft giggle April gave pushed any lingering thoughts out of her mind as she finished getting dressed.

Several minutes later, she followed April into the kitchen. Looking at the large clock in the shape of a black cat, its white tipped tail swinging back and forth, she realized she had just enough time for a quick breakfast.

"Good morning, girls." Mr. Needen offered, not making eye contact with either of them. He made his way from the kitchen with a coy grin on his face. Isolde looked over at April, now sitting at the table, as the girl shrugged.

"Made you girls a couple of breakfast sandwiches. Something told me you'd be down a lot later than this." Mrs. Needen turned and made her way to the table, a plate containing the food in her hands. "Figured you lot would need something to eat on the go as it were. Enjoy, and make sure you," she had turned and was looking straight at Isolde, "get to work on time."

April was already holding one of the sandwiches, bacon and eggs on fresh biscuits. Isolde looked and saw the purple jam oozing from the other, just how she liked it. As she made her way to the table, she heard Mrs. Needen stop at the door, clearing her throat.

"Now, before I go, I do rightly got one thing on my mind to hash out real quick." Both girls turned to face the woman, Isolde noticing the look of concern, no, the look of fear on April's face.

"Have myself a pretty good idea of the news you girls have to share later, and," she turned to look at April, her features softening, "don't worry hun. Who you love is who you love, no one's right but you and yours to judge."

The fear on April's face faded, as Isolde just shook her head. Of course they would have figured it out, she thought. "Just, do us old timers a favor," Isolde took her first bite as the woman spoke. "Be a little less, intense, with the loving next time, ok?"

April's face was as red as her own felt as Mrs. Needen left the kitchen, and she tore into her breakfast, eager to clear the embarrassment.

Finishing her breakfast, she rushed upstairs for a quick date with her toothbrush before she set off. As she passed her room, her thoughts were focused on how to gently persuade April to be a little more reserved the next time they shared a bed.

APRIL GAVE ISOLDE A hug on the front porch, still not yet comfortable kissing out in public as she watched her girlfriend ride off. She looked over at her own house and dreaded the coming drama. Drama she knew was now on her own head as she had been the one to seal her mother's legal fate.

Guess I've finally outdone you, Cassie. She thought as she made her way back inside the Needens' house. Pulling her phone from her pocket, she powered the thing on as she made her way to the living room.

She gave Mr. Needen a nod, and a "good luck at work," as she passed him in the small hallway. She felt the phone buzz several times in her hand, indicating several notifications as she took a seat on the couch.

She swiped through them, ignoring the several from Rachel, and focused on the one from Jessica. She leaned back on the couch, a big smile on her face as she read, glad to once again be on speaking terms with the girl.

"OMG GRATS BITCHES! Guess this means my vacation from you girlies is over, huh? Oh well, kinda boring anyway, so HMU ASAP."

She fired off a response, letting Jessica know she was going to meet Isolde on break, and later after she gets off work. She made sure to add in a demand to meet them there. She shut the phone off and sat there, relaxing.

"Right scared of the pot you set boiling at home sweetie?" She looked up, seeing Mrs. Needen sitting in her recliner across the living room. She wondered if she had dozed off, having not heard the woman enter the room.

"Honestly?" She began to answer, pausing to gather her thoughts. She was worried, both of the fallout of her mom's arrest and more so the revelation of her new relationship. "Yes and no." She finished.

The older woman sat there, looking confused, so April elaborated. "Yeah. I'm worried how they're going to take it when they find out about, you know." The warm smile that crossed Mrs. Needen's face pushed out the encroaching embarrassment. "About me and Isolde."

The woman gave a soft chuckle, and a reassuring look to April. "But if I'm being honest with myself? I've spent so long thinking of ways to help them, my family. To help my Mom" She found herself sighing, as she took another few moments before continuing.

"I don't know what it was. Maybe it was Rachel betraying me, maybe it was getting attacked, I don't know. Maybe it was finally having the courage to go for what I've been wanting with Isolde." Once more she felt the tinge of embarrassment tinting her cheeks.

"Whatever it was, it made me finally realize." She looked over at the window, across the small walkway between the houses at her own home. "Realize just how toxic they really are. How much, how much they've held me back. How much pain they've caused me."

She felt the burn in her eyes, as she closed them, hoping to stave off the tears. She felt the couch shift as though someone sat next to her, and felt an arm around her shoulders.

She let go, and felt the shudders run through her as she began to weep, thinking of all the pain she had tried to hold in, to bury over the years.

"Let it all out, sweetie. No use in holding it all in anymore." She reached up and clasped the woman's hand, thankful to have someone, to have a motherly figure to talk to who actually cared.

"Now, I reckon I've told you this before, but take it to heart. You are always welcome here, sweetie." She squeezed Mrs. Needen's hand, before drying her eyes.

She spent the next couple of hours talking with her neighbor. Talking about her family concerns and acceptances, and her new relationship status, before she said her goodbye, and began making her way to the Diner, eager to catch Isolde on break, and get some lunch thanks to her new girlfriend's financial generosity.

Chapter 21

WEDNESDAY JUNE 23RD Early Afternoon.

ISOLDE CLOCKED IN HER break, eager to get back out to the lobby, to April. In her rush, she almost ran into Daisy, stopping herself at the last second. The older woman had a warm grin as she looked at Isolde.

"Well, I don't reckon what's got you in such good spirits, but I must say it marks a welcome change, girl." Daisy said, as she moved aside to let Isolde out of the employee room. She gave her boss a thumbs up, and headed out to the lobby.

Clara was already delivering their order, as she made her way to the table. She was glad to see April had put the BBQ sandwich order in as well, as she found herself with a larger than usual appetite.

"Like damn, it's so good to see you girl. Been a hell of a busy morning today." She noticed April's hand resting on the table as the girl was taking a drink of tea, and placed her own on it. She found herself puzzled at April's reaction, as the girl pulled her hand away and looked around the crowded lobby.

"Ditto. But umm, I'm not ready for any public displays just yet. Sorry." April looked down at the table, a look of guilt on her face. Isolde lightly tapped the table to get her attention.

"No, no, no. You got nothing to apologize for, girl. We'll take things as slow as you need." The gigantic smile that swept across April's face was all the reassurance she needed that her girlfriend was going to be ok. She picked up the saucy sandwich, the sweet and tangy scent was almost intoxicating as she took the first bite.

April had once again ordered a chicken salad, and was busy digging into it. "Still trying to maintain that lovely figure, I see? Noticing a lack of chips though." Isolde couldn't help but tease her friend, thinking back to the first time the two of them had sat across from one another,

"You know it." April patted her belly, drawing forth an involuntary laugh from Isolde. " And nah, not in the mood for any chips today." Isolde shook her head, unable and unwilling to remove the beaming smile she wore as the two ate in silence for several moments.

"You know, if only you weren't, you know, technically still on the clock. This might count as a first date." April said, surprising Isolde with the amount of confidence the girl spoke with. *Not ready for public physical displays, but I guess she's fine with verbal ones.* She decided to keep the thought in mind going forward.

"Like, nah. I already got that planned out for us. Just, we gotta wait a bit for umm. Technical reasons." She couldn't help but notice the look of curiosity on April's face, and felt a little bad that the place she wanted to go wouldn't be open for a few more days.

"Don't worry though, I know you'll love it." She added, taking another bite. April shook her head, clearly intrigued but admitting she was "willing to wait and trust you." She had finished her sandwich and was checking her phone. Her heart sank as she noticed she only had five more minutes before clocking back in.

"You know, maybe I should apply for a job here some time or," April's sentence was interrupted by her phone notification. Rolling her eyes, she picked it up. "Probably Jessica again or."

Isolde felt her heart sink even more at the look of concern that now rested on April's face. She asked if anything was wrong, worrying something might have happened to Jessica.

"Well it wasn't Jess," Isolde let out the breath she wasn't aware she had been holding. "That was Rachel." April sighed as she slammed the phone down. "Mom's getting released later today. Something about some kind of plea deal or something."

April's fears about public displays of affection didn't stop Isolde from reaching over and putting her hand on the girl's shoulder, giving it a tight squeeze. "Like, don't worry. I'll be right there with you and we'll totally face whatever she throws at you together."

April gave her a warm smile and nodded her head, as Isolde removed her hand from April's shoulder. She sighed, knowing she had to cut their time together as she was due back on the clock, her break, ever short as always was now over.

"Time to go back already?" April had a note of sadness in her voice as she asked. Isolde nodded, as she saw Clara making her way over.

"Yup, yup, yup. Don't worry, I'll be off in a few hours and we'll have the rest of the night to hang." Isolde relished the smile her words put on April's face, and she started to make her way back to the employee room. She stopped abruptly, and turned back to April.

"Like, you should totally go over to Jessica's. Been too long since either of us have actually seen her." She took April's thumbs up as a positive sign and made her way back to clock-in.

APRIL PAID FOR THE meal, and waved goodbye to Isolde as she left the diner. She checked her phone, relieved that Rachel hadn't texted her again. She pulled up Jessica's contact and fired off a quick message, asking if she was free to hang out.

She hadn't even gotten her bike lock key out of her pocket before Jessica's reply came in. "Better believe it. GTFOver here ASAP." She smiled, sent off a text saying she was on her way and proceeded to unlock her bike.

Several minutes later, she was pulling up to Jessica's house, her friend already out on the porch waiting. Jessica was waving her down as she pulled up to the porch, hopping off her bike as she came to a stop.

" Well if that ugly mug isn't a sight for sore eyes." Jessica ambushed her with a big hug, once she felt no desire to avoid returning. She heard Jessica sniffing loudly. "You smell like," she moved her head around April, sniffing in an exaggerated manner, "like diner. And candy cane waitresses. Couldn't resist stopping in on your new girlfriend already huh?"

April found herself chuckling. Still the same old goofy wiseass she knew and loved. "Better believe it. Actually considering applying for a job there myself." She couldn't tell if the look of shock on Jessica's face was genuine or another of her wiseass mockeries.

"Well hell, dad's been pestering me to start applying to places as well. Maybe I'll join you in that idea. Not like me and the candy cane haven't talked about it before and all." Jessica said, as she sat back on the porch steps. April followed suit, taking a seat beside her friend.

"Well you got my vote. Imagine the three of us running rampant in there, the terrible trio together again." Jessica let out a hard laugh at the old nickname her father had given the three of them years ago.

"Speaking of together again." April balled up her fist, and punched Jessica in the arm. Not hard enough to actually hurt the girl, but with enough force that she'd feel it.

"Ow, what the hell was that for?" Jessica was rubbing her arm as April smirked. *Guess I don't know my own strength. Oh well, serves her right.*

"That was for ditching us for a week. I get it, you warned us and didn't want to be caught up in our drama but still. That hurt." Jessica stopped rubbing her arm, and placed it around April, pulling her in for a hug.

"Yeah, sorry about that. Not the brightest idea I've had. Regretted it after the first day, but you know how stupid stubborn I can be." April once more found herself chuckling, her smirk growing in size.

"But enough about me. Let's talk about you. Like, you seriously got threatened by a cop?" April nodded, and gave Jessica an overview of the events of the last couple of days.

"Damn. Well, you did a good job with the makeup." Jessica was eyeing April's face up. "I can see the bruise if I'm up close and looking at it but from a distance? Good job covering it up." April touched the side of her face, it was still sore but didn't hurt anywhere near as bad as it had the day before.

"Yeah, Mrs. Needen helped me with that before I left to go meet Isolde on her break, so I can't take all the credit." Jessica cracked her own grin and shook her head.

"Figures. You never were all that good with make-up. Better than Isolde though." Both girls found themselves laughing at the comment. She thought back to the first time she had seen Isolde wearing self applied makeup. It had been a disaster, with Jessica making the joke that she looked like the bad guy in a horror movie where a prostitute ran crazy killing people.

"Can't disagree with that. Glad you were able to teach her some tricks and techniques. Ugh, can you imagine how I'd feel walking around with the bride of Frankenstien for a girlfriend?" Jessica burst out laughing at the imagery.

"Stop it, you're killing me Smalls. That purple hair she keeps would just make the look too." April found Jessica's laughter infectious and joined in. "Anywho, Rachel did more to help than I did after all."

The mention of her sister's name drained any joy and laughter April had. Seeing the shift in tone on April's face, Jessica also stopped laughing, asking her "what's wrong girlie?"

April gave her a rundown of her suspicion that it had been Rachel who betrayed her trust, Jessica confirming what she already knew that she would never do such a thing.

"Wow. I always thought she was the normal one in your household. Guess both of your sister's are pretty toxic." April shook her head, wishing her friend's comment wasn't true, but finding no faults with which to argue against it.

"Yeah. She swore she wouldn't say anything to anyone, but that boy, that Brandon clearly knew. So someone had to have been talking." Jessica shook her own head, a frown on her face.

"I don't believe she did, just making that clear but you did ask Isolde if she had done it, right? I can't imagine you running off and ignoring her didn't hurt like hell." April shook her head, a chuckle breaking her dour mood.

"Not a chance. Yeah, I asked and she said no. Not that I needed to though." Jessica had a look of confusion on her face. "You should have been there the day we ran into Rachel and her friends. Brandon was there, staring at my tits." She shuddered from having to recall the event.

"Me and one of Rachel's friends had to basically hold Isolde off the guy or she might have killed him." She couldn't help but wonder how things would have gone differently had she not held Isolde back that day.

"Got that right. Love the girlie, but man, does she ever have a temper." April found herself chuckling once more, glad that Isolde never turned her anger towards other people unless they deserved it.

Her phone notification went off again, and she checked it. Another text from Rachel, wondering if she was planning on coming back home today or not. She replied letting her sister know that she didn't know yet.

"Not her biggest fan anymore, huh?" Jessica was reading the phone as April texted. "Can't say I blame ya. If Sarah betrayed my trust like that, I wouldn't talk to her for a month."

April smiled, not really feeling the joy behind it. Something deep within told her she would be going a lot longer than a month without properly talking to Rachel.

"Yeah, I'll give it a decade and see if I'm ready to talk to that bitch again." As the two girls continued talking, counting down the hours until Isolde got off of work, April found herself startled by the sound of a car backfiring.

She looked down the road, as a faded red pickup truck pulled out onto the street and drove past. She found herself wondering if that had been the same one that drove past her, scaring Brandon off.

Her moment of curiosity passed with the truck, as she turned back to Jessica and the now much more lively conversation.

WEDNESDAY JUNE 23RD Late Afternoon

April and Jessica pulled up to the small backlot behind the diner, eager for Isolde to get off work in a few minutes. Looking around, April spotted Isolde's bike locked up, and walked her own blue bike over towards it.

She flipped the red milkcrate over, and took a seat, as she watched Jessica move her own bike over to the other two. April checked the time, three-fifty-five, and felt her anticipation rising.

"Few more minutes, and I get to see the happy couple together, huh?" Jessica was kicking at some small pebbles on the concrete. "You two aren't gonna start making out as soon as she walks through that door, are you?

April wasn't sure whether to take the question as a joke, or see it as Jessica having some problem with this new change. A concern that was quickly erased by Jessica's next comment.

"Cause honestly, that'd be kinda hot." Jessica began making some mock kissing gestures and a few of the fakest moans April had ever heard. *If only you had heard us last night.* The thought caused her to laugh, and blush a little at the same time.

Jessica's antics were interrupted by the employee door opening. April's smile felt like it was going to tear her lips apart as it grew the moment she saw Isolde. A painful reminder of the now mostly healed cut on the inside of her cheek.

"Like, look what the cat drug out of hiding." Isolde marched over to Jessica, and wrapped her arms around the girl in a big hug. "Was kinda worried we'd never actually see you again, you jerk."

Jessica looked like she was about to let loose another wisecrack when Isolde balled up her fist and punched Jessica in the arm, the same spot April had hit earlier.

"Ouch, dammit." Jessica was looking between Isolde and April while rubbing her arm. "Geez, I get it, you two don't have to break my damn arm over it." April couldn't help but burst out laughing at the scene.

"Like, guessing April gave you one of those as well huh? Good. Could have really used a friend this past week you know." Jessica spent several minutes apologizing to the others as April sat on the milkcrate smiling.

"Yeah I get it. I get it already. It won't happen again, just leave my poor arm alone." Isolde was now teasing Jessica, pretending like she was going to punch her again. "April, can you call off your attack-girlfriend or something?"

Jessica sprinted around to stand behind April as Isolde walked towards them. As much as she was enjoying the teasing, April felt it best to intervene, so she stood up and hugged Isolde.

She felt at peace with Isolde in her arms, despite the gnawing fear that sat in her gut like a heavy stone. She looked around the nearby streets, not seeing anyone, and leaned in and gave Isolde a quick kiss.

"Like wow. Not that I'm complaining but." April put her finger on Isolde's lips to silence the girl. She was in too good of a mood to ruin it with any kind of drawn-out explanation.

"Just go with it babe." Isolde shrugged and walked over towards the bikes, and began to unlock her own.

"Guess you girlies really are lovebirds huh?" Jessica asked, a big grin on her face. April turned to Jessica, her own grin beaming. "You better believe it. This bitch is mine." One more glance around confirming there was no one around, and April reached over and smacked Isolde on the rear.

"Yeah, shoulda known the way you were ogling that same ass at the river." Isolde was the one who let out a heavy laugh this time. "Like, yup, yup, yup. The greatest ass in the world and it's all yours, baby." April gave Isolde another warm smile as she walked over to get her own bike.

"Geez, am I gonna have to head home? I couldn't cut the sexual tension in the air with a razor blade factory." All three of them burst out laughing as Jessica grabbed her own bike.

"Like, you sure you're ok with this? I mean, with us?" Isolde had genuine concern in her voice, catching April off guard.

Jessica smirked, and nodded. "Of course. If anything, I'm even happier this happened than either of you two are." April and Isolde shared a look of doubt, before Isolde told Jessica to "prove it."

"Well, first things first," Jessica put one hand on her hip as she cocked it to one side and raised a finger on her other hand. "Like you said in your text. You two are now girlfriend and, well, girlfriend. That means you are no longer best friends. Ergo, I've just gotten a double promotion to being both of you girlies' best friend."

She raised a second finger on the hand she held in the air as Isolde was giggling. "Secondly, I now have a whole new can of wisecrack worms to open on you two going forward." Jessica finished her mock show-off by putting a grin on her face, sticking her tongue out and tilting her head to the side.

"Like Jessica? You are a dork. Big time." Isolde had to stop to catch her breath multiple times as she spoke those few words between the laughter.

"You take that back, right this instant you damn candy cane." Jessica had her hands on her hips, trying to hold some kind of an authoritative pose.

"Like, nope, nope, nope. You're a big old dork, dork, dork." Isolde hopped on her bike and pedaled off a few feet before turning back to them, her own tongue sticking out.

"Oh yeah? Well at least I'm not obsessed with some dumb kid's movie. Who the hell even likes dinosaurs anymore anyway?" April took offense at Jessica's words.

"Excuse you?" The tone of her voice caught both Jessica and Isolde's gaze. "I'll have you know I very much like dinosaurs still. And for your information," April walked over and poked Jessica in the chest, "miss teddy bear pajamas. The Land Before Time is a damn classic, so you watch your mouth about my favorite movie or I'll make you watch all the sequels." Jessica's mouth hung open as Isolde was busy snickering.

"No way. All of them?" The idea of being subjected to a marathon of any movie series was enough to put a little fear in her friend, so April capitalized on it.

"Yep, all thirteen of them. In order." She gave a harrumph as she turned from Jessica and climbed on her bike. "And I happen to like Isolde's little habit, thank you very much."

Isolde's snickering had once more erupted into full blown laughter as the trio began to pedal away from the lot. "Yup, yup, yup. You tell her baby."

They hadn't gotten very far when April's phone started ringing. She came to a stop, with Isolde and Jessica pulling up beside her as she answered it.

"What do you want?" April didn't bother trying to put on an air of civility towards her sister, as she put the phone on speaker.

"Rude, remind me again what I did to you? Anyway, Mom just got here and Cassie's already started. Mom wants you home, now." April felt her chest tighten at the news. She'd been dreading this all day, despite knowing it was coming.

"Fine, I'm down by the diner. I'll be there soon. Bye." She ended the call before Rachel could get another word in. She felt both Isolde and Jessica's hands on her shoulders, and reached up and clasped both of them.

"You better believe we're coming with you girlie." Jessica's words filled her with a renewed sense of strength that was only emboldened by Isolde's "Like yup, yup, yup. Count on it."

The trio rode off, as April began running ideas of how to handle the upcoming drama through her mind.

Chapter 22

BY THE TIME THEY ARRIVED at the house, April had worn out her resolve. She was now scared to go inside, and had her friends not been there with her, would have just left.

As the trio was putting their bikes on the porch, Rachel opened the door, letting Buster run out into the yard. "Hey, sis. In case you didn't hear it coming down the street, Cassie is in one of her worst moods yet."

April shook her head, not surprised by the news, as she could hear the girl screaming something. What did surprise her though, was just how little she cared anymore. She made her way inside without acknowledging or even looking at Rachel.

Isolde hung back, saying something to Rachel but April didn't care enough to stop and listen as she and Jessica headed into the living room.

The arguing stopped the moment she entered the room. Cassandra's face was red, and the girl was clearly not blushing. Rachel wasn't kidding about her mood, the girl was going to burst something in that volcano of a head if she was not careful. The thought did little to lighten her mood.

She looked towards her mother, who looked disheveled and had been doing a lot of crying. A moment of happiness at the lack of any booze containers was replaced by the sting of pain as her mom turned away, not making eye contact.

April let out a sigh as she heard Isolde and Rachel rejoin the group. Rachel walked over and sat beside their mom on the couch, as Isolde stood to April's right side, just behind her.

"So, which of you fucking retards was it who ratted Mom out?" Cassandra would of course be the one to break the silence. And of course, she'd have an insult in the mix. Jessica started to say something, but April put her hand up to silence her friend.

"I did. Gave them the video I took when I caught Mom in the act for good measure." Cassandra took a step forward, her fists balled up, but their mom reached out a hand to stop the girl.

"Why? I mean, what made you do it?" This time it was Rachel to speak. Unlike with Cassandra, April chose not to give Rachel the dignity of looking at her as she spoke.

"Why? Simple." She took a moment to gather her composure, steeling herself for what she was about to say. "I love you, all of you. Some of you much less than others but still." She couldn't help but notice the fear she held earlier was gone. Everything was gone, now that she thought about it. A deep calm filled her in the moment.

"For as long as I can remember, things around here have been a nightmare. A whirlwind of anger." She looked at Cassandra. "A wave of alcoholic neglect." This look went to their mom. "And backstabbing betrayal." Once more she refused to look at Rachel, turning back to Cassie.

"Day in and day out, all you do Cassandra is throw your little shit-fits over every little thing." Cassandra began to speak, but April silenced her. "Shut up. Just shut the hell up for once."

April heard gasps all around the room, as Cassandra did as she was told. The look of shock on her face was something April hadn't expected and wasn't sure how to feel about.

"Do you really think you have it any harder than us? Do you think we don't hurt because of her? Because she's too stupid to let go of Dad?" April was realizing the calm she felt had to be some kind of defensive mechanism, as she could feel the world of pain just beneath the surface.

"I'm sorry, sis. I'm sorry that our mom is a failure. I sorry that she killed our father and then fucked us all up because she couldn't get the fuck over it." Another round of gasps, with Rachel giving a "what the hell, April?"

"Bullshit." Cassandra shouted. "What the hell is wrong with you? Dad died in a car crash, you know that."

April just shook her head, as their mom finally spoke up, begging April to stop, to leave it alone. But she wasn't going to. Years of pain at the hands of her family, her violent, neglectful, dysfunctional family left her numb to the pleas.

"No one ever told you, Cassandra. I only found out a couple of weeks ago when Rachel told me." Cassandra shot Rachel a questioning look. "The crash that killed Dad? Who do you think was driving?" She looked at her mother, who was now crying.

"Mom? But you always said Dad was driving? Why the fuck did you always lie for if you were driving?" Cassandra turned back to April, rage on her face. "And why the fuck do you blame her for? So what if she was driving, it was an accident."

April felt bad, a heavy weight in her chest as she was about to drop the bombshell she'd held in for far too long, but Rachel beat her to the punch.

"Mom was drunk. She lost control of the car, killing dad and almost killing me because she was drunk driving." Cassandra sat down on the chair she had been standing in front of and looked at the floor. Tears were rolling from her face as for the first time, April could see no hint of anger on the girl.

"No, Mom? Please, say they're lying. You, you didn't." She felt terrible for her younger sister, knowing she was going through the same pain she had felt when Rachel confided it to her.

"She only got out of prison time because of you, Cassie. The officers that arrested her lost," Rachel held up her fingers in air-quotes as she said the word lost, "the evidence so the charges were thrown out."

Cassandra was staring at their mother, tears streaming down her face. "They figured losing her license for the latest accident was enough, and didn't want to break up another family. They were already dealing with another broken family at the time," Rachel looked at Isolde as she spoke, and April couldn't help but feel numb. Rachel hadn't ever mentioned that part, though thinking pack it did track.

"Trying to figure out what to do with another little girl whose mom had died shortly before her father abandoned her. Guess they didn't want to see us in the same parentless predicament."

Cassandra also looked over towards Isolde. "Wait, your dad abandoned you? I thought your parents died or something?" April followed her sister's gaze. Isolde looked like she was going to cry, leaving April regretting that she got dragged into this.

"Like, sort of. My Mom died from cancer when I was a kid, guess it was around the same time your dad died. My dad stuck around for a few months, but ditched me at the police station and no one's seen him since." April reached over and rubbed Isolde's shoulder.

"I'm sorry to hear that, you didn't deserve that." April was taken aback as Cassandra walked over and gave Isolde a hug before returning to her seat. Another round of gasps made the rounds as Cassandra did so. *Wow, she's actually capable of being nice?* The thought shocked April. Clearly it had shocked everyone, including Isolde, who mumbled a "thanks, appreciate it."

The momentary silence was broken by April's mother clearing her throat. All eyes were now on the woman.

"Are you done trying to destroy me, or is there some kind of point you'd like to make?" April let out a sigh, realizing she let Rachel and Cassandra sidetrack her.

"Yeah, there is a point. A damn good one to make." She took a deep breath, held it for several moments, and released it. "The point is this, Mom. You are already destroyed. Dad wasn't the only one who died in that crash. You died with him."

The words felt like broken glass as they left her mouth. A realization she had made some time ago but had never let herself acknowledge.

"Whatever good, whatever decency, whatever it was in you that cared? It died with Dad." Her mom looked down at the couch, more tears flowing. "Look, Mom. Take a damn hard look at your daughters."

She took a step forward, pointing at herself. "Look at me. How many times have I stayed next door over the years? Almost more than I've stayed here. Not because of how awesome Isolde or the Needens are. But because of how toxic this family is."

She took another deep breath before letting it out. "I've been a burden, leaning so hard on my friends for so long because of you. Because I have no idea how to deal with the pain of seeing you like this every fucking day of our lives." As much as she wanted too, she chose not to look at either girl behind her. "So much of my life has been spent living in the shadows of your neglect, of your alcoholism." Her voice began to crack, "your failure as a mother."

The anger taking over again, she pointed at Rachel. "Look at Rachel." The first time since she arrived home, she looked at her sister. "For years now, she's busted her ass to keep us fed, to help keep the damn lights on. So much of her youth wasted doing your fucking job. Being more of a mother to us than you ever were." Despite the anger she felt for her sister, she couldn't deny the respect she still held as she now pointed at her younger sister.

"Look at Cassandra. Look what you've done to the girl. We all nearly had heart attacks because she said something nice. Something so out of character that I'm still not sure if this isn't a damn dream. A moment of human decency, a break from her constant rage was enough to bring us all to shock because of how bad you've fucked her up." She felt bad putting her sister on the spot, but needed to drive her point home.

"Simple human decency that should be the norm, but is it? No, because the only thing Cassandra has ever known from you is neglect. The pain of neglect, and suffering watching you ruin what little of a life you had with a thousand thousand bottles." All eyes were on her as she spoke, a silence that felt deafening as she stopped to take a breath.

"The point, Mom, is exactly what you said. To fucking destroy you. I ratted you out, because I knew you were never going to stop, never going to change on your own." She felt her own tears welling up, the pain breaking through the calm she felt earlier.

"Seeing you come home, beaten and bruised? Worrying if we would ever see you again every time you disappeared for hours at night?" She wiped away the tears, as her anger was coming back. "I'd ask if you even care about how much that hurt, how bad it fucked all three of us up. But we all know that you don't."

Despite thinking it for a while, actually saying the words hurt like hell as she continued. "Yeah, I ratted you out. Because hurting you, even tearing our family apart? Is better than doing nothing and letting some sick freak rape and beat you. Better than being terrified every time my phone notification went off, petrified it was a text from Rach that someone found you. Dead... Murdered or worse." She felt herself shaking, and her friend's hands on her back.

"You didn't think there might be a better way to go about that?" Rachel's words only strengthened her anger, sharpened her pain. She glared at Rachel, before turning to look at Cassandra, who looked lost, even broken.

"No, I don't think there was. In fact, and I'm sure my friends here will be happy to confirm my memory isn't completely faulty, but I do recall us all sitting around trying to figure out how to do exactly this very thing not too long ago." She felt a sense of smug satisfaction at the look on Rachel's face as she looked down, defeated.

Once more the ensuing silence was broken by her mother. "April, Cassandra, Rachel? I'm sorry." She looked up towards April. "You are right. I'm broken. I've been broken for so long, that I never could see what it was doing to the three of you."

April felt another round of tears coming, the pain in her mom's voice was tearing at her heart. "I've got a serious problem, and I let it ruin our family. But not anymore." The words gave April a small sense of hope. One shared by her sisters as they all looked at their mom.

"I got out of any charges, by taking a plea deal. In addition to testifying against my, um, client. I'm being forced to submit myself to rehab, every day for the next three months." The small spark of hope was now shining bright.

"But what about us? Who will take care of us?" Cassandra asked, her voice still shaken. Their mother pointed at Rachel. "The Sheriff and a few deputies are collecting food and some funds to help out, and Rachel will be taking charge of the household while I'm away." April stifled a giggle at the look on her sister's face.

"So, April." Her mother was now looking at her directly. "I don't think I'll ever be able to truly forgive you for this, but at the same time? Thank you. I hate it, but I needed this wake up call." She turned away, looking back at the couch, as April felt Isolde's arm around her waist, pulling her in close and placing her head on her shoulder.

"Ugh, gross." Cassandra turned away, as April felt a bolt of fear. She tried to shift out of Isolde's embrace before any more attention was drawn to them. *Dammit Isolde, there's been enough drama for one day, this can wait a while.* She thought, hoping to avoid any further issues with her coming out at the moment.

Rachel's laughter was enough to sink that hope in one shot. "See you and Isolde worked out your little lover's quarrel? Congrats on the new girlfriends, both of you." She felt Isolde's arm tighten around her, embracing the acknowledgment.

"What the fuck? You're really a faggot or whatever girl fags are?" Cassandra's words were a dagger through the heart, as she lowered her head. "Like, no way in hell am I staying here, not with those freaks around. Disgusting."

She felt Isolde's arm slip from around her, as Rachel tried to talk Cassandra down. The pair bickered for a few minutes, with Jessica chiming in on Rachel's side, mentioning her own lesbian sister to no avail. The bickering ended when their mom cleared her throat.

"April. I'm happy that you've found someone, even though I don't agree with this, this lifestyle." April's heart sank even further, as she could hear the disgust in her mother's voice. "I don't. Between the betrayal, and this? I don't think I can deal with it anymore."

April braced herself for what was coming, as painful as she knew it would be. "I think it would be best for your sister, for me, and for you if you left and never came back."

Her mother turned away once more, and April shot her right arm out to the side, just in time to stop Isolde from escalating the situation. It hurt, every bit as much as she expected. But more so, there was something liberating in it.

"Fine. If that's what you want, I'll go pack my things and leave. Just promise me one thing?" Her mother looked back at her, despite not making eye contact. "Promise me that you'll see this rehab through. That you'll do better by Cassie."

Her mother turned to look at Cassandra. "I promise. Rachel, go clear out anything alcoholic in the house for me, please. "April watched as Rachel happily set off to fulfill the request.

"Come on girls, we got some packing to do." April found her voice was strangely neutral for how turbulent her emotions were inside, as she led her friends upstairs to pack what they could.

THE THREE GIRLS PACKED clothes, accessories and the few stuffed animals that April had in backpacks, grocery bags, and an old suitcase they found in April's closet.

None of them spoke a word, as the oppressive silence in the room was broken here and there by Cassandra shouting something downstairs.

"Like, I think that's about as much as we're gonna get, baby." The pain in Isolde's voice was evident as she broke the silence. April was stuffing her undergarments into a trash bag, while Jessica was sitting on the bed.

April finished her task, and turned to face Isolde. "Yeah, I think that's true. Gonna grab a few things from the bathroom, and we can take this all next door." April's voice trailed off, causing a sharp pain in Isolde's core.

She felt terrible for the girl as she watched her girlfriend walk off. She turned to Jessica, who was likewise not looking to be in any kind of joyful or wiseass mood.

"Like, can you believe April's mom? I mean, I get that April might have gone too far rating her to the cops and all but still." Jessica nodded, and stood up, picking up the suitcase as Isolde started grabbing bags, with the backpack on her back.

"Guess that explains why April was so scared to get with you, huh?" Jessica had a point. April had told her about her fears of bigotry after the diner incident, but she hadn't believed those fears would actually happen.

The thoughts were broken by April's return, carrying a small box of assorted toiletries. She sat it on top of another trash bag as she picked both up and the three of them set out, making sure they had left nothing behind.

Isolde and Jessica carried their loads outside while April stopped to return the house keys to Rachel. Isolde noticed Mr. Needen pulling in, and that he had taken notice of the odd scene.

Jessica was already carrying her load next door when Mr. Needen got out of the car and waved Isolde over. She followed suit and dropped the bags off on the porch.

"There some kind of fire sale at the neighbors or something, ladies?" The man looked between the two of them, realizing the gravity of the situation as April was walking up, crying. "I'll take that suitcase, Jessica. Grab those bags and you lot come on in."

The three of them followed Mr. Needen in, leaving the bags by the stairs as instructed. Jessica pulled Isolde and April to the side, hugging each of them.

"I'm sorry girlies, but I gotta get gone. Dad's already gonna blow a gasket, don't wanna make it worse. I'll bring your bikes over, don't forget to lock them up." The three girls hugged once more, as Jessica left, Isolde locking the door behind her.

Isolde led April to the living room where the Needens were sitting in their recliners. Isolde and April took seats on the couch.

"So, sweetie, what happened?" Isolde reached over, pulling April towards herself to comfort her as she told the Needens what had happened, up to her being kicked out.

"The nerve of that woman, to kick your own flesh and blood out like that?" Mrs. Needen looked between the two girls. "Guess you two have more in common than we reckoned." April was shuddering as she wept in Isolde's arms.

"April, sweetie?" Isolde helped April sit up, and wiped her eyes for her. She started rubbing April's back, knowing how much she always loved that, even back when they were just friends.

"Yes?" Her voice sounded normal, but Isolde figured it was just her trying to put on a brave face.

"You remember what I told you? About you being welcome here?" April nodded. "Good," She looked over to her husband, "Hun, you and Isolde help the girl take her stuff up to the spare bedroom." She looked back at April. "Your new bedroom, sweetie."

April broke off the embrace she and Isolde had been sitting in and walked over and gave Mrs. Needen a big hug. Isolde followed her foster father to the hall, to help move her girlfriend in. She told April to go lock the bikes up, tossing her key to April before she headed upstairs with several bags.

Chapter 23

April was pacing around the backlot behind the diner, waiting on Isolde to get off of work. She stopped to look around, the summer heat was here and in full swing as she wished she'd taken a bottle of water with her.

She heard the employee door open and turned around as fast as she could. She let out a long sigh when she realized it was only one of the employees carrying out a trash bag. She kicked a small rock across the lot, not sure if it was out of frustration or boredom.

Wiping the sweat from her brow she noticed her makeup was smearing off with it. Letting out another sigh, she pulled a hairband from her purse and began putting her hair up into a ponytail, regretting not doing so before leaving the house.

Despite the heat, the mix of boredom and frustration she now felt waiting, she was more at peace than she had been in a long time. The last few days had been amazing. Being able to sleep in without worrying when the next nuke was going to go off downstairs or worse right outside her bedroom door was something wonderful.

She began making another round of pacing as she thought. Thought of how perfect life was right now. Not just being able to spend so much time with the girl she loved, the closest friend she'd ever had. But how welcoming, how loving the Needens were as she had settled right in at her new home.

As she was pulling her phone out to check the time, the door opened once more. This time her eyes lit up as Isolde walked out, and towards her. She took the few steps to make up the distance between them, and threw her arms around Isolde, giving a long, tight hug.

"Like damn did I need that." April could feel the tension leaving Isolde's body as she broke off the hug. "Next time I decide to swap shifts with Alicia, sit on me or something so I can't leave the house." April let out a laugh, but the look on Isolde's face showed she wasn't joking.

"That busy today?" She asked, curious how Isolde's first Saturday shift had gone. Isolde nodded, unlocking her bike. She walked over and squeezed her girlfriend's shoulder.

"Busy, busy, busy, baby, doesn't even come close to describing it. Like, I think Daisy needs to hire another dozen waitresses for Saturday shifts alone." April chuckled at the mental image of a dozen candy cane looking waiters running around the small dining area throwing out that horrid greeting.

She mounted her bike and began to follow Isolde. "So, umm, you never did tell me where we're going." Isolde laughed, and turned back to look at her.

"Like, you'll see. Told you I had a special place in mind for our first official date, remember?" April found herself pedaling harder not only to keep up, but out of her own excitement. "Sorry I had to work today, but you forgive me, right, right, right?"

Laughing and sweating, April shouted that she "might think about it," as she followed her girlfriend down streets the two hadn't ridden down much before. Her legs were getting sore so she slowed down, letting Isolde get some distance on her before she too slowed down.

"How much farther is it babe?" She asked after Isolde had come to a stop. The pair of them had not been in this part of town in a long time, so she had no idea what there was around here, let alone what would make a good date.

"Oh, like, only a few more feet. Take a look." April did so, looking at the restaurant they had stopped in front of. No, she realized, it wasn't a restaurant but an ice cream parlor. She followed suit and locked her bike with Isolde's.

"Been waiting for over a week for this place to open, and today's the big day. I mean, in case the big ass grand opening sign over the door didn't give that away." April laughed, following Isolde inside.

"Yeah that it did. Think you've been spending too much time with Jess, her smartass is rubbing off on you." The pair of them laughed and talked as they waited in the fairly long line before making their purchases.

April followed Isolde to one of the few open booths, amazed at how busy the place was this late in the afternoon. Remembering how hot it was outside, she figured ice cream was as good a way to cool off as any.

She sat her order, a large root beer float with cherry chocolate chip ice cream rather than vanilla on the table. She waited for Isolde to place her own order, a double scoop of mint chocolate chip and rocky road down, before she leaned in close and gave Isolde a quick kiss.

She quickly sat down on the opposite side of the booth, as Isolde took her own seat. Sensing Isolde's confusion, she reached over and grasped her hand.

"I'm done caring what other people think, and doubly done with letting fear keep me from showing my love." She felt Isolde squeezing her hand as took a large sip of her float. "Speaking of other people, Jess's mom is back in town. She wants us to swing by in a day or two, something to show us."

Isolde rolled her eyes, taking a spoonful of ice cream in her mouth. "Like, she probably spent all night working on some corny ass jokes again." Both girls laughed, as April took another sip of the drink. The bittersweet almost medicinal taste of the soda paired well with the tart cherry ice cream.

"Well, keeping the news flowing, Got some of my own." Once more she felt Isolde squeeze her hand. "Talked to Daisy today. She's fine with me keeping weekend shifts here and there during the school year."

April smiled, her feelings as bittersweet as the soda she was enjoying. She knew Isolde was happy working there, and was, in turn, happy for her. But she couldn't deny her disappointment at how much it would cut into their free time over their senior year of high school.

She kept her eyes locked with Isolde's as the pair held hands, enjoying their treats and lots of small talk. Despite what it had cost, having not spoken to any of her family since the drama, and likely wouldn't anytime soon she was happy. For the first time in her life she was truly happy as she looked forward to the last several weeks of Summer. At how magical they would be.

SUNDAY JUNE 27TH MORNING

"You ready, babe?" April asked Isolde, not turning from the mirror as she finished brushing her teeth. She could hear Isolde getting dressed behind her as she rinsed her brush off.

"Like almost. Jess loves to wait til the last minute, doesn't she?" Laughing, April turned around and gave Isolde a quick kiss. "Yeah, she's like that, you know. I'll be outside waiting on you, so hurry up." She made her way out of the house, and sat on the porch waiting for Isolde. Jessica greeted her as she stepped outside, and the two sat on the porch steps to wait.

As the two had some light conversation, April couldn't shake the feeling that someone was watching her. She looked around, but couldn't see anyone around. The only thing she saw was an old beat-up and faded red pickup truck on the far end of the street. Something seemed very familiar about it but her attention was broken as Isolde arrived.

"Like I'm here, here, here. I'm tired, and here, so what's this big surprise, girl?" Despite her words, Isolde's tone of voice was cheerful as April watched Jessica climb on her bike.

"You'll see, come on girlies, first one to my house is the winner." In true Jessica fashion she took off, before the other two had even unlocked their bikes. April looked over at Isolde, who was rolling her eyes.

"Jess is always gonna be Jess I guess." She followed suit and unlocked her own bike as she and Isolde took off towards Jessica's house. April couldn't help but notice the red headed woman in the truck as they passed, swearing she recognized the woman from somewhere.

A short while later, the pair arrived at Jessica's place, where their friend was already waiting on them. She was wagging her finger and shaking her head.

"You girlies are just too slow. Yall need some better wheels." April shook her own head, looking down at her single-speed bike. The one thing she definitely missed from her old home was being able to take Rachel's bike.

"Like, look who's talking girl. That bike's worse than April's, and she doesn't even have any gears." Once more April found herself the odd one out as Isolde and Jessica tossed ever increasingly irreverent jokes at one another.

"Oh yeah well it doesn't matter how many gears your fancy pants bike has, it'll never catch this." Jessica turned, pulling something from her pocket. April recognized it as the garage door remote as Jessica began opening it.

Her jaw dropped as she saw not only the old jeep Jessica's father drove, but a shiny black classic muscle car. She picked her jaw up off the ground, and looked at Isolde, who had a look of envy on her face.

"Like, no way. Is that? I mean it's the same year?" Isolde was mesmerized. Something about the car was familiar to April, she was certain she'd seen it, or at least one like it somewhere.

"Yup. Sixty-seven, fully refurbished, and freaking mint, my own Baby." April's stupor faded as she joined her friends by the car. The comment had triggered her memory. This was the car from their favorite tv show. Despite her disinterest in watching tv, she made a note to sit down and watch the show with Isolde sometime.

"Wait, Jess? Is this yours? How?" While Isolde was more interested in the car itself, she was more concerned with how and when their friend had gotten a car in the first place.

"Mom. Apparently, it's been her little project for the last couple of years, getting it fixed up for me." April was stunned, looking at the thing there was no chance this didn't cost a fortune, especially for a full refurbishment. *Just how loaded is her mom?* April thought with amusement.

"Like, damn girl. Wait, wait, wait, you got a license to drive it?" Isolde managed to get out, still mesmerized. Jessica pulled the small card from her pocket, a giant grin on her face. Isolde now had an equally massive grin.

"You have no idea how hard it was keeping this a secret from you girlies. But yeah, Dad broke down, no thanks in part to mom's nagging and helped me get it. Been working on it all summer break so far. Passed my test Friday and there you go." Jessica opened the door, standing at the driver's side.

Isolde climbed in the passenger side, looking like a moth drawn to the flame. April walked over and stood next to her, watching her girlfriend's excitement.

"Man Jess, I totally hate, hate, hate you. You do know that right?" Isolde looked up at April, who couldn't help but feel her heart melt at the look on her girlfriend's face.

As she watched her best friend and her girlfriend talking about the car, she couldn't help but think once more, just how happy she felt. She looked out of the garage, up into the clear blue sky, wishing the summer would never end, while being excited all the same for whatever was to come next.

To Be Continued

Epilogue

MONDAY AUGUST 16TH Morning

Isolde had to push April's arm off of her in order to reach and silence her alarm. Laying there, April half on her and the blanket long since kicked off the bed, she let out a long yawn.

Though it was now the fourth time the two had shared a bed, it was no less awkward, nor any less enjoyable this time. What was unenjoyable, was having to get up and more so, having to wake her girlfriend up.

Sighing, she began to do just that, shaking April softly. "Like, rise and shine, baby." The joy she felt as April opened her eyes, those wonderful brown gems looking up at her made getting up all the more worthwhile.

"Morning babe. Guess it's that time again, huh?" Isolde couldn't help but laugh as April climbed off of her and the two got out of bed.

"Yup, yup, yup. First day of school. Senior year too, isn't that crazy?" They began gathering their clothes, Isolde from her closet while April's were hanging on the desk chair. Brand new uniforms for the school year, though they looked exactly the same as last year's.

"Yeah, it is. Think about it, next year we will be out of school. Hell, you'll legally be an adult by the time we graduate, and we'll finally be able to get out on our own."

Isolde felt bittersweet at the idea. Though the two of them have been discussing it for a while now, it still felt wrong somehow. The Needens were amazing people, the way they took to April, letting her live here was something Isolde would cherish about them forever.

But leaving them? As much as she knew it would soon be the time, it still felt wrong all the same.

The two made their way down to the bathroom where they enjoyed a quick shower together before making their way to the kitchen. Mrs. Needen was there to greet them, a pair of plates loaded with scrambled eggs, bacon, diced fried potatoes and toast. Plenty of jam on Isolde's, she noticed happily.

Something else caught her eye as the pair sat down at the table to eat. Something Mrs. Needen picked up on as she brought the small plastic baggy over.

"Fresh baked cookies for you sweetie. None of the processed stuff for your first day back to school now, you hear?" Isolde smiled, taking the treats with a big hug for the woman.

"Cranberry oatmeal. May not be as sweet as you rightly expect my cookies to be but I'm sure you'll love them all the same." Mrs. Needen gave her a kiss on the forehead before leaving the girl's to enjoy their breakfast.

"Guess you won't be enjoying any oatmeal creme pies today, huh babe?" Isolde laughed at the words, as true as they were. She could go a day without any snack cakes, especially with these cookies.

"Like guess so. Anyway, we got bigger things to worry about. Like getting this delicious food down in time to not be late." April smirked at the comment as the pair finished their meal with some light conversation.

Having cleaned their plates, brushed their teeth and said their goodbyes to the Needens, the pair were outside unlocking their bikes. Isolde took a deep breath, excited for the new day, their newest journey in life as she mounted her bike. What didn't excite her was just how hot and humid the air was despite how early in the morning it is.

"Like ugh, riding to school is going to suck in this humidity." She waited for April to mount her own bike before they started off.

"Thinking of the wrong thing, babe. This is going to be fun and games and a wonderful time, compared to the ride home." April spoke with a side of mockery as the two girls rode.

"Ugh, like did you really have to go and put that into my head? Gonna be thinking about it all day now. Thanks." April burst out laughing at the comment as the pair made their way onto the school grounds, locking their bikes together at the end of the now full rack.

Jessica joined them as they headed for their homeroom class for the year, a pleasant surprise that they all three had the same one for once, as the first school bell of the day rang.

Next Time, Book Two

WEDNESDAY JUNE 22ND Morning

Isolde bolted upright, the shock of the latest dream still fresh in her mind. She untangled herself from April, climbing to the edge of the bed before grabbing her phone from the nightstand.

Seven-forty in the morning. No point in going back to sleep, she thought, climbing out of bed as she made her way to the mini-fridge. She liberated a can of grape seltzer water, before walking over to the window.

She stood there, enjoying the fizzy and fruity drink while staring at the street below their apartment. The dream was still heavy in her mind as she took another drink.

Ever since she began realizing her feelings for April, these dreams, ones she'd had all her life had become more intricate. More involved, and, she ran her fingers along the scar beneath her left breast, somehow more dangerous.

She traced the thing, the fear over how she got it as fresh in her mind as the day April had pointed it out to her. While the larger of the two cuts had healed with no issue, the smaller one had been deeper, and left her with a thin scar.

She looked back out of the window, crushing the empty can as she worried just how much worse things were going to get in that weird dreamland, as the latest dreams had become so much darker, so much more serious. So much more dangerous. The thought terrified her, before she shook her head to clear them out.

No, she had more important things to do than dwell on freaky ass dreams. She looked back over at April, still blissfully asleep as she made her way over to the girl.

She took a seat on the edge of the bed, pulling her phone off the stand once more. She loaded her ticket app up, once more confirming they were there. Afterwards, she checked the reservation she had made at a fancy restaurant a good ways outside of town in a major shopping area.

She texted Jessica once again, reminding her for the fifth time what time schedule they were working on, before shutting her phone off. She laid back on the bed, stretching before looking to face April.

Like, today is going to be perfect baby. The thought brought a warm smile to her face. What better way to use her newfound wealth than on her girlfriend, after all.

She reached over, gently shaking April awake as she leaned in close to the girl. As always, April looking up at her melted her heart.

"Like, good morning baby. Time to get up and get ready." She leaned in and the two shared a long and passionate kiss. "And happy anniversary." The smile on April's face confirmed it all over, today was going to be perfect.

MONDAY JULY 1ST AFTERNOON

Jessica slammed the phone down on the seat next to her. "What the hell happened, girlie?" She said it aloud, despite being alone in the car. The tears were rolling as she drove. The pain in her heart was almost too much to bear as she flipped the wipers on, the rain beginning to pick up outside.

She reached up and wiped her own droplets from her eyes, as she found herself stomping the breaks due to a poorly timed red-light shift. She sat there watching as several other cars drove past, waiting on the light to change once more.

She looked over at the phone, the text once more racing through her mind, along with the fear and the pain. "Why? Sarah? What the fuck were you thinking?" Once more she found herself speaking aloud to no one in particular.

The light finally changed and she floored it, desperate to get to the hospital, to see her baby sister. She had never been religious, having never seen the appeal, but in this moment? In this moment she found herself praying to whatever God might answer that Sarah made it through this intact.

The phone began ringing. Not even looking away from the road she reached over and answered it, hitting the speakerphone button as she did.

"Like hey, April just told me the news. Oh my god girl I'm so sorry to hear it. Do they know what exactly happened?" Hearing Isolde's voice had a calming effect on Jessica, as she relaxed the iron grip she had on the steering wheel.

"Yeah, Sarah was a fucking idiot, that's what happened. I'm on my way to the hospital now. Mom said she still hasn't woken up yet."

Despite the calming effect talking to her best friend had, the anger at Sarah's mistake was taking over.

The two girls had some heavy conversation as Jessica made her way to the hospital, Victoria General and began looking for a place to park. She said her goodbye to Isolde as she was exiting the car, before noticing her father standing by the front doors, waving her over.

She took several deep breaths as she locked the car, to try and calm herself, and steel her nerves for whatever sight awaited her.

Don't miss out!

Visit the website below and you can sign up to receive emails whenever Damion Thaxton publishes a new book. There's no charge and no obligation.

https://books2read.com/r/B-A-UIRZ-HVDMC

BOOKS 2 READ

Connecting independent readers to independent writers.

Milton Keynes UK
Ingram Content Group UK Ltd.
UKHW010710140823
426838UK00001B/121